hot sauce

hot sauce

hot sauce

scott pomfret & scott whittier

WARNER BOOKS

NEW YORK   BOSTON

This book is a work of fiction. Names, characters, places, and incidents are the product of the authors' imagination or are used fictitiously. Any resemblance to actual events, locales, or persons, living or dead, is coincidental.

Warner Books

Time Warner Book Group
1271 Avenue of the Americas, New York, NY 10020
Visit our Web site at www.twbookmark.com.

Printed in the United States of America

First Edition: June 2005

Library of Congress Cataloging-in-Publication Data
   Pomfret, Scott.
      Hot sauce / Scott Pomfret & Scott Whittier. — 1st Warner Books ed.
         p.   cm.
      ISBN: 978-0-446-69431-5   ISBN: 0-446-69431-2
      1. Gay men—Fiction. 2. Fashion designers—Fiction. 3. Boston (Mass.)—
   Fiction. 4. Cooks—Fiction. I. Whittier, Scott. II. Title.
      PS3616.O58H68   2005
      813'.6—dc22   2004030271

Book design and text composition by rlf design
Cover design by Brigid Pearson
Cover illustration by Lisa Henderling

acknowledgments

The authors would like to give special thanks to the following people whose generous contributions, creative genius, and enduring support made Romentics possible: our photographers (Bob Ward, Blakely Crawford, Amy O'Connor, and Marilyn Humphries); our design team (Rob Tighe, Jamie Allison, and Alla Litovchenko); our agent, June Clark; our editors, John Aherne and Emily Griffin; and our official Romentics artist, Michael Breyette (http://www.studio1088.com).

hot sauce

hot sauce

1

Brad Drake woke up to a wet dream: Troy Boston stood at the foot of his bed. His torso was bare. His hair was wet. He was wearing nothing but a plush red towel wrapped around his waist.

Droplets strayed down between his broad shoulders and into the small of his back. As he ran his hands through his thick dark hair, his shoulder muscles rippled. The reflection in the full-length mirror at the foot of the bed showed Troy's broad chest narrowing in a V to a tiny wasplike waist a gay man half his size would have killed for.

Two years ago, a vision of Troy at the foot of his bed might have been a masturbatory fantasy or an idle daydream. Impossible and unattainable. Something Brad had cooked up to get himself off after another night in the bed alone.

It wouldn't have crossed Brad's mind back then that he could get a piece of Troy Boston—or anyone even half as hot. He had pretty much given up trying. In fact, in those dark days, Brad had sworn off gay men forever, believing each and every one to be a liar and a crook, shallow and cruel. They were living, breathing, walking advertisements for the joys of a celibate life.

Troy continued to fuss with his thick, coarse hair in the mirror on the wall at the base of Brad's bed. He slicked his palms with gel and ruthlessly shaped the mane that—he complained—never obeyed him. It took him a full five minutes of work before he was satisfied.

To Brad, Troy looked just fine—before, after, or during the arranging of his hair. It didn't make a bit of difference to Brad. Troy looked hot every which way. Any time of day.

As he tugged the last recalcitrant locks into position, Troy caught Brad's lustful look in the mirror's reflection. He flashed a half smile at the mirror. Then he turned toward Brad, who sprawled comfortably in their bed. A sheet was twisted around one arm as if he was in bondage. His brown hair was tousled. One of his feet stuck out beneath the covers at the bottom of the bed.

A rush of guilty pleasure raised the bedclothes like a tent over his crotch.

"You peeking?" Troy teased.

Brad nodded. He had never been much good at hiding his feelings. His body betrayed him: his anger, his passions were all right on the surface, raw and available.

He couldn't help it. He was a chef, and being a chef was all about display, about revealing the secret flavors that lurked in food. He was not one of those cool cucumbers who wore a mask twenty-four-seven.

Troy let the towel on his waist drop. The morning light falling into the room put his abs and pecs and nipples into perfect relief.

Brad gasped, as if it was the first time he had seen what was hidden beneath. Troy was a magnificent specimen of manhood. At thirty-three, three years older than Brad, he had the firm, hard stomach of a high school athlete. His muscles were naturally lean and ropy; he was strong, but he had none of the false bulk of a steroid queen.

Troy playfully let a hand drop to his crotch. Although they had been together almost two years, the size of Troy's member never failed to surprise Brad. Troy tensed. His cock twitched obediently.

Brad's mouth went dry. His penis throbbed. Hunger rose up from a place deep inside him, an animal hunger, basic and carnal.

The muscles of Troy's belly wrestled one another like animals under a blanket. And the thin treasure trail from navel to crotch seemed positively alive.

All thought rushed out of Brad's head. He threw back the covers. "Quickie?"

Troy laughed. He picked up the wet towel from the floor and threw it at Brad.

"Not today, sweetheart. It's Friday. I've got a breakfast meeting with the investors and a dog-and-pony show this morning with the mayor to talk about the Club. Only three months until the target date for our grand opening, remember?"

Being business partners and opening a club together were exciting developments in their relationship. But Brad wished they focused as much on their romantic connection as they did on being business partners.

Troy's fine, firm ass pranced into the hallway and disappeared. Even though they didn't officially live together, Brad had turned over the hall closet to Troy to store a few things, so that he did not have to go home every morning to change. Brad was looking forward to the day when they would share a bedroom with enough closet space for the both of them. That would be the day he would have the luxury of watching Troy dress each morning, bare-ass in the sunlight.

Brad touched himself beneath the sheets. The thought of sharing a home contented him. It was a feeling less urgent than the animal desire that had just coursed through his veins. It possessed a richer, fuller flavor. A long, round finish. Hints of chocolate and berry. Pinot noir. A whiff of something evergreen.

Brad often thought of love and sex and relationships in terms of flavors. Sharp, piquant encounters on the beach in the summer with a new friend were a kind of sweet mango salsa. The return to the bedroom of a comfortable ex-lover for a little backsliding was slow comfort food with hot barbecue sauce. The bruising yelp of being with a big man had all the subtlety of a thick piece of beef, nearly raw, and tender on the inside.

Brad closed his eyes, dozing in half sleep, laughing at himself for being so goofy.

What was Troy, he mused, in this world of flavors? Red-hot Creole? Succulent lobster? Braised lamb with mint at the end of a tired day?

All the labels fit to some extent. But none was quite right. Brad had not found the culinary match that captured Troy Boston. Troy was elusive that way. Making love with him was like making love with many different men, all with the same face and perfect body. Brad never knew what the flavor of the day might be.

All he knew was that Troy had the ability to make him randier than a high-school cheerleader at homecoming. And at the same time, to make him feel like the most important person in the world. Brad was—in a word—crazy about Troy Boston.

"You dreaming about food again, pretty boy?" Troy whispered. He was leaning over the bed, his lips to Brad's ear. His breath sent little electric sparks all over Brad's skin. His distinctly male scent at close range brought Brad fully awake. "It's giving you another hard-on."

Brad's eyes popped open. He had dozed off.

"I was thinking of you."

"Liar."

Troy trapped Brad in the bedclothes. He stroked Brad's head with his large, strong hands. The palms were cool and smelled of cologne and soap. He put a finger on Brad's lips and Brad suddenly opened his mouth and bit it, gently, holding it between his teeth.

"I don't know how you stay so skinny when you think about food every second of the day," Troy wondered. "And night. I would be a fat-ass if I did that."

It was a lie. Troy Boston would never be a fat-ass, no matter how long he lived or what he ate. He could swallow six Big Macs and never gain an ounce. And he could go without food for three days and never notice the difference.

And, Brad thought, I am not exactly skinny. Not fat either—well-toned and developed, a little stocky, with good shoulders and, he prided himself, a flawless gymnast's chest. And Tour de France thighs. But unlike Troy, Brad had to work his ass off in the gym to get and keep the body he wanted.

"Why do you think I was dreaming about food?"

"You get this fat lusty baby look on your face," Troy teased. "Drooling. Content."

"Sounds sexy."

"Trust me, honey. There's enough sexy about you to make a half dozen boys happy."

Troy kissed him on the forehead and stood. Brad glowed, and ran an appreciative eye over his boyfriend. Troy was hot naked, but he could peg the mercury in the thermometer even when he was fully dressed. Today, he was wearing a charcoal pin-striped three-button flannel suit that perfectly complimented his slim, muscular figure.

"You look hot."

Troy nodded. His confidence was not arrogance. He had designed the suit himself, so it damn well better look hot. It was part of the Troy Boston label and would have cost a mint at retail in one of Troy's stores. Troy prided himself on never wearing another designer's clothes, although he made an exception for Prada.

"You going to come over tonight after work?" he asked.

It was not really a question. One of Troy's great talents was his ability to get people to follow his commands without even knowing they had been commanded.

Brad nodded.

Troy smiled, turned, and then blew a quick kiss over his shoulder. "Wish me luck."

"Luck."

Then Troy was gone. He bounded down the stairs of the condominium two at a time. The outside door slammed shut behind him with a sound that rattled the whole building. The apartment was suddenly as still as the dead, as if Troy had taken all the energy in it away with him.

Brad sighed. "Luck" was not what he would have preferred to say as a last word when they parted in the morning. Brad would have liked to say, "I love you." Or better yet: "Be late to meet the mayor and make love to me."

But "I love you" was an expression they never used. If Brad had pushed him for a declaration of love, Troy would have gotten all squirrelly. Troy spoke eloquently enough with his body and lips and hands. He was quick with a compliment and a reassuring touch. He might have pointed out that actions were more important than three words that were easy to say but hard to mean.

Troy never mentioned love. He never said so much as "You make me happy." He never revealed a trembling lip or eyes filled with tears. He was focused, hard, and exquisitely controlled. His cheekbones were dark and angular and his forehead was honest, but his penetrating eyes never gave up a secret. He was a fortress, absolutely impregnable when it came to his feelings.

This sexy unavailability only made Brad want him all the more. He plotted constantly about how he would taste that forbidden fruit hidden inside the walls that surrounded Troy's heart.

Someday, he vowed, Troy would surrender control, break, and confess his love. And that day, Brad would be waiting to embrace Troy and be his forever.

Brad snuggled into the flannel sheets, which were as deep and soft as blankets. He tested the pillow beside him for a quick hit of Troy's animal smell. He inhaled deeply, and again won that deep contented feeling that told him he was the luckiest man in the world. Everything he wanted would come. Spring in Boston was right around the corner. He just needed to give Troy time. The two years they had been together were not (yet) enough.

Brad rolled over to try to get more sleep. Unlike Troy, four hours' sleep was not enough to tide Brad over. Fifteen hours would have been nice. Followed by breakfast in bed and a full-body massage by six sculpted members of the United States swim team in their tiny blue Speedos.

2

Seconds later, the alarm bleated six inches from Brad's head.

BEEP! BEEP! BEEP!

Brad groaned and swatted at the clock. He knocked it clear across the room, where it bleated in the corner, happily unchecked.

"Make it stop!" Brad cried out, holding his pillow around his ears to drown out the sound. His wish did not come true.

Finally, with his body screaming for more sleep, Brad hauled his sorry carcass out of bed and kicked the alarm off. Then he dragged himself in front of the mirror, where Troy had stood hours before, and contemplated the damage to his body that had been done by aging overnight.

It could have been worse. Years in a steamy kitchen had not yet put a line in Brad's good skin. (The secret was eye cream, applied religiously, morning and night.) He had broad shoulders and Popeye forearms, a powerful wrestler's build, and a lean-meat body, courtesy of regular torturous workouts with a personal trainer who had interned at a Siberian death camp.

Brad's hair was brown and naturally spiked from sleep, and he again decided he would put some color in it for the summer. He regularly decided this, year after year, spring after spring, and then chickened out when summer arrived. He calculated that an inch or two of extra height would have been nice, but to his chagrin the night's sleep had not produced such a change.

Despite his general satisfaction, Brad thought he detected a little pudge that had not been present the day before. It was right there, above his hip. And chubbing around toward the back above his boxers.

Before the fat could get hold, he decided, he needed to destroy it. Four hundred sit-ups. Four sets of pull-ups. Four hundred push-ups. And dumbbells. By the end, his shoulders and arms hung dead at his sides like slabs of beef in a meat locker. It was only after this whole process that Brad permitted himself even to look at his refrigerator.

Troy constantly teased Brad about his kitchen because—although Brad was the top-rated chef in Boston and maybe the country—his own kitchen contained only a case of springwater, a can of tuna, and some stale high-protein cereal. Nothing more. The refrigerator was a desert. The granite countertops were immaculate and the utensils were in perfect order on racks to the right of the commercial-grade Viking stove, but this tidy, stainless arrangement only emphasized its barrenness.

Brad would have loved to get more use out of that kitchen. He would have loved a long Saturday to cook a meal that only he and Troy would share. To light candles and decant a fine Barolo into the flared crystal Riedel decanter that was stored upside-down and unused in its rack. Serve up a meal personalized and seasoned with his love for Troy.

But even if Troy had had the time, Brad could not spare a Saturday. He had three restaurants to run—Jean-Baptiste, Cheval, and Coriander—and was busy consulting with Troy on a fourth restaurant that was part of the new Club Troy. These restaurants needed more maintenance than the worst of boyfriends. Indeed, even as Brad took a break from his workout, his cell phone chortled, right on schedule.

A quick glance at the number showed him it was Turner Page, Brad's best friend and business partner. Turner was a big, soft-spoken, religious African-American man. People tended to respect him on sight. He was generally warm and open, with a craggy smile and an immense, playful intelligence.

But Turner was a very private person. The moment a stranger innocently probed too far into his private affairs, he became perilously still and completely expressionless. His face went dead calm and grave, and—always with glacial politeness—he would simply decline to answer the too-intimate questions.

Only with Brad did Turner permit himself the comfortable gossip and dish of two old friends, who were as close as brothers. Even though they no longer shared the same roof, like they had during the early days at Borneo Bistro, they did share the same business, and Brad trusted Turner as he trusted no one else on earth, even Troy.

"Yo," Brad said.

"Yo yourself. You want the bad news or the real bad news?" It was the same thing Turner said every morning. He lived for pessimism, a habit Turner felt he had earned, the way things tended to turn out.

"Give it to me straight, bro."

As Brad munched a couple of handfuls of protein cereal and washed it down with water, they went through the morning routine. Personnel matters, purchasing, and the multitude of other obligatory details of running a restaurant that Brad hated because they took his mind off the food.

If Brad was the heart of his kitchens, Turner provided the brains and muscle. He was manager, minority owner, and all-around hard-ass. He was tireless and exacting, as fanatical and obsessive as Brad himself. Brad ensured that not a single dish went to the dining room floor until he had inspected it and made sure it was flawless. Turner handled the other end of the process. Nothing entered any of Brad's kitchens unless Turner had given his personal approval that the goods were fresh and of the highest quality.

Bored by the discussion of budgets and projections, Brad picked a dumbbell up from the floor and grunted as he worked through a set of curls.

"Am I interrupting you?" Turner snapped. "If you need some time by yourself . . . ?"

"Just making sure the pipes look good. You never know when the UPS man is going to show up with an urgent package," Brad joked.

"You're so hung up on that man of yours, you wouldn't know what to do with a UPS man if he threw himself on you."

Turner could see right through Brad, and they both knew it, but Brad wasn't going to let Turner get the satisfaction of showing him up.

"I can take Troy or leave him," he lied.

Turner laughed out loud. "It's been what? Almost two years of taking, as far as I can see, hasn't it? That's all you do."

"Two years last month," Brad said proudly. "And I don't just take it, Turner. Sometimes Troy's the bottom."

"Whoa, mister. WTMI. Way too much information. I don't need no full-color glossy pics, you know what I mean?"

"Deal. So long as I don't have to hear anything about pussy from you."

Turner laughed his deep, comforting laugh, which had not changed in the ten years they had known each other.

"So . . . Last month, eh? You been together two years. Well, time flies, doesn't it?"

"Yeah . . ."

"I mean, one day you're in here bragging about how you finally conquered your dream man who can't do no wrong, and now it's two years later and you come in every day bitching about where this relationship is going."

"I do not!"

In fact, Brad had been complaining to Turner that he did not know where he stood in his relationship with Troy. But this was just garden-variety bitchery. About as necessary to a gay man like Brad as breathing. It meant absolutely nothing. In fact, Troy was, as far as Brad could see, devoted to their relationship, certainly above and beyond anyone else he had dated.

It wasn't perfect, of course. The absence of "I love you" or any other tangible sign of long-term commitment was a problem. And that's why Brad had been venting.

Brad understood, of course, what he was fighting against: Troy was damaged goods. Troy had already been in love, and it had ended badly. Kurt Tamweiler, the man Troy had lived with for five years, had been killed in a polo accident when he was thrown from his horse. And Troy never spoke of Kurt.

Instead, Troy made periodic speeches about how you had to plant your own garden because no one else was going to bring you flowers. Brad would never hear from him the words "I can't live without you."

If Brad harbored any romantic ideas that Troy was his true love and destiny, and vice versa, he had to keep them on the back burner. He had to acknowledge that Troy might already have had the love of his life.

Or maybe work was the love of his life. Maybe Brad was only third. However much it hurt to comprehend this, it was a concept he had to face if he wanted to stay with Troy. Troy might not want anything deeper than an amiable companionship, a deep friendship with benefits. It remained to be seen.

But that was too much serious thought this early in Brad's morning, and he knew Turner was only busting his balls.

"When I bitch about my boyfriend, Turner, it's just to make you feel needed. I know you straight people. You always need to live vicariously through us gays, because our lives are much more fabulous. Now, what about that order of new stemware you said was coming in from Ireland?"

"You changing the subject on me?"

"I'm just saying—"

"You trying to hide something from me, Brad?"

"No, I—"

"I think you are," Turner accused playfully. "It's that you didn't invite Jacqueline and me to your anniversary party, isn't it? We aren't good enough to get an invite now that you are hangin' with all the rich white folks your boyfriend *does* love? I'll remember that."

"There was no anniversary party," Brad retorted. "It's next month, Mr. Know-it-all."

"Next month? I thought you said last month was your anniversary. What's up with that?"

Brad sighed. "Yeah, well, that was my reaction. But Caroline was busy then. She operates on her own schedule. So if Caroline wants to change the date of our anniversary, it gets changed."

Caroline Treadwell was Troy's mother. She had long since accepted—even prided herself on—the fact that her son was gay. Her problem was that she had never met a man who was good enough for Troy—except for Kurt Tamweiler. And Caroline was not shy about showing it. In fact, there would have been no celebration of their anniversary at all—by Troy or his mother—if Caroline didn't pounce on any excuse to throw a party.

Turner grunted. "You sound whipped, son. By your mother-in-law of all people."

"Yeah, well, maybe. But I figure, when you're gay, how do you measure an anniversary anyway, right, Turner? I mean, is it the first time you met? When you fucked? It's all arbitrary anyway, since we couldn't even get married until recently. Personally, I mark the anniversary as the time when you moved in together."

"Well, that explains it," Turner crowed triumphantly. His voice was filled with satisfaction at having solved some mystery.

"Explains what? Why is it every time you sound pleased with yourself, I feel like I've got to start worrying?"

"It explains the rumors."

"What rumors?"

"Rumor has it," Turner insinuated slowly, "that you and Mr. Big Shot are going to be moving in together any day now."

Brad panicked and bluffed. "No. No. Nothing to that rumor. I don't know where you get your info, Turner."

"So, it's not true?"

"Hey, don't worry, Turner. I'll keep you posted if something like that ever happens. You know how Troy is."

"I know how you are, too, mister. You don't quit until you get what you want."

Brad sighed. "I might have to accept second best on this one, Turner."

"Bullshit!" Turner bullied. "You haven't accepted squat. I heard you were up in the South End looking at penthouse condos like you were already hitched! You're still going for the whole nine yards."

Damn! Brad thought. He complained, "Stop throwing these football analogies at me, Turner. I'm gay. I don't understand them. You know that."

Brad was speechless at being found out so quickly. These excursions around the South End had been his own little secret fantasy. His planning ahead. Maybe wishful thinking.

He hadn't the courage yet to mention househunting to Troy. Or Turner. Or his faghag Chessie. Or a damn soul, except his real estate agent.

But it was impossible to keep anything from Turner. Turner had connections to everybody in Boston. No matter what the field or line of work was, Turner knew someone on the inside—including real estate agents, apparently.

But Brad was not going to admit a thing.

"Troy and I are hitched at the waist, Turner," he joked. "That's about it. Trust me, I know how these things go." Brad had to pretend everything was cool, so as not to jinx it. The last thing he needed was to do the Troy-go-round again, which had kept him up enough nights.

"Man! I thought we had an agreement that I didn't need to be hearing about anything below the waist?"

"It must be your lucky day."

"So, seriously, man, you sure we should not be expecting any wedding bells soon?"

"Turner, drop it. Please. I promise—you'll be the first to know."

"Fair enough. Good things come to those who wait. So, when's the party? Are me and Jacqueline going to get an invitation to the big anniversary celebration?"

"Yeah, unless Caroline succeeds in the meantime in her long-standing plan to break up Troy and me."

"No way, man. I'm sure she's proud to have you in the family. You're a real catch."

"Trust me, Turner. Not in Caroline's eyes. No one's good enough for Troy."

"You're worth a hundred Troys," Turner said loyally.

Brad didn't object. "Maybe. But regardless, Caroline does like parties, so she's commandeered this one. It's out of my hands. Caroline is in charge. It's probably best that way."

"You don't sound so sure."

"Well, hell, Turner, if I was planning it, you and Jacqueline— and maybe Chessie—would be the only people I'd invite."

Turner chuckled softly. "Well," he said. "You want equal rights, you got 'em—wouldn't be the first mother of the bride to take over a wedding."

"I told you, it's not a wed— Oh, damn!" Brad caught sight of the kitchen clock. "I'm gonna be late! Caroline's never going to let me hear the end of it."

3

Club Troy was Troy's idea. All the best ideas were. Ever since Troy transformed his family's staid clothing business into a multinational fashion empire at the ripe age of nineteen, he had been at the cutting edge of the Boston scene. Millennial raves. A fashion boutique on Boston's toniest retail thoroughfare, Newbury Street, where he was nestled between Armani and DKNY. An Internet presence, mail-order marketing to the gay.com crowd. Troy Boston was an exclusive, upscale brand—New York with touches of New England and Milan—and always at the front of the pack.

Troy's latest venture, Club Troy, had been built in an old opera house that in the sixties and seventies had been an X-rated theater in Boston's old Combat Zone.

The lurid history inspired Troy. He had preserved as much of the red-velvet atmosphere as he could. They'd torn out the seats and terraced the sloped floor that led to the stage.

Troy had designed a hip restaurant with live music and a martini bar in the early evening. Brad was to be the executive chef of the restaurant. At 11 P.M., the tables would glide away and a rack of club lights would descend from the ceiling. The DJ would take up a spot in one of the old opera boxes on the second tier so the glitterati could party until dawn.

Critics thought it was an unlikely combination. But Troy had spent the last ten years proving time and again that nobody spotted trends sooner than he did. And he enthused privately to Brad, "I've been looking for ways for us to work together. How great would that be!"

Now that the club's opening was imminent, the key was to reassure City Hall that Club Troy was really a desirable thing in that up-and-coming neighborhood. There were palms to press and campaign contributions to promise and egos to stroke.

No one did that better than Troy. Flattery and social skills were both a God-given talent and a fine art to him. He had been born to the life of the rich and powerful. His family had a long pedigree in Boston politics. They were one of the few old blue-blood Yankee families that had managed to retain some political clout in a city overrun with colorful Irish Catholic political powerbrokers, who could charm and ruin you in the same breath.

The matriarch of Troy's family was Lady Caroline, Troy's mother, who was already seated at their table in the Carlyle Restaurant in the Copley Hotel.

"Oh, *there* you are, Brad dear," she said pointedly. Her voice dripped with petulant, highbrow condescension. She managed to convey contempt more clearly than if she had spat in Brad's face. "We had been wondering whatever happened to you, that you would keep us waiting for half an hour. We were *so* worried."

He was, of course, only five minutes late. But Caroline took some perverse pleasure out of embarrassing Brad. It was what she did for a hobby. Even this meeting at the Carlyle was one of her insulting games: Brad's restaurant, Cheval, was only two blocks away. Some people collect stamps; some people read romance novels. Caroline tortured her son's boyfriends.

"Hello, Mrs. Treadwell."

Without rising from her seat at the table, she let Brad give her an air kiss. A waft of her perfume, delicately applied, was like a whisper in his ear. As always, she looked stunning. Her face had only the faintest lines and her breasts and calves were firm. She wore a skirt and smart jacket with a belle époque silhouette that looked like signature Troy Boston. It would have been a lot easier to hate her if she gave him more material to work with, but Caroline was the personification of perfection. Right shoes, right hat, right son.

"Brad," Caroline said, "this is Aria Shakespeare. He is going to be the creative director on this new campaign for the opening of Club Troy."

For the first time, Brad glanced at his other lunch companion. He immediately wished he had not.

Aria was exactly Troy's type. He looked about twenty-five years old, his skin as unblemished as a twelve-year-old's, with the red bloom of youth in his cheeks. He wore a tourniquet-tight, long-tailed, long-sleeved shirt. The shirt's main body and piping were navy blue but the sleeves were bright orange. His pants sagged and hung loose. His hair was skillfully untended, bleach-blond. He wore a pair of square-rimmed black glasses to try to make himself look older, artsy, and more sophisticated.

"Haven't we met?" Brad asked. Something distinctly familiar about the boy's face jogged his memory. He thought: I've met a hundred boys like you. Dime-a-dozen, dishwasher-safe white trash.

Caroline snorted. "Oh, I don't think so. Aria does not run in your sort of circle, Bradley."

"My circle?"

She had the grace to blush. "You know. Food service."

"Pleased to meet you," Aria said, extending a limber hand. His manners were those of a boy who had been raised in a fancy suburban country club.

"Likewise," grumbled Brad.

"You're older than I thought."

"And you're younger."

"Thank you."

"What do *you* know about marketing?"

"Bradley," Caroline gushed. "Really. Aria is an *expert* in marketing. He comes highly recommended. All the best people use him. And his family is the best. Absolutely wonderful woman, his mother. We were at Smith together."

"Oh," Brad said. He stared at Aria again. "Are you sure we haven't met?"

Aria met Brad's look with a level gaze, interrupted only by the cocktail server, who breezed up to the table inquiring whether they might wish for another drink.

"That's it," Brad said, and slapped the linen-covered table, startling the cocktail server. He pointed an accusing finger Aria's way. "I *knew* I'd met you before."

For the first time, Brad thought he saw the slightest bit of alarm in Aria's chilly, pale blue aristocratic eyes, and it made him feel good. He continued on. "You applied for a position at Coriander. Last month."

Brad remembered that he had turned Aria down. He did not hire trash. Flirts, yes. Attitude, no.

Aria flushed but did not immediately answer. He ordered a Pellegrino and only then deigned to take notice of Brad. "Did you say something?" he asked.

"I was just remembering that you had applied for work at one of my restaurants. Coriander."

"Not me, sister. You've obviously mistaken me for someone else. You wouldn't catch me working at Coriander. No offense."

Aria sipped from his drink, and there was no doubt the offense was intended, the remark made to sting.

"My bad," Brad grumbled, pretending he did not give a shit. He lowered himself into his seat. "It must have been somebody else."

"Must have," Aria said.

Inside, Brad's stomach churned. He was proud of what he did, it was a noble calling, and fuck Aria if he did not see it, these god-damn rich kids pissed him off to no end, what the fuck did they know?

Brad ordered a cocktail. Caroline raised her eyebrows but said nothing. Instead, she pointedly requested a mineral water. While they waited for the drinks, Aria and Caroline gossiped about people Brad didn't know.

The whole exchange pissed him off. That was the thing with rich people: You could not get under their skin. They were so god-damn sure of their own superiority, you could be rubbing their face in their own shit, and still they could shoot a look that made you feel six inches high.

Aria was animated and charming. He whispered naughty things that made Caroline feel attractive. He touched Caroline lightly on the forearm from time to time as they talked, and shared gales of laughter with her at the stories she told in her ferocious Boston Brahmin deadpan.

But even as he watched the performance, Brad felt like there was another face to Aria Shakespeare. He felt sure that the applicant they had turned down at Coriander had been him. It must have been him—Brad made a mental note to check the files of résumés and applications, to see what the story was.

As they sipped their drinks, Aria produced a sketchbook. He set it on the table between him and Caroline and began to explain the various concepts he had come up with for a Troy-Brad "brand."

Brad tuned out. He had already decided that this partnership between him and Caroline Treadwell—and her fancy country club designer boy Aria—was not going to work out.

Instead, Brad slugged back his Scotch and soda and scoured his competitor's menu from top to bottom. He was pleased to see that his own menus at Cheval, Jean-Baptiste, *and* Coriander were generally superior. Still, he bowed to his competitor's tarte tatin, which, he allowed, sounded scrumptious.

"Are you listening, Brad dear?" Caroline asked imperiously.

Brad looked up, startled. "Of course, Caroline."

He folded away the menu. Aria turned a bemused smile on him, as if he had caught Brad masturbating.

"This is *important*," Caroline stressed. She spoke to him as if he were someone else's unpleasant and incorrigible child.

Before Brad could dispute the point's importance, the waiter arrived. The timing was good, he thought. If there was any topic that he had a better command of than Caroline did, it was food and wine.

Brad made a show of quizzing the waiter on the origin and preparation of the sea scallops with pequillo pepper brandade and parsley puree. He ended up ordering a Galway oyster broth with dill and tomato instead, as well as a grilled portobello mushroom tower and a broiled steak in wine sauce. He paired these with a glass of Nozzole Chianti Reserva.

Caroline ordered a garden salad. "No dressing," she advised with pursed lips, not bothering so much as to grace the waiter with a glance as she handed him the menu.

Aria made the same choice. Both of them looked back at Brad pointedly, as if their spare choices were more virtuous than his.

The bitch, he thought. She wasn't even going to bow to his superior knowledge in the field they could all agree he knew better. Not Caroline. If she was not at the top of the class, then the class was not worth taking.

Brad swirled the ice cubes in his cocktail glass. As Aria turned the pages of his sketchpad for Caroline, they amused each other with untempered enthusiasm for all his ideas. Brad would never have thought that he could share a café table with two people and still feel as if he were in a different time zone.

Caroline suddenly burst out in a peel of controlled laughter. "Did you hear that, Brad dear? Isn't Aria brilliant?"

"No, sorry." Brad smiled with tight lips. "I missed it."

Caroline frowned. Aria looked smug.

"I was telling Caroline that a Trojan Horse would be the perfect emblem for Club Troy." When Brad failed to be impressed with Aria's brilliance, Aria pressed, "Get it? Troy? Trojan? *Trojan?*"

"He doesn't get it," Caroline explained.

"Horse? Cheval?" Aria persisted.

"I get it," Brad snapped. "I was just trying to decide if I liked it." Actually, he did like it. A lot. But he was damned if he was going to give Aria the satisfaction. Or Caroline.

"It's all right," Caroline consoled Aria. "It's absolutely the thing. The very thing we need." She glanced at Brad, and then back at Aria. "It would be so much better for the club if you were more involved, Aria."

Aria adopted a look suitable for a puppy that was being stroked on its tummy.

"You have that innate sense for what works. Your mother," Caroline concluded, "brought you up just right."

"Well," Aria allowed, "of course I am available as you and Troy need, Caroline. It's the least I could do." Their eyes met conspiratorially. And then Aria added, "And, of course, you, too, Brad."

"Hey, don't put yourself out on my account," Brad shot back.

The oyster broth came and went. It was delicious. The broiled steak had been rubbed with sazon, paprika, salt, and lemon pepper, doused in wine, and broiled rare. The food was a welcome distraction from his dining companions, who did not seem interested in his opinions in any case. He concentrated fully on gorging himself.

"Brad, dear, slow down, we wouldn't want you to choke," Caroline admonished. But she sounded as if she would not mind if he choked just a little.

It was a pleasant interruption to the stilted conversation when Brad was finally recognized by someone on the staff. The Carlyle's chef—Brad's fiercest competitor, Paul Jenkins—swept out of the kitchen in too-white toque and apron. He wore a bold, triumphant, shit-eating grin.

"I'm glad to see you've finally discovered Boston's finest dining experience," Jenkins said, smirking.

"Nah, just slumming."

"Bradley! How rude!"

"Caroline, please. We're old friends, that's how we talk in the biz." Caroline sniffed loudly.

Encouraged by Caroline's interjection, Jenkins introduced himself. Neither Aria nor Caroline could be bothered to muster more than a polite smile for him. They quickly turned back to their urgent conversation, like a pair of conspirators, and pretended that Jenkins was not lingering.

Embarrassed by the snub, Brad pulled Jenkins aside. He complimented him on the food and exchanged a little dish on the restaurant business. It was a much-needed relief from the company of Caroline and Aria.

Jenkins, however, kept looking over his shoulder, his feelings obviously hurt.

"Who's the twink?" Jenkins asked. "I thought you were hot and heavy with Troy Boston."

"I am," Brad explained. "It's business." Then he rolled his eyes, indicating Caroline, who was chewing out the waiter for some imagined slight. "That's Troy's mother."

"His mother!" Jenkins rolled his eyes. "You're a brave man. She's a goddamn ice queen."

By the time they were done talking, Caroline and Aria had gathered up the sketches and their coats and bags.

"Well, darling, I think we've got some great work to start with here." She beamed at Aria. "As usual, Aria."

Aria did all but offer her a little curtsy.

Then Caroline turned her eyes on Brad, and they rested heavily there, full of judgment.

After a moment, she said, "Aria and Troy were at Drovers together. Although, of course, Aria is *much* younger. And Aria's mother is a dear old friend. We were at Smith together."

"You told me that."

"Did I?" she asked vaguely.

"What's Drovers?"

Caroline sniffed and laid a hand on Aria's forearm for balance, as if she might faint from shock. Brad had known many drama queens in his day, but Caroline topped them all.

"Drovers?" Aria volunteered. "It's only the most prestigious riding school in the United States."

"Oh."

"Haven't you even heard of it?"

Brad shook his head. Where he was from, you learned to ride in your backyard, if at all. He knew nothing about fancy riding schools. Hell, he had not even known that Troy rode horses. Apparently, Brad reflected, there was a lot of Troy that Brad did not know as well as he thought he did.

Troy had certainly never mentioned Aria. Or, for that matter, said much about any of the many lovers who must have preceded Brad at Troy's side, least of all Kurt Tamweiler.

With Troy, it was don't ask, don't tell. And this was even after Brad had spilled the beans, going through the litany of bad boyfriends that had been his life.

Finally rising from his seat, Aria said, "It was a pleasure to meet you, Brad. I've heard, um"—he flashed a look at Caroline—"*so* much about you." It sounded like what Aria had heard was not very impressive. And that the real-life experience had not even lived up to that low standard.

Turning to Caroline, Aria put the gentlest of kisses on her cheek. "Good-bye, Mrs. Treadwell. So good to see you again, dear. I'll give Mum your best."

"Do that . . . and remind her we've got a tennis date next Thursday!"

Caroline watched him leave the room with her hands clasped in front of her ample chest. She sighed. "What a lovely boy! He's like a son to me, you know."

"No, I didn't know that." Brad reached for the folder containing Aria's various sketches and proposals, which still lay on the linen tablecloth.

Like a cat, Caroline pounced on them before he could.

"Not so fast, Brad dear. It didn't look like you were particularly interested in Aria's work. Why don't I take care of explaining it to Troy? I don't want to trouble you with too much information. I mean, you've got your *cooking* to do."

She made his vocation sound as unappealing as dishwashing. Then she smiled grimly and marched off, barking something to the coat-check girl. By the time Brad managed to control his impulse to tell her off, she had slipped into a cab and driven off.

Brad sighed.

Troy, he thought, you better be glad I love you enough to put up with *that* bitch.

4

There was no Drovers where Brad came from. His hometown was Durgin City, Iowa. Population: 1231 souls. Sixteen separate churches and a hundred or so functioning farms. The greatest celebrity in Durgin City was the local minister, and Friday night, high school football was the primary source of entertainment.

Never having fit in with the 4-H crowd, Brad bolted town at seventeen. He had made his way east with a duffel bag and no fixed plan, taking rides from dirty old men who wanted to get in his pants and lonely Christian truck drivers eager to give him a lesson on God and life and everything in between. Brad had ended up in Boston, primarily because Route 90 came to a stop at the Atlantic Ocean and there was no way to hitch a ride across the sea.

He found a room at the YMCA and got himself a job bussing tables at a restaurant called Borneo Bistro. After a few weeks, one of the other bussers, a black boy his age named Turner Page, felt sorry for Brad and offered him the spare couch in his mother's apartment.

Brad's only ambition in those days was to make enough to give Turner's mother something toward the rent. If he had anything left over, he blew it on gay and after-hours clubs with coworkers from Borneo. At the time, Brad's only glimpse of the lifestyle that Troy lived was when guests drifted into Borneo, draped in smart suits, diamonds, and fur. They casually sipped their cocktails and dropped a month of Brad's take-home pay on dinner.

During the four years he worked his way up the ladder at Borneo, Brad often listened to the conversations at the rich people's tables. He heard talk of jewels and benefits and yachts and corporate raids and stock deals.

To Brad, they seemed like something not human. Not like him. They seemed self-possessed and sophisticated and knowledgeable in ways Brad did not think he would ever be. He was scared to death to be around them. He tried to be as small and unobtrusive as possible, going about his business clearing the tables and filling water glasses in a nearly invisible way.

It never occurred to Brad at the time that some of these rich older people were gay. Or that they might have any interest in his corn-fed Midwestern body. And he thereby squandered opportunities to win extra tips just by throwing an extra smile an old man's way. He worked with his eyes glued to the floor and tried to avoid being noticed.

That is, until he laid eyes on Troy Boston that first time nine years ago.

Brad would never forget it. He had been out back having a smoke. The maître d' sat Troy and four or five other men at the best table in the house. It was near the window and commanded a view of the whole restaurant.

Each of the men with Troy was immaculately groomed and handsome. Their hands were powerful yet manicured. Troy was seated facing away from the kitchen door. His fabulous ass was hidden by the jacket slung over the back of the chair, so he had not immediately caught Brad's attention when he came back from his break.

It was only after Brad cleared a table on the far side of the one where Troy sat that an uproarious laugh made him look up. His eyes fixed on Troy's face. Fixed and held.

The smooth, unlined brow. The high, angular cheekbones. The strong chin. The dark eyes that were like mirrors and that possessed a maturity that belied Troy's then-twenty-four years.

Troy was the most beautiful man Brad had ever laid eyes on. He was so damn beautiful that Brad fumbled with the serving tray. A teapot clattered to the floor, making a resounding hollow crash that brought conversation throughout the entire restaurant to a stop.

When Brad bent to retrieve the errant teapot, his towel fell from his apron to the floor. And yet, despite his horror and embarrassment at the commotion, Brad was unable to remove his eyes from that stunning, obscenely beautiful face. He fumbled around on the dining floor, blindly seeking the items he'd dropped.

Most of the restaurant's patrons looked at Brad's noisy clattering with disdain. But not Troy. Troy was used to being looked at and fawned over. He simply reached over from his seat, scooped up the lost towel, and tucked it playfully back in Brad's apron with a wink and a kind smile.

"Thanks," Brad managed to say.

Troy inclined his head. "You're very welcome."

Brad stood frozen and rooted for what seemed like an eternity, until Troy returned to the conversation at his table. Humiliated and thrilled, Brad scurried back to the kitchen. He felt as if he had not drawn a breath in a full three minutes.

"What's wrong with you, man?" Turner asked. "Even for a white boy, you're pale as a ghost."

"I can't believe he spoke to me."

"Who?"

"My husband. My future husband." Brad pushed Turner up to

the kitchen's swinging door, budged it a crack, and pointed out the beautiful rich young man sitting at Borneo's best table. "Isn't he gorgeous? I think I'm in love."

"Oh, for God's sake, you're always in love," Turner snapped. And it was perfectly true. Since he had moved to Boston, Brad had been in virtually constant love, one after another, with guys who weren't worth it.

But Brad liked being in love. He liked being gay, now that he had left Iowa behind. And sooner or later, he decided, he would fall in love with a man that would love him back. And he was fully ready to dream that man was the man at the table at Borneo, even though he did not yet know his name.

Francesca DeMotta passed with a loaded tray. Francesca, who called herself Chessie, was a Borneo waitress. She was a sexy, lithe, dark-haired nymph. Brad would have been in love with her if he had been straight. She looked at the object of Brad's affection and laughed.

"Don't you know who that is?"

Brad shook his head. Back then, he did not know much about fashion; he was dressed in an apron fifteen hours a day and aspired to a chef's hat and checkered pants. He hadn't a spare dime for so much as a pair of decent club shoes.

Chessie patiently explained who Troy Boston was. And where he was going.

"The man owns Newbury Street," Turner added. "He's got a shop at each end, and his corporate offices high over the city in the Franklin Street Tower."

"Is he married?" Brad asked. "He can't be, he's too young."

"Married? No, man, he's gay."

"He's gay????! You sure?!"

Brad rushed back to the kitchen door and propped it open for another look. It was a dream come true: there was no ring on that manicured but powerful hand. He was gorgeous, absolutely gorgeous.

And gay. Gaygaygaygaygay.

Brad did a little dance in the kitchen and took Chessie on a long tango from one end of the freezer to the other, terrorizing all the Mexican help.

The news and the view would be worth a month of nighttime fantasies. Fantasies of Troy plucking Brad out of his busboy life and bringing him home and being the hottest sugar daddy on the face of the planet.

"Just don't interrupt me in the middle of the night," Brad warned Turner.

Turner looked disgusted. "Don't you make a mess of my mom's couch, bro."

Brad laughed.

And then Turner slipped in the dagger: "But from what I hear he might as well be married, man. Been with a guy for years now. They say it's true love."

All the hopes that had been raised came crashing down among them right there in the kitchen like a trayful of dishes. Brad numbly surrendered Chessie's hands. It was utter heartbreak, and all the sous-chefs made fun of Brad's crestfallen look for many days after.

Brad obsessed over Troy Boston and his own bad luck for weeks, realizing he would never be Troy Boston's boy toy. He plunged into an adolescent tailspin, followed by yet another series of disastrous dates and hookups. When there seemed to be no more boys left in Boston to date and get burned by, Brad poured himself into work instead.

The supreme ruler of the kitchen at Borneo, Chef Jean-Baptiste Roulard, asked Brad one day if he wanted to learn something about food and life. He was a big old queen, and Chessie and

Turner used to joke about Chef Roulard's crush on the much younger Brad.

But Chef Roulard was sweet and nice with Brad rather than creepy. He respected the difference in their ages and experience without relaxing the strict discipline of the kitchen at Borneo a moment. Chef Roulard took Brad under his wing.

Brad used to come into the restaurant early and stay late. He finished all his usual tasks as a busboy, in addition to the lessons he took from the cranky and sometimes contemptuous Chef Roulard. Chef Roulard taught him about food and wine and the pairing of the two. He taught Brad how to use a knife.

Eventually, Chef Roulard demoted Brad from busboy and made him a prep cook. Full-time. At the time, Brad was the only prep cook who spoke passable English, and Chef Roulard browbeat him mercilessly, but he had Brad's best interests at heart; he was cultivating in Brad the taste for perfection that would serve him well when he had restaurants of his own.

After a long trial period, Chef Roulard promoted Brad. When the time was right, he recommended him for culinary arts school and even footed the bill. Before Chef Roulard died of complications from AIDS, he had secured Brad a position as executive chef in one of Boston's better restaurants.

It was the jump start to a meteoric career. Brad was designated a rising culinary star in national magazines. He won the James Beard award for Best Chef Under 30 one year, and the very next he was named the top chef in every category. He socked away cash, splurging only to outfit the kitchen of his humble apartment in the city's South End with a professional stainless kitchen. And he superstitiously fattened his bank account, in case one day the dream was taken away from him by a terrible taste-bud disorder that rendered him unfit to cook.

It didn't take long for the financiers to come looking for him. Boston was a city sadly in need of great restaurants, and Brad soon had one of his own. He called it Jean-Baptiste to honor the man who'd made it possible, and he presided over its kitchen like a little dictator, just as he had been taught to do by Chef Roulard.

The results spoke for themselves: he opened more restaurants, and each was as successful as Jean-Baptiste. There were plans in the works for a cookbook and a line of specialty foods. Invitations to appear on television and talk shows were routine.

But for all that success, something was missing. Brad's life was like bland soup—it needed something more, that key ingredient that would tie in all the other flavors and make it more than just the sum of its elements. Waves of loneliness came and went. Sometimes he thought he would always live alone and his career would be enough to keep him reasonably content. Other times, after all the meals were prepped, and the staff trained, and he could relax a little, he craved a companion so badly that his teeth itched and his groin ached. It was all he could do not to break his vow and resort to a quick fix on the Internet or in the nightclubs.

On one of those tempting, desolate nights, two years ago, Troy Boston had marched into Jean-Baptiste, Brad's flagship restaurant, past the protesting maître d', past the waiter's station. Leaving a trail of hard, hungry gazes and turned heads, Troy marched right into the kitchen, Brad's inner sanctum.

It was hard to fault Troy for his presumption and disregard for etiquette. Though Brad had seen him around Boston after that first time in Borneo, he was surprised all over again by how devastatingly, weak-in-the-knees handsome Troy was.

Troy humbly and apologetically introduced himself by his full name—as if Brad would not be familiar with Boston's most eligible gay bachelor and the ubiquitous founder of the Troy Boston brand. He waxed so poetic about the food at Jean-Baptiste that he made Brad blush, and he held Brad's hand just a little too long after shaking it.

Brad was disconcerted by this barrage of attention. He felt naked. Exposed. He wanted to fend off that burning intensity with a good-sized fry pan. It seemed to him that Troy had somehow divined that Brad had been using him for his masturbatory fantasies since he was twenty-one.

The heat from the stoves made Brad acutely conscious that he had not properly showered, nor even bothered to comb his hair. Brad's eyes kept wandering to Troy's chest, and his mind was actively helping Troy slip out of his shirt. He had to keep dragging his attention back from Troy's body to his face, and he heard hardly a word that came from Troy's mouth. It was all just the ocean-rushing sound you get in a conch shell on the beach.

None of this stopped Troy, who wound up his enthusiastic spiel with a bald pitch to have Jean-Baptiste donate dinner to some nameless charity event of which Troy was the host and emcee.

Brad choked out agreement like a sock puppet. He had no choice but to agree, to agree with everything Troy said, so long as he won his approval. So long as Troy kept talking to him. Actually, Troy did not even have to talk. So long as he stood there and looked beautiful, that was enough for Brad.

Brad couldn't muster the ghost of an engaging response. Regardless, before he left, Troy bluntly asked Brad for his phone number.

"Please," Troy insisted, as if anyone in their right mind would have refused Troy Boston his phone number, "you've got to come out with me some time."

Brad gave up the number eagerly. Brad was a good boy. He did what he was told.

It was not that he had regained any faith in gay men. And he certainly didn't dare believe he had found his husband. He was not as naïve as he'd been years ago. And since Troy had lost his youthful love, Brad suspected he was a live wire—unattached, the kind of man who never dated more than a few days, then showed up with a new and prettier boy every night of the week.

Not that Brad had any direct evidence that Troy was basically a big slut. But the way people talked, and the way Troy looked—it was enough right there to convict Troy of being a man who could not be contained to a single bed. How could anyone that beautiful not be a slut? Troy Boston could have his pick of men, a different one every night. If that was what he wanted.

It certainly was not what Brad was about. Not by a long shot.

Once Troy left, Turner jeered, "Sucker. He totally played you. Pick your lower jaw off the ground now, and put that tongue back in your mouth and wipe up the slobber, wouldja? We'll have health code violations."

But Brad accepted the invitation when Troy Boston called the very next day. He allowed himself to be seduced, even though he knew Troy's reputation. He tried to pretend that he did not mind when Troy disappeared in the morning.

And he utterly failed to pretend he did not care when Troy rang his bell again with breakfast and roses a few hours later.

5

The Friday night crowd at Cheval was in full swing when Troy Boston strode through the massive oak doors like a conquering hero. Hips forward, shoulders back, chin up.

He stopped in the entryway. He surveyed the crowd as if he expected a round of applause. His eyes started little fires everywhere he looked.

To one side, women in mannish pantsuits and clinging turtlenecks were draped over a line of bar stools near the door. They were drinking apple martinis and cosmos, and sneaking approving peeks at themselves in the mirror behind the bar, while they waited for the sought-after tables to become available.

Handsome stockbrokers and traders crowded around these women. They had shed their jackets and loosened their ties. They were trying to impress one another and the women with tales about their high school sports exploits and sexual conquests, and loud jibes passed back and forth among them. At least some of the women seemed amused.

On the other side of the host's podium, to Troy's left, was a second sunken bar, which fell three steps down from the main floor. This bar was not intended for waiting. It was closed off from the rest of the restaurant like a cave, and plunged in moody blue light. Brad had staffed it with little sylphs, sleek boys and young women, experts in chatting up the single guests, but discreet with the couples.

The staff moved about like silverfish, quick and, sometimes, Brad acknowledged, hard to catch. Brad made no bones about the fact that he hired pretty waitstaff. In his restaurant, nothing ugly would ever show its face.

But Troy made the staff pale in comparison. His appearance was like an announcement over a loudspeaker. Conversation stopped. Heads turned, men's and women's alike. In both bars. And on the dining room floor.

His self-possession was immense. It seemed to demand attention. The candlelight from the tables brought out a naughty, wet sheen in his eyes. The baked Tuscan ambiance of the restaurant lent a summer's glow to Troy's brown skin.

He had shed the morning's suit for a pair of black pants and a vintage-looking wool vest that emphasized his athletic shoulders and narrow waist. They often said that Troy Boston had become such a successful designer because all clothes looked good on him.

And no clothes looked even better.

Having won everyone's attention, Troy resumed his journey across the dining room floor. He passed the host's station with a discreet wave at the maître d'. Behind it, a narrow, railed platform brought dinner guests from the two bars into the oval dining area. It was like a drawbridge over a moat and everybody watched Troy cross it with bated breath, almost as if they expected something disastrous to happen, the bridge to collapse.

Troy turned down onto the main floor of the dining room, where the most visible tables were arranged. Here, under a two-story vaulted ceiling, Boston's powerful and rich were on display. The waitstaff moved among them fluidly, as if choreographed. Nearly all of them were strong men with hairy forearms and barrel chests, who inspired deference.

Troy loped among these tables and their guardians like a tiger through a jungle—untiring, predatory, dangerous. He had the kind of erotic everyday confidence that made people want to be close to him.

As he passed various tables, acquaintances beckoned him to stop and talk. Without a break in his stride, Troy graciously deflected these offers. He made a beeline for the kitchen.

Brad still got a thrill from thinking that no one in that whole dining room—TV newscasters, politicians, high-powered attorneys—was as important as Brad was. No one in the whole world.

The smell of shark bacon and fresh andouille sausage, cornbread and pistachio-roasted venison loin produced a dizzying, disorienting sensation of crowds and plenty. And the lustrous ambiance had blown away Brad's pique from lunch with Caroline like a cleansing summer storm breaks the heat.

He was bursting with pride as he watched Troy skip yet another table of high-wattage friends. It was like they were the only two people in the room.

Troy was good this way. Brad gave him credit—he was a master at making him feel special. Troy never entered a room Brad was in without acknowledging him first. Never spoke to anyone else without first supplying Brad with a reassuring touch, a quick word, a wink, or a smile.

Even in a crowded room, Troy had a preternatural sense for where Brad might be, and he gravitated immediately to that place. It was as if he was drawn irresistibly to Brad by some higher force, like iron filings to a magnet, or a planet to gravity.

Troy hopped up the three steps to the landing in front of the kitchen's swinging doors, and Brad pushed away from the door frame and into his path.

It was like walking in front of an oncoming train. Troy pressed his body close. He cupped his hand around the back of Brad's neck and pulled Brad toward him with elegant violence.

Troy's mouth closed over Brad's lips, and Brad closed his eyes. The fireworks inside were enough to light up the room. Who needed candles? Who needed electricity? The world was a bolt of lightning.

Brad surrendered himself, acutely conscious of every electric patch of skin where Troy's hands rested. He sought and found Troy's chest, running his hands over it, down around the back, where the two columns of muscle ran down his spine toward that magnificent ass.

Which he cupped. And groped, and shaped. And then pried himself away, so he could feast his eyes on Troy.

The surge of raw excitement hadn't diminished a bit since the day they had begun dating. The mere sight of Troy made Brad ache with want. His fingers itched for Troy's chest, his ribbed belly, his hard and tremendous crotch. He loved the dimple in Troy's chin, the angle of his hip, the firmness of his muscles, the rank smell of his manhood.

Troy smiled, and Brad struggled to control his trembling body. He wanted to press up against him and rut right there on the floor of his restaurant. And he hoped his struggle to restrain himself was not as obvious from the outside as it felt to him. It just was not cool to be so exposed, so vulnerable, so scandalously affected by another human being's presence.

The power Troy had over him was not something Brad cared to acknowledge. It was a frightening feeling. It made his life feel precarious and unstable. Everything that he'd achieved felt like it could go up in smoke at any moment when Troy was around. Brad would do anything for him, anything at all.

It was a dangerous, delicious, dizzying feeling, addictive and threatening. It could be triggered by the slightest suggestion of the man's presence—a piece of cloth, a whiff of cologne, a handwritten note.

Brad struggled to regain control and master the blood surging through his veins. He searched for a topic of neutral conversation. Troy looked at him in amusement, knowing full well his effect on Brad. Troy was not cocky, just exceptionally well-pleased with himself.

"How'd it go with the mayor?"

"Did anyone ever tell you you're beautiful?" Troy replied, not relenting for a second. His tone was husky, like a diva's at a piano bar. It was filled with a bedroom grunt and thrill.

Brad's efforts at composure were undone by Troy's words. He stuttered and blushed furiously. Like a coy schoolgirl, he looked around him to see whether anyone else had heard.

Troy laughed.

This, finally, was enough to pique Brad's competitive instincts. He did not like to be laughed at. And Brad was damned if he was going to let Troy get the upper hand.

"As a matter of fact," he joked, "you're about the sixteenth person to tell me today. What's up with all you boys? Don't you have something better to do than gawk at me?"

Troy's smile broadened, and he released Brad from the most muscular elements of his penetrating gaze. His eyes danced.

Then they focused again. Troy let them run over Brad's body like a starving man who had set his eyes on a full meal. Troy licked his lips, and the corners of his mouth turned in a wolfen snarl.

"Can't blame 'em for good taste," he said.

Brad felt a twinge of chagrin. It would have been nicer if Troy had shown a hint of jealousy. But he would settle for the heat of Troy's gaze as it passed over every inch of his body, exploring every bulge and muscle. The look made Brad dizzier and more excited, as if he was losing his balance at the edge of a steep cliff, and then drawing back. A sickening stomach plunge, a little thrill in one's crotch.

"It's a good thing I'm wearing an apron," Brad declared.

Troy arched his brows questioningly.

Brad answered his question by looking down at the surging erection Troy had given him.

Troy laughed, his body animated over every inch of its six-foot-one-inch length. He clapped Brad on the back, and shook him a little as if he didn't have words enough for his affection. As if it was beyond words, in the realm of magic. Troy pinned Brad against the wall, stole a kiss, and then slid in alongside him, as if they were two of a kind.

Together, they turned back toward the tables, Troy's arm around Brad's shoulders, the royal couple surveying their vast domain.

A second helping of pride rushed through Brad's bones, and he stood taller. He watched Troy's eyes pass over his restaurant. His baby.

Troy's approving, inquisitive gaze began with the power tables in the center of the room. Then it shifted, moving outward to the concentric ring of more intimate booths that lined the restaurant's oval perimeter. The booths, tucked into spaces against the exposed brick walls, circled the main dining floor. Beams ran up the walls, half-plastered and rustic, and the ceilings over these tables-for-two were low, to hold in the romantic secrets and to give the meal the feeling of a sultry breakfast in bed.

Glints of recognition lit Troy's eyes like pops of a photo flash. He saw people he knew, as usual. Troy knew people everywhere, successful people in art, politics, theater, and of course fashion.

Troy had grown up on Beacon Hill and attended Choate and Harvard. He had learned how to mix a martini before he was twelve. He could effortlessly chat up a senator's wife, had met presidents and kings, and hadn't ever done a stitch of his own laundry.

Brad followed his gaze from table to table. To Brad, all these people were just a blur of sparkling glitterati, one indistinguishable from the next. Rich people's faces. Composed, proud, austere.

Even after two years of dating Troy, they did not seem quite human. Not like him. They seemed possessed of themselves and sophisticated and knowledgeable in ways Brad did not think he would ever be. Even now that—by every measure—he was himself a big success.

At one table, Brad caught a quick glimpse of a familiar face under a shock of platinum hair, but when he looked more closely, the face had disappeared.

Troy remarked, "We're going to get approval for the Club, I'm sure of it. Hell, we may get the mayor and his 'lady companion' up to the opening, if we play our cards right. I hope you and Turner have been brainstorming and coming up with a menu that's on the far side of fabulous, sweetheart."

With his left hand, Troy poked Brad in the ribs. Then he withdrew his arm and shuffled from foot to foot, filled with the eager energy of a boxer before the fight. Playful. Disarming. And somehow belligerent at the same time.

"Don't you worry about me," Brad assured him. "The menu for Club Troy is going to destroy the critics. They'll set up a little church to worship me. I've got it all worked out."

Troy laughed. "Where's my sweet humble boyfriend gone?" he asked, lifting up a nearby tablecloth. "Come out, come out, wherever you are . . . !"

"When it comes to cooking, he takes a powder. You know that." Troy nodded. He knew that.

"You going out?" Brad asked.

It was a superfluous question. Except for the nights when Troy was holed up in his studio in a creative frenzy, with the doors locked and the phones switched off and pizza boxes stacked outside the door, he went out nearly every night.

To dinner. Maybe to a party, or theater. Or drinks late-night at a martini bar. Maybe to a gallery opening. Or a benefit. But always somewhere where it was hip and exclusive and fabulous and Iranian princesses in exile and heirs to vast fortunes were bound to show up.

"Yeah," Troy confirmed. "I've got a dinner party with some potential clients. Big names. You'd know them, but I can't tell you who they are. Or I'd have to kill you."

You could not keep Troy restrained. And you would not want to restrain that kind of enthusiasm. That jet stream. It was one of the things Brad loved about Troy. Loved, that is, as long as Brad got his share of Troy's attention.

Troy was already strategizing which of the tables he needed to stop by on his way out and which he could pass by with merely a nod and a smile. He was a consummate politician, with perfect pitch for social niceties.

"That's why I've only got a moment. But I thought I'd stop by." Troy's gaze swung around to Brad with a sudden predatory violence, like a bird of prey swooping down on its dinner with open talons. "I was horny as a dog, and needed a fix of this."

Again, Troy touched Brad with a pointed finger and the spot burned. Brad leaned into him, taking Troy's hand in his and stroking the exposed hair at the wrist.

"So who's your date tonight?" Brad asked. Brad rarely got home before 2 A.M. on nights when he was working, so they had come to an arrangement: Troy could have other "dates"—usually one of his endless supply of fantastically beautiful female friends.

Troy mentioned the name of a local model, and Brad gave a grunt of grudging approval. Better a beautiful woman than a beautiful boy. Of which there was also a limitless supply available to Troy.

If Troy had wanted any of them, he'd only have had to crook his little finger. Boys were constantly and shamelessly throwing themselves at him, hoping to get lucky, to score, to show up Brad Drake.

The thought of these pretty, vacant club kids and hairy sugar daddies made Brad's stomach clench with anger. He could not bear the thought of someone else running hands over Troy's body. That belonged to him alone.

Brad did not mind sharing Troy with the occasional supermodel for the evening, but when it came to the bedroom or the heart, he would not share the prize. Ever. The moment Troy showed an interest in any of these beautiful boys was the day Brad hit the road. He had made this vow to himself. He was pretty sure he would keep it.

Aggressively, Brad leaned toward Troy and took a kiss.

"What's that for?"

"For being sweet. And irresistible. And mine."

"I can't argue with any of that!" Troy replied, with a sly grin. Again, his whole attention was focused on Brad, and Brad alone. The heat was like standing beneath a spotlight. Troy had a knack for using his brown eyes to see down into Brad's very soul.

This could be infuriating. Sometimes Brad did not want to be looked into. Sometimes he wanted to be mysterious and cryptic and Troy not to be so damn sure of himself.

And sometimes Brad wanted to see into Troy's soul, the way Troy saw into him.

But it was no two-way street. Troy's eyes had "no trespass" signs up. They were as reflective as a pair of mirrored sunglasses. Brad had never been able to detect a damn thing going on in Troy's head unless Troy let him.

It drove Brad crazy. And not always in a bad way. It was alluring, enticing, magical.

Troy grinned. Brad grinned back. And they might have gone on grinning at each other all night had not Turner burst through the kitchen's double doors. He barged between them and snapped, "Break it up, loverboys, we got hungry mouths to feed."

Troy grinned and rolled his eyes. Turner's pretending not to like him had become a game between them.

"Bitch!" he mouthed after Turner had passed and descended into the main dining room.

Turner bellowed over his shoulder, "I heard that!"

Again, Troy grinned. He loved to play games with Turner. And that made Brad happy. He liked to see his lover get along with his friends.

Troy suddenly clapped himself on the forehead. "Jeez, I almost forgot . . . How did it go with Caroline? I'm sorry I couldn't be there."

Brad groaned. "Bloodbath. Don't even remind me. No offense, but Caroline takes some getting used to."

"None taken, trust me. I've spent thirty-three years trying to get used to her. And I'm still only halfway there. Did you guys at least come up with anything you liked?"

Brad shrugged.

"Because she said you had picked out some concepts together."

"*She* picked them out. Not me." A vision of Aria's smug little mug crossed his mind, and a thrust of jealousy struck him to the core. He added with a sneer, "She and *Aria*." As he said the name, Brad focused on Troy's face. Not a shadow crossed it.

Troy asked lightly, "Who's Aria?"

"Caroline said you knew him. Knew him well."

Troy frowned and then shrugged. "Nah. I don't. You know I never forget a name. Who is he?"

If he was pretending ignorance, he was awfully good at it, better than Brad would ever have been. Which made a little shiver of cold run down Brad's spine. If Troy chose to cheat on him, he would never know for sure. He might feel it in his soul, but he would never know.

Brad shook his head and dismissed the thought. It was unfair. No one ever really knew. Part of love was a leap of faith, and it did not do too much good to dwell on it. Making it work was hard enough without inventing reasons for fear. For holding back. Still, if he ever had rock-hard proof . . . that would be a different story.

"Aria Sha— Oh, never mind. He's just the guy who did the designs. No one you need to meet if you don't know him already."

Troy grinned like a devil. He raised his eyebrows. "Is he cute?"

"You would think so," Brad said reproachfully. "He's cute in an arty-twinkie sort of way."

Troy laughed and cupped Brad's cheek and jaw in his palm. "If I'm so smitten with arty twinks, what am I doing spending my life with a stocky, ripped, hot muscle boy who, unless you can eat it, hasn't a clue about art?"

He leaned forward and kissed Brad's forehead.

"Temporary insanity," Brad groused gloomily. But inside, the words of praise had done their magic. And he ceased to be jealous of anybody in the world. "Spending my life with" Troy had said. "Spending my life with"—what beautiful words to hear. Was that what Troy thought they were doing?

Brad was charmed. He felt light and silly inside, like a schoolgirl. Troy had let the words slip so casually, as if it should have been obvious. No doubts. A given. The casually dropped phrase was more powerful, Brad thought, than an overt, horns-blasting, high-definition declaration of undying love. It really meant something.

Chastened, he felt his knees weaken, and all the tides in him inclined toward Troy. His suspicions about Aria Shakespeare seemed ludicrous. He again wished, more than anything in the world, that he could take Troy home right then and there, and tear the clothes off his body, and press himself up against that chest and crotch.

At that moment, one of the sous-chefs poked his head out the kitchen door and urgently requested Brad's assistance. Troy took the graceful hint, even if Brad was reluctant to let him go.

"Go put out your fires," Troy directed. "See you at my place tonight?"

He goosed Brad in the butt and kissed him on the neck before surrendering him.

"Sure," Brad agreed, wondering quietly where he was going to take a cold shower so that he could get back to the business of cooking.

6

At 2 A.M., Brad finally finished up. Turner had long since gone home, since he rose at dawn to get the restaurant ready for the day. The waitstaff had disappeared, bubbling with excitement about the after-hours club they were all headed off to.

Brad was the last to leave. Whining compressors and the ticks of a tired building were the only sounds.

He surveyed the kitchen to make sure every last knife had been put away, and took pleasure in the last, lingering smells of the meals that had been prepared and served. This was Brad's favorite time of night. His tired mind was loose and his creative powers at their height. Some of his finest creations had been concocted on this wrong side of midnight, after the rest of the staff had gone home.

Brad loved spice. He had no fear of fat, at least not when he was cooking for one of his restaurants. He was a culinary slut, drawing on a dozen different traditions. His sole goal was to ravish his diners' palates by any means necessary.

Duck livers, foie gras, bacon, apples, brandy, shrimp—you name it, and it had been in the mix, one way or the other. And even after washing up, the scent of each of the flavors was in his clothes and hair, on his skin, indelibly seared into the kitchen's very air.

Brad drew out a pad of paper, which was crosshatched with his scribbles and notes. The pad contained his ideas for the menu at Club Troy that he had been working on. He wanted a menu like none other in Boston. Daring, cutting-edge food and ingredients rendered in conventional, all-American guises to encourage people to try them. The exotic flavors hidden inside like the men in the horse at Troy: blue cheese in meatloaf, white sorbet made from skinned tomatoes and topped with a dry cracker filled with a squirt of surprising olive oil, a chicken croquette that contained its own liquid consommé, ravioli pasta made from a skin skimmed from a pot of boiling milk and flash-chilled. To conquer people, you had to deceive them. That was the theme of his menu.

A knock at the front door of the restaurant prevented Brad from getting very far with his work. It was Chessie DeMotta, his faghag and best female friend in all the world. They exchanged a quick kiss and then she planted herself on a bar stool.

Chessie was a strikingly slim girl, given to bare bellies, hip boots, and a dirty mouth. She was just under six feet, and had a face so full of life that it could be dazzling at close range. Men were always falling in love with her.

Chessie had a knack for showing up now and again at Brad's restaurants, just after the bars had closed, when she still had a good buzz she wasn't ready to surrender. They would sit under the dimmed lights in the blue of the bar at Cheval and dissect the day, and their lovers, and sometimes their dreams.

Some nights, Chessie would have a man in tow. They would stay only a few minutes. Other times, she settled in for the night and exhausted Brad, though he hardly noticed until she was gone and his watch said 5 A.M.

Tonight was a short visit. She was headed to after-hours at a club called Rise, but she wanted to hear all about the lunch with Caroline, and the latest ideas for the menu at Club Troy. Brad gave her the *Reader's Digest* version, which she punctuated with all the right curses, and some characterizations of Caroline that were so startlingly obscene that Brad would not have thought of them in a million years.

Chessie reserved her strongest disdain for Aria. She unleashed a string of obscenities that seemed to go on forever. Like Brad, Chessie was a working-class girl and nothing got under her skin like a spoiled rich kid.

"As if that fuck-pig Aria could possibly have *anything*—brains, beauty, anything—on my sweet Brad Drake. I promise you, if I ever see that guy, I'll take his balls off and wear them around my neck like a crucifix!"

After Chessie left, Brad closed up. He folded away his Club Troy recipe notebook and locked it in the restaurant safe, to which only he and Turner had keys. Then he turned the bolt on the front door and headed home.

The traffic was light. The streets of the financial district were deserted. Beacon Hill was almost a ghost town. The only action was a line of taxis double and triple parked to accept the Burberry-coated drunks piling out of the bars at closing.

Brad expertly maneuvered around these hazards, and turned his Honda Civic up one of the steep, narrow roads that led to the statehouse. It didn't embarrass him at all that his Civic was by far the most modest vehicle in these golden streets of Lexuses and Porsches and Mercedes. Brad could not see the point in wasting money on something he did not care about.

About halfway up the hill, toward the Gold Dome of the statehouse, was Troy's town house. It was a stately corner building, with a brick façade and large bow windows in two directions. The penthouse had two cupolas, each topped by a spire and weather vane, and the short, sloped roof that led to the roof deck was blue-green Virginia slate.

The library was visible through the parlor windows. Its shelves were made of warm fruitwood, and the walls had been painted a rich, blood-red shade. The fireplace opened cavernously, shoulder wide, and the ceiling showed perfectly preserved decorative moldings from the prior century.

Best of all, the ornate gold-leafed mirror which hung in the library did wonders for abdominal muscle definition beneath the kind overhead light.

Brad pulled into the garage entrance that was tucked under one of the parlor windows. It was one of the few private underground garages on Beacon Hill, and Brad was thankful not to have to try and find parking in this crowded neighborhood.

Although Troy's car was in ahead of him, the town house was quiet. The library was empty and cold: tepid lighting from the overhead tracks bathed the paintings. Brad bypassed the bedrooms and went to the third floor, a massive open room with a fireplace at each end, a comfortable lounging nook in each cupola, and a dining room off to the side, where the stairs led to the roof deck.

Brad, of course, made a beeline for the kitchen. Whenever he came into his own apartment or into Troy's house, he always sought out the kitchen first. It grounded him, made him feel centered and whole, relaxed and comfortable.

He poured and downed two full glasses of water without taking a breath. He was dog-tired from a night in the kitchen. The restaurant's commotion and rich languid flavors sometimes masked the supreme effort Brad put out every night. The race to get the timing correct, the hustle, the rich smells—it was all a constant rush.

Only when the crowds had melted away, and the staff took a cigarette break, to detox and dish and laugh about the night's crowds, did the exhaustion fall on Brad like a tidal wave. A sweet exhaustion. Not unlike, Brad thought, the aftermath of good sex.

Brad peeled off his shirt. It reeked of sweat and leeks. Garlic was embedded in the pores of his skin. He dragged himself off to the shower, standing beneath the matching heads as the water cascaded down around him. He was looking forward to getting horizontal in the plush sheets on Troy's bed and sleeping until noon.

Brad closed his eyes and let the steaming hot water cascade over him. The steam made his hair stand on end, and the water passed over his ears, making a sound like you'd hear in a seashell if you held it to your ear.

Brad did not notice as the shower door popped slowly open. A hand reached toward him, and it was quickly followed by a hard, ripped male body. Confusion passed over Brad's face, as his nose took in Troy's familiar animal scent among the soap and shampoo.

Still, Brad jumped a mile as the large warm hand closed on his ass, and another slid around to his chest. And then, without opening his eyes, he relaxed into the familiar crotch pressing insistently against his buttocks.

The first kiss tickled the spot behind his ear. The hard cock was a firebrand against his backside. Troy's breath was hot on his neck.

The kisses whispered down along his spine. An electric sensation ran all the way to the base of his tailbone, down his hamstrings to his feet.

Brad felt himself already hard. He let his hands reach back. He pulled the fine, muscular thighs up against his. They were rock-hard and lean, with a coarse layer of hair made slippery in the wash from the shower.

Slicked with soap, Troy's hands moved one circle to Brad's chest, one on his right hip. Gradually the circles grew closer and closer to Brad's crotch, as the kisses reached the point farthest down his back.

Troy was crouching behind him. His tongue flickered at the

base of Brad's spine. He nipped at Brad's ass, and the sharp, short pain of each nip was like an electric shock. Troy's tongue probed and fluttered and then thrust. Brad gasped, the heat of the shower, the rush of his blood making him dizzy. He was ready to weep, to be taken.

He tried to turn, but Troy would not let him. He tried to hold out, but his throat moaned without any prompting. He surrendered entirely to the pulsing tongue, the fingers spreading and kneading his flesh. Now inside him. Now out.

When Troy finally turned him, still crouching, Brad put his hands on Troy's powerful shoulders. He let himself be taken into Troy's mouth. The pleasure was as sharp as a bite, and then it expanded to fill him.

Brad saw himself in Troy's mouth. His attention focused on the thick lips, the beads of shower water on Troy's eyelashes and his face streaked with water.

He was a god; he was beautiful. His hands on Brad's ass were big, broad, strong. It was like being held in the hands of God.

From the very inside of Brad's being, the honey poured out, filling him, arching him back against those hands, pressing his manhood into that mouth. He tried to hold back. But the effort only raised the pleasure to an unbearable pitch.

He arched until he broke, and shuddered, and his knees went weak. He felt as if he was held upright only by that mouth and those wide hands. He clasped his own hands thankfully around that sopping head.

Troy released Brad from his mouth. He looked up from where he was kneeling on the tile floor of the shower.

He was grinning, but there was no amusement in his eyes. His face was a mask of lust. His eyes moved up and down Brad's body, lighting those familiar fires here and there. Brad felt exposed and raw before that appetite.

Troy stood. He was the taller of the two, and his impossibly long arms reached around back down to Brad's ass and yanked him against him. Brad's post-orgasm penis was so sensitive that the touch made him jump.

But Troy refused to let him go. His soapy finger went in and out, fingering, touching, spreading. Brad turned to the glass wall of the shower. Like a man arrested, he placed both his palms on the glass, spread his legs, lowered his butt slightly.

First there was a finger, then two.

And then he felt it. Hot and rigid. Probing, spreading, insistent.

Brad let himself loosen and the cock found its mark. The head slid in, then out, then in a little farther, then out, with a gentleness that was an absolute necessity to accommodate such manhood.

Brad let his whole body go slack, and Troy took him up on the invitation. The cock was finally all the way in, touching a dull place deep inside. A hard, rippled breath came from Troy's mouth.

Troy crooned Brad's ear, "You have such a sweet, sweet, sweet little ass." His voice broke as he said it, as if he were crying.

And then he stopped speaking and his body went convulsive and hard, and the thrust was deep, and Brad braced himself as Troy's strokes followed, one after the other, as if they would never end. All gentleness was gone. And it was a pleasure for Brad to let Troy take so much pleasure from him.

Finally, when Brad did not think his body would last any longer, Troy came, convulsed, emitting a hard, leonine bark. He slumped a moment against Brad. Then gave a last shudder like the dead.

And then, as he had at the start, his hands were making circles over Brad's hard abdomen. He was murmuring, "Mmmmmmmm."

For a long time they stood there in the gushing wet of the shower, and then Troy reached around Brad and turned off the faucet. He led Brad by the hand out of the shower stall, pulling a plush thick towel from a heated rack.

Troy toweled Brad down from head to toe. He spread cocoa butter all over Brad's body, until his skin was like a baby's.

They stopped in the kitchen on the way to bed. By mutual agreement, they indulged in decadence. They shared a pint of Ben & Jerry's, feeding each other, laughing softly and giggling. Not a serious word had passed between them since Troy arrived home.

When they lay in bed and Troy spooned him, his lithe body pressed up against every inch of Brad's skin. Their legs tangled and Troy's hands folded over Brad's heart.

Brad's exhaustion had left him. He felt as if he could go completely without sleep. Every nerve was awake, even as he felt Troy go slowly limp. Troy's hands shuddered and jerked as he entered sleep.

Brad could not sleep. Mentally he touched all the points on his body that Troy had touched. He felt used and raw and delicious. He smelled the clean soap of Troy's skin, the faint alcohol on his breath, the shifting of his muscles, the sweetness of the ice cream on his lips.

Brad thought: I am lost to this guy. He owns me. It had never been like this before Troy. And it was not just one night. It was every night, again and again.

Fear bloomed in him like a flower. He felt as if he did not deserve such luck. And he was ashamed of himself, too. He suddenly felt like he had made it too obvious. Been too easy. Fallen so completely.

He should have been cooler, he thought. Should have played games. Should have been coy and careful. Protected his heart. It was dangerous to have exposed himself like that.

Troy stirred in his sleep and gave an animal purr.

Brad's doubt rushed out the window. And a rich, contented feeling flowed through his belly. He pressed his fingertips into Troy's palm.

In some ways, he thought, it was also a relief to admit to himself how far he had surrendered his heart. A relief to tell Troy about it, to have no secrets.

And one day, he hoped, Troy would give himself entirely back to Brad. Troy would love Brad, and admit that he did.

At this point in their relationship, it was still too early. Troy was just too polished to be believed. The words he said were the right words at the time, and the details he remembered—the way Brad took his coffee, the way he liked his clothes folded and arranged in his drawers, the particular spot on the back of Brad's neck that, when touched, could send goose pimples in a star shower down his spine—were touching. Troy was a thoughtful, imaginative lover, and so affectionate at times that he made Brad feel almost embarrassingly grateful for the attention.

But there seemed to be something missing. Troy was too contained. Too careful not to lose control of his feelings. Too protective of what was inside.

Sooner or later, Brad vowed, he would open Troy up. Troy would feel the same way about Brad as Brad felt about him. And he would admit it, at least once, in their most private moments. Of that, Brad had no doubt. Even if it took the rest of their lives.

7

Saturday morning, when Brad woke, the bed was empty. He could hear the comforting sounds of Troy at work in the kitchen on the floor above.

Troy was an enthusiastic but undisciplined cook. He was singing along to a Cher CD and banging around pots and pans and occasionally, judging from the footsteps, doing the cha-cha-cha. His preparation was punctuated with good-natured curses and the crash of cascading metal bowls as he endured one culinary disaster after the other.

Brad grinned. He was glad his fame and skill did not inhibit Troy in the kitchen. In fact, Troy often cheerfully challenged Brad as to who made the better frittatas.

Troy's weak spot was his lack of enthusiasm for cleaning up afterward. Following one of his whirlwinds, the kitchen was a federal disaster area. Cabinets were opened, pots were stacked eighteen inches high in the sink, and a fine coating of flour dusted every surface. Brad sighed at the thought of confronting this mess. But Troy's appearance at the door made the prospect instantly worth it.

He was carrying a tray on which rested two plates, each piled high with eggs. He was wearing only an apron, and his butt hung out the back, as it would have hung out of a hospital johnny or a pair of chaps.

It was a great butt. Firm and round. Not too skinny, the way many gay boys wore their butts.

"Hey! Are you ogling me?"

"A little," Brad admitted. He dragged his eyes back to the heaping plates. He frowned. "That doesn't look like it's fat-free," he said with mock disapproval.

Troy set down the tray. He stood tall, grasping his two buttocks in his own hands. "This? Not fat-free? What are you trying to say?"

"I meant the eggs, smart-ass."

Troy grinned and hopped in beside him under the sheets, nearly upending the tray.

"It is, trust me. One hundred percent fat-free. Scout's honor," Troy said.

For a moment Troy adopted a pious and silly expression, and then broke into a happy grin. He doled out the eggs in generous portions, pulled four slices of toast from the apron's pocket, and attacked his eggs with the same robust lust that he had directed toward Brad's ass the night before. (From which treatment, Brad reflected, his ass was pleasantly sore, in a rough velvet sort of way.)

Brad loved Troy because he was not one of these gay guys who starved himself. He came to his leanness naturally, and he loved good food, eating with appreciative noises that sounded distinctly like sex.

"This needs only one thing," Brad proposed.

Troy stopped in mid-chew, narrowing his eyes as if he thought Brad were going to critique his cooking.

"A bloody Mary."

Brad raced upstairs naked, and in no time had whipped up a pair of Cajun Marys. He dumped in pickled okra and beans and plenty of Worcestershire and horseradish, Tabasco and cayenne pepper.

They gulped the Cajun Marys, and a fine sheen of sweat broke out on Troy's nose and forehead from the spicy heat. Troy shoveled a bit of egg on his fork and fed Brad. Brad promptly returned the favor.

Then Brad turned to digest another kind of morning meal. Making short work of Troy's apron, he lifted the flap and found more satisfying meat beneath. Any exhaustion in Brad's bones had been driven away by desire.

He licked and tongued and consumed, making a home in Troy's crotch. Troy slid down the bed as his large hand guided and supported the back of Brad's head.

"Oh, yeah. Oh, yeah," he cried in a guttural whisper. His orgasm rumbled in like a freight train. Brad washed it back with a slurp of Cajun Mary. Smiling, he touched the salt on his lips with his tongue and reflected that there was more than one meal that went well with tomato juice.

The day passed, with chatter and music, intermittent dozing, and sex. They left bed only to refresh their drinks and use the bathroom. In the drawer by the bed was all the lube and massage oil and condoms that an army of horny men could need.

The soporific Cajun Marys eventually lulled them into a long afternoon nap. When Brad woke, he found a haze of dust motes falling like snow in the low light of late winter and early spring.

Troy's fingertips on his back started almost as light. A brushing. Then he readjusted himself, straddling Brad's butt. He drove his fingers deep into the flesh of Brad's neck and shoulders, kneading and rubbing, finding every knot and dissolving them in his hands.

Like my heart, Brad thought. It was like he reached all the way through my skin, my ribs, and reached my heart. And dissolved it. And Brad trusted him to do it, trusted him utterly.

Half asleep, he thought: it's beautiful to trust.

Beautiful and rare.

The next time Brad woke, it was his turn. He put two beads of oil on his palms and rubbed them until they were slick and warm. Under Brad's hands, the tension drained from Troy's body. His legs emptied and turned pliable. His muscles went loose in Brad's hands.

He worked his way up from Troy's feet and over his lean calves. He followed the coarse black hair on the back of Troy's thighs, until they rounded to a firm melon butt. He traced the crack to the small of Troy's back, along the twin columns of sturdy muscle that bordered his spine.

When he turned, Troy was entirely pliant. Submissive. And Brad worked the reverse side, down from the shoulders, down over the firm pecs, down to the belly.

By the time Brad reached Troy's manhood, it was tumescent and twitching. It slapped hard against the hard flesh of his belly. With another touch of oil on his hands, and the practiced skill of a master bread maker, Brad brought Troy to another tremendous orgasm.

And then they slept some more. The room smelled of sweat, spunk, and contentment. Only when they finally decided that their laziness was bordering on terminal did Brad and Troy rouse themselves from bed.

While Brad cleared dishes and lotions and condom wrappers and the other detritus of love, Troy picked out clothes from the closet for Brad to wear. Troy had a perfect sense for what items best flattered Brad's broad shoulders and muscular thighs. And he dressed Brad every chance he got.

Troy set out various articles of clothing on the bed, layered them on top of one another and then decided that something was missing. He ransacked the closet he had set aside for Brad, diving nearly headlong into it so that only his rounded butt was visible in the door frame.

Admiring it, Brad asked him what he was looking for.

"You need an ascot."

"No, I don't," Brad objected.

"Well, you need a silk jacket, then."

"I have a silk jacket at home. In the condo."

Troy withdrew his head and shoulders from the closet. "You do?"

"Yes. Don't act so surprised."

Troy considered it a moment, and then dove back into the closet. "Doesn't help us now. We're not there now."

This comment made a phrase flash in Brad's head: If you lived here, you'd be home now.

The phrase came from a sign that hung over a set of condominiums in the West End of Boston, which was visible from the gridlock on Storrow Drive, the highway that ran alongside it. It was supposed to persuade all the suburbanites to exchange their long commutes for the convenience of city living.

"If we lived together," Brad said, "we could have all our stuff in one place."

As soon the words were out of his mouth, Brad reddened. For weeks, he had been planning to propose to Troy that they give up their separate apartments and move in together. He had imagined this proposal taking place over dinner, with a rose and candlelight. But now he had blown it. He had gone and blurted the idea aloud in a ham-handed way that suggested the higher spiritual purpose of their living together was to be sure Brad had access to a full supply of boxer shorts. What a dumb thing to say!

Although he hoped that Troy was too intent on rifling through his wardrobe to have heard him, he could not have been more wrong. Troy backed out of the closet and gave a funny little smile.

"Was that your way of suggesting we move in together, Bradley?"

Brad stuttered and blushed, hemmed and hawed. He loved it when Troy called him Bradley.

Finally, he squeaked out, "No, I—just saying, I mean, well . . . Yes."

Troy's smile grew broad. "I accept."

"Really?!"

"Sure."

For a moment, a delirious champagne happiness spilled over Brad. It was amazing, sudden, and beautiful. Like winning the lottery. Brad could hardly believe this luck was his.

And then, as if nothing should get in the way of a good evening's outfit, Troy turned back to his hunt for a silk jacket. He added, "It would be so much more convenient for us to get our own place. And we'd save with just one mortgage payment."

The fizz went out of Brad's mood until it was as flat as ginger ale left out overnight.

"Mortgage payments?"

"Yeah." Troy reached deep in the closet and retrieved a shirt. He held it up against the light, frowned, decided against it, and returned to the closet.

"You're such a romantic, Troy."

Troy again withdrew from the closet and raised his eyebrows. He had begun to sense that his response was not what Brad had been looking for.

"What?"

"Oooh! Mortgage payments. It's enough to set a boy's heart a-flutter." Brad pressed his hand to his chest.

"Um . . . this from the guy who was talking about the consolidation of closet space?"

"Yeah, but the difference is, *I* didn't mean it."

For a moment, Troy looked as if he had something important to say. A real bombshell. But then the look left his face, replaced by a long, inscrutable gaze that revealed nothing.

Brad's heart lurched. There were moments he did not understand Troy, when he felt there was a whole part of Troy's life from which he was excluded.

The thought made him crazy with sudden jealousy. Troy could be absolutely maddening. Brad wished that just once, in some moment of weakness, Troy would admit that he was passionately and mortally in love. Preferably with Brad. If Troy admitted it *just once*, Brad swore to himself, he would carry it to his grave and never ask again.

Then Troy reached out and traced a finger on Brad's lips and face. "Don't look so sad, sweetheart. I don't always say the right thing. But my heart's in the right place. Trust me."

Brad fought it. He wanted to pout and bitch. But he could not help but yield. It wasn't fair. Those molten brown eyes of Troy's brimmed with a heat that Brad just could not resist.

He let his lips part and took Troy's finger in his teeth. He bit it gently.

Troy smiled, pulled him close, nuzzled at his neck. The day's scruff scratched at Brad's skin in a pleasant way. Then Troy released him, and slapped his butt playfully.

"Now, let's get our asses in gear. We've got a busy night ahead. And we've got to go retrieve that silk jacket from your apartment."

8

It was an average Saturday night for Troy Boston: he and Brad were scheduled to attend two separate parties at different ends of town, including a benefit for homeless youth at the Harvard Club. Drinks with Troy's musician friends would cap the night.

On most Saturday nights, Brad was excused from some or all of the festivities. In the restaurant business, Saturday was not a day off. But on this particular Saturday, Troy had cashed in one of the Brad-All-Night cards that Brad had given him for his birthday. So the restaurants had been left in Turner's capable hands while Brad did the rounds with Troy, dusk to dawn.

The first stop was the Harvard Club on Commonwealth Avenue in the Back Bay, Boston's most upscale neighborhood. Two ferocious stone lions guarded the door. Inside, a fire burned brightly in the fireplace. Butlers relieved Troy and Brad of their overcoats, and hushed waitstaff in black tie circled among the guests. A live piano tinkled in the background. In the main room, the table groaned under the weight of hors d'oeuvres, including an enormous ice sculpture that housed oceans of peeled shrimp.

Caroline Treadwell met them at the door, swooping from a conversation with swanlike grace to embrace her son. To Brad, she offered a cold hand.

Caroline emphasized the glamour and pocketbooks that accompanied the guest list. All of the guests, she explained, were interested in getting some money into the Troy Boston financial juggernaut.

"I thought you were trying to benefit homeless kids," Brad mentioned, not without malice. Troy's agreeing to move in with him made him giddy and aggressive.

"Well, we are, dear . . . Just leave your check with the man at the door and don't upset the guests," she advised.

With that, Caroline left Brad in her dust, oblivious to his brimming excitement. She swept Troy into the next room, where she expected that he would seal the deals for which she had smoothed the way. Homeless kids were all fine and good, but Troy's financial success was the clear priority in Caroline Treadwell's books.

And Brad did not entirely begrudge Caroline her view of the world. It was nice to see a mother so interested in her son's well-being. And so protective, even when her son was thirty-three years old. Brad wished he himself had had such a mother. It just would have been nicer if Caroline had not seen Brad as one of the forces against which Troy needed protecting.

Brad lost track of Troy in the warm hum of the crowd. Left to his own devices, he plucked a shrimp from the castle of ice, doused it in cheap cocktail sauce, and scanned the room.

Old Yankee money had gathered clannishly at one end. New finance millionaires compared portfolios in the area immediately surrounding the fire. A few young dot-commers were sprinkled in-between. They all seemed to know one another. The Harvard Club was the home of air kisses and rigidly feigned expressions of pleasure as people exchanged greetings and introduced their better halves.

Brad sighed and checked his watch, already bored by the festivities. He resisted the urge to lob a second shrimp into the air and catch it in his mouth.

Brad still wasn't used to parties like this one. Cold New England manners and rich people priding themselves on giving away a pittance were not his idea of a good time. They only made him want to do something outrageous and naughty.

Back when he and Troy were first dating, they had attended a dinner party Caroline threw. Despite her suspicious eye, they had managed to find time to take refuge in her palatial bathroom to grope and tussle, fighting to maintain control and silence, only to lose it at the last moment, when one of the guests knocked on the door, and they dissolved in giggles.

And at dinner, Brad had slipped his stocking foot into Troy's crotch beneath the table. Troy had maintained a perfectly controlled face, but Brad had felt his growing excitement under the dinner table.

"Why did you stop?" Troy asked later.

"I was afraid, Troy, that everyone else would discover what I was doing when your cock jacked up and upended the table, and the centerpiece slid into your mother's lap."

"Don't I wish my manhood were that big," Troy had replied modestly. But Troy liked to be flattered this way. It gave a boyish pleasure to his face that was the opposite of the sophisticated, cool mask he wore all day long.

Brad had never seen Troy offer this look to anyone else but him. It was a look that belonged to Brad alone. Hungrily, he hunted for Troy among the other guests, as if he might now win one of those looks, or a chance to do something naughty in a corner of this ornate mansion.

His progress from room to room was delayed by the other guests, who were solicitous and inquisitive. He had no sooner shed one elderly sophisticate than another bent his ear. They all feigned tremendous interest in Brad's restaurants and complained vociferously about all the other restaurants in the city. But none of them really seemed to mean it. Or to care whether Brad believed they meant it. In fact, Brad doubted whether, except for events like this benefit at the Harvard Club, they had been out to a restaurant in years.

That was what killed Brad about these socialites. They were very nice, but every word out of their mouths was, at bottom, absolute bullshit. Why did they not just say what they meant?

Of course, when several of them proposed recipes Brad might want to try at Jean-Baptiste, he reflexively served up his own well-placed bullshit. He lied and promised to give the suggestions serious consideration.

After an hour or so, Brad couldn't muster any more patience to fake and pretend and force politeness with people he did not care about. The impact of the realization that he was moving in with Troy was building up inside him like an oncoming train. He was a balloon full to bursting with good fortune, excitement, pride, and love.

He and Troy were going to get a place together. He and Troy were going to share a life.

Troy himself had put it that way, unbidden. "Share a life." It was hard for Brad to believe that somebody as fabulously wonderful as Troy would want to be with him forever. For all the half-assed awkwardness of their discussion, Brad realized he had gotten exactly what he had always wanted.

Maybe he was an incurable romantic, or maybe it was because he had abandoned his family in Iowa when he was young. But Brad still thought of this shared house as a castle, where he would live forever with his knight in shining armor, with a moat and drawbridge to keep them secure when they wanted to be alone.

And it would soon be his. And Brad was positively vibrating with a desire to share the news. He did not think he could possibly go another minute without telling *someone*. But none of these wizened old Yankees seemed worthy recipients of such a heady announcement. He ached instead to call Chessie or spread the news to Turner. They were the only two who would really understand, who knew how long Brad had been waiting for this.

Brad snatched a glass of champagne from a passing tray and drifted off toward the back of the room to enjoy the glass and his own happy thoughts alone, where no one would bother him until it was time to go.

He was surprised to find that he knew the piano player. Before Brad had met Troy, he and the piano player had dated for a month or two. It hadn't worked out, but they had parted on good terms, and Brad was pleased and relieved to find someone he could talk to.

"Hey, Mike!"

Mike smiled. "Hey, Brad . . . I've been trying to get your attention all night."

"Really?" Brad pointed at the keys. "And here I thought you were trying to put me to sleep."

"What's wrong with this?" Mike asked, continuing the swirling, amorphous Frenchified sounds that filled the room like a honey *jus* that was too damn sweet.

"Well, it's not that I'm looking for techno, but . . . something in this century—even early this century—would beat that crap."

Mike blushed. He did a little flourish on the keys for Brad's benefit, and then returned to the soporific sounds he had been playing. "Yeah," he admitted, "it sure as hell is not DJ Victor Calderone, is it?" He shrugged. "But it's what they pay me for."

"You want a drink?"

"I'm not sure they'll let me . . ."

"Nah . . . you can take a break. Five minutes."

Mike glanced around. "Oh, sure, all right, twist my arm."

Drinks in hand, the two of them fell into a conspiracy in the back of the room, dishing about this and that, and taking apart the guests good-naturedly. It was the first time that Brad had relaxed since he walked in the door.

Mike congratulated him on Troy Boston. "Nice catch. Wish I could find a boyfriend like that."

The smile punctured the silence Brad had been trying to maintain. He couldn't contain his pride, as the mixture of easy camaraderie and champagne brought him to a heady euphoria. He gushed, "We're moving in together, you know. Getting rid of our places. We decided just tonight."

"Really?!"

"Yeah, really."

"Congrats!"

"Thanks, I guess I really lucked out. Call me a princess. Call it a silly dream. But I've bought into the fantasy, hook, line, and sinker."

"No, I totally get it. I only hope it works out for me someday." There was a twinge of sadness in Mike's voice. It was like he did not really have any faith that it would happen. Like he believed he would always be lonely.

But he didn't dwell on it. Mike mustered up a good mood and clapped Brad on the back, and said, "Well, you're a long way toward getting what you want. I mean, you even have the wicked stepmother."

Mike nodded at Caroline, who was regarding the two of them from across the room with a baleful stare.

Brad laughed and nodded.

"Of course," he added, happy to talk to somebody who understood it all, "*my* medieval fantasy has a gay twist: a dash of urban fabulousness, wonderful dinner parties, exposed brick, Sub-Zero appliances, mango-painted walls, and a strawberry Louis XV divan next to a glass armchair by Coulon. It's going to be heaven."

"Here's to heaven." Mike raised his glass.

At that moment, like a bucket of cold water, Aria Shakespeare barged between them. He leaned back against the piano like an exhausted diva, declaring loudly, "Heaven can wait, ladies. I prefer the more earthly pleasures."

He batted his eyelashes at them, and Brad sensed Mike's immediate interest in this pretty young doll that had joined them. He seemed to have forgotten Brad's presence as he surveyed Aria from head to foot.

Aria was dressed for the occasion to Brooks Brothers perfection. His rep tie was knotted in a full Windsor, his blue blazer was well-tailored, and his cheeks had an appealing boyish redness that could only have come from a compact.

He looked from Brad to Mike and back again, obviously enjoying the attention. No one took so much pride in being noticed as Aria Shakespeare.

"Pick up your jaw off the floor and put your eyes back in your head, dude. This body's not for the likes of you," Aria said. "Aren't you supposed to be working?" Aria persisted. "We pay you, don't we?"

"*You* don't pay me a damn—"

Before Mike could finish, Aria turned his back on him. He said to Brad, "And you, darling? Are you enjoying your moment in the sun?"

"I didn't know you were invited," Brad said. It seemed like he was running into Aria everywhere.

"*I* don't have to be invited, honey. *I'm* at home here. Remember?"

It was true. Cherrywood trim and Oriental carpets and paintings of nineteenth-century Boston and portraits of railroad barons and the sound of a subdued moneyed drawl were what Aria had grown up with. He was a country club boy.

"Look around!" Aria encouraged. "Take your time."

Brad did not look. He did not need to look. He only watched as Aria glanced around the room, naming off the guests one by one.

It was like a catalog of the names of Boston's public buildings: Winthrops and Lowells and Saltonstalls, powerful families, whose ancestors had once graced this same room. Their names fell off Aria's pouty lips with an undeniable naturalness.

"Maybe it's you who doesn't belong here," Aria suggested.

"I'm with Troy."

"Well, of course. But do you really think it will last?" Aria's voice was loaded with condescension and false earnestness and pity. The remark stung.

"Troy loves me."

"Mmm . . . ," Aria murmured. "Yes, well, you're not the first bit of fluff that's caught Troy's attention. And you *certainly* won't be the last. He's got a thing for the, um, working classes. No offense."

Brad was as angry as if Aria had spit in his eye, and Mike—who had been visibly shaking with fury—was not far behind.

"Why you son-of-a . . . !"

But before either of them could lay a finger on Aria, Caroline swooped in between them. She planted a kiss on each of Aria's cheeks and held his hands as if he were her long-lost son.

"*So* glad you could make it, Aria!" she gushed. It was a tone warmer than any she had ever used with Brad Drake. "Are you drinking?"

Aria nodded humbly, and shot each of his antagonists a smarmy look.

"Brad, dear," Caroline commanded imperiously, without bothering to look Brad in the face, "why don't you fetch us a couple of Campari and sodas? Or have your friend do it." Then Caroline hooked her elbow under Aria's and led him away to another end of the room, saying, "I was just telling everybody the wonderful things you were doing for Troy."

Mike stared at their departing backs. His face was beet-red with anger.

"Don't they make a wonderful couple," he snapped.

"Bitch. Grade-A consummate first-class bitch!"

"More power to you if you can put up with *that*."

"Amen."

They clinked their glasses. There was nothing more aggravating to either of them than a pretty boy who thought he was God's gift to gay men, or a rich kid who thought birthright alone made him worth his weight in gold.

"I loathe that dude," Mike said.

"Me, too. And he hates me right back."

"He's jealous of you."

"No, I don't think so. I'm beside the point. It's Troy he wants. Trophy Troy."

Brad raised his glass to his lips, and felt a hand slip up under his jacket and snatch at his butt. He jumped and spilled the drink down his shirtfront.

"Speak of the devil," Mike said.

Brad turned to find Troy Boston beside him, the offending hand covering an "oh" of fake surprise. Grinning sheepishly, Troy said, "Sorry, but that butt was crying out to be grabbed and I figured I was just the guy."

Troy shifted to Mike with the kind of heated gaze that made the recipient feel afterward like he had to take a long cold shower.

Troy said, "I can tell when you get bored at a party, Bradley, because you end up tracking down all the hottest guys in the room." He stretched out a friendly hand and said, "I'm Troy Boston."

"I know who you are," Mike said. "Everybody knows Troy Boston."

Mike did not relinquish Troy's hand. He was obviously quite impressed by Troy Boston in the flesh. Who wouldn't be? Troy was decked out in a blood-red blouse and leather trousers of his own design. His famously recalcitrant hair had been allowed to remain spiky and unkempt on top, giving him a boyish, rakish air.

Still, Mike managed to retain his composure. "So you think I'm among the hottest guys in the room, eh? Well, since this room is mostly elderly women, that's not necessarily much of a compliment."

Troy grinned wickedly.

"But thanks for saying so," Mike added.

"Your mother . . . ," Brad interrupted.

Troy's grin collapsed into chagrin.

"I know, I know. I'm sorry," Troy said. "She was threatening to come over to see you a few moments ago, but I got trapped in a conversation with the lieutenant governor, so I couldn't rescue my damsel in distress." Troy affectionately dusted Brad's lapels and said to Mike, "Brad always gets this flustered look when my mother is done with him."

"I do not!"

"He just needs to be petted and soothed, and then he gets happy again."

Brad jabbed his boyfriend in the ribs. Despite Caroline's fresh outrage, his spirits soon fell prey to Troy's affectionate teasing. Troy sealed the deal with a kiss. He had gauged perfectly how he could both make Brad feel better and amuse Mike with humor and affection. He was just too exquisitely perfect.

And now that he saw he had softened his crowd, Troy turned up the wattage. He inquired into Mike's career, his interests, his love life, where he lived, who his friends were. He complimented his suit and his piano playing.

And then Troy added, "You should come by Club Troy when it opens. Call my office. We'll get you a pass."

He slipped Mike a business card.

Mike flushed, overwhelmed by the friendly assault. He looked at Brad guiltily, and then accepted Troy's card. The line between flirt and business was so fine with Troy that people often got confused. That's why he was so good at what he did, whether he was working the gay boys or the old ladies or the local politicos. Mike would, no doubt, turn out to be a loyal customer at Club Troy, even if he only came for the scenery that Troy's appearance provided.

"Hey!" Mike said, examining the card. "That's cool!"

He indicated the graphic design alongside Troy's name and the club's name and address. It was a modernistic depiction of a Trojan horse, rendered in only a few swooping flourishes. The horse itself had a tiny, maniacal, high-energy leer on its face, and one of its eyes contained fire.

"Lemme see that." Brad took the card and examined it. "That *is* cool. Where'd it come from?"

"Didn't you see it?" Troy asked. "Caroline told me it was one of the designs you picked out the other day. From the graphic designer."

Then Troy glanced at his watch and announced it was time to go and make their excuses. Mike returned to his piano a little flushed, another in a long line of conquests by Troy Boston. As they headed for the door, Brad thought he could hear an extra flourish coming off the piano keys. Troy Boston often had that effect on strangers.

Caroline intercepted them at the coat check. Her nose was wrinkled as if she had stepped in something nasty.

"Do you think it's really appropriate," Caroline asked, "in a room with dozens of potential investors to be spending time chatting with the *help*?"

Brad flushed at the contemptuous tone she reserved for Mike. He was a nice guy and didn't deserve to be treated that way.

Troy, however, did not argue with or engage her. He had spent a lifetime knowing when to pick battles with his formidable mother. He kissed Caroline on the forehead, disengaged her from his arm, and thanked her for inviting them to the lovely party.

Caroline's face fell, and she looked like a forlorn little girl.

"You're going already?" she asked. She looked at Troy with pleading eyes as if she could not bear to be left alone.

Brad sighed. Caroline's one redeeming feature was that she so obviously loved—and was furiously proud of—her son. It was lucky they had that it common—in fact, it was the only thing they had in common. He was almost envious that Troy had a mother like this, and he would have liked to have been friends with her, instead of the object of her scorn and contempt.

"Sorry, Mother," Troy said gently. "Things to do, people to see." He returned a loose lock of her gray hair to its place and again kissed her good-bye.

Like a scorned woman reasserting her pride, Caroline stood straight and tall, as if she didn't give a damn in the world if they left her and never came back. As they put on their coats, she declared loudly, "I bet the next party won't be as good as mine."

"No one throws a party like you, Caroline," Troy assured her.

These words seemed to appease her, and they escaped onto the street in a gale of happy giggles. Brad was thrilled to be released finally from the confines of the Harvard Club. Elegance had a short shelf life, as far as Brad was concerned, and the pretense was grating.

To Brad, manners were supposed to make an occasion more enjoyable, not less so. But somehow Caroline's parties never worked out that way. As far as he was concerned, Aria Shakespeare could have the whole lot of Brahmin friends that he had so casually named.

Except Troy, of course. Troy Brad intended to keep.

Their next stop was much less intimate. It was the convention hall of one of Boston's waterfront hotels. A huge Trojan horse, in the same style as Troy's business card, hung from the second-story window and down over the door.

They swept through the open door. Troy's eyes scanned the crowd inside, offering a smile here, a nod there. He was like the queen of England, or a woman throwing beads from a Mardi Gras float.

"We're Boston's gay First Family. You know what I mean?" Troy murmured in Brad's ear. "Every liberal wants to see a gay couple succeed."

He was right. In a liberal city like Boston, you could instantly win a label for tolerance and style by including Troy and Brad on your guest list.

"But it might not last," Troy cautioned, "so we've got to make the most of it. It's really a boost for our careers. There are young guys coming up who want our places."

Troy faced Brad. "How do I look?"

"Fabulous. As always."

Troy smiled wolfishly, kissed him, and dove into the crowd. Social occasions were to him like a championship series. Like Mike the piano player, people were mesmerized by his manicured masculine hands, his tempered voice, his ability to focus on you as if you were the only person in the world and everyone else pure distraction.

Watching him, Brad thought: Give Caroline credit for this. She had raised him on cocktail party chatter and finger foods. Troy's manner was effortless, because his life had been one long social engagement.

Brad skirted the edge of the room, moving toward the bar. A beautiful woman tapped him on the shoulder as he passed. Her lipstick was slightly smeared and her eyes were a bit muddy with alcohol.

"I don't know how you stay around him twenty-four-seven," she said, looking like she would not mind being around Troy twenty-four-seven. "It must be exhausting."

"Sometimes," Brad admitted cheerfully. "You get used to it." The woman was paying him no attention, so he added, almost to himself, "You've got to get used to it if you are going to be with Troy Boston. You've got to learn to share."

Before he had met Troy, Brad would not have been caught dead at a function like this. It was pure marketing. Pure glitz. Not Brad's style.

Only because Turner had told him it was necessary for the restaurant business had Brad learned to meet with the press for each of the openings of his restaurants. And then he had only wanted to talk about food, when the press had wanted to talk about celebrities who had eaten or would eat at Cheval or Jean-Baptiste or Coriander.

The plasticity of public relations turned him off. It was like processed food. You lost all the natural flavor, and replaced it with bubble gum.

That was not what Chef Roulard had taught Brad, and it was not the way Brad operated. Brad was far more reserved by nature than Troy. Troy let the phoniness wash off his back like water from a duck. He maybe even enjoyed it a little.

Troy was the one with the hundreds of friends. Brad had only Turner and Chessie. Two close friends were all he needed.

As if he had summoned her from a netherworld just by thinking of her, Chessie burst out of the pale crowd and struck a pose in front of Brad. She invited him to admire her, which he promptly did.

"You look scrumptious."

"I don't," she demurred. "But it's sweet of you to say."

She kissed him and all but sat in his lap to whisper, "Now if you could only convince the straight guys how scrumptious I am, that would be doing me a big favor. Have you ever seen so many hotties in one place in all your life?"

"Troy's events always bring them out of the woodwork."

Chessie's lustful expression turned into a scowl. She was no fan of Troy Boston.

"It's not just his event," she said. "It's yours, too. Your restaurant is what's going to make or break this Club Troy. I honestly don't know why you let *him* get all the credit."

"Um, have you considered, Chessie, that I don't give a shit?"

She locked her eyes on his. "Yes. I have. You probably don't. Can I help it if you're plain crazy?"

She gave him a cockeyed grin. Chessie had been known to be a little crazy herself. She was wound tight, with a hair-trigger temper and a habit of falling in love with professional assholes, in Brad's humble opinion. She couldn't help herself; bring a misogynist into the room and she would be hopelessly smitten.

Chessie had first impressed Brad the day they were hired at Borneo. She had vomited the free meal provided to the waitstaff on purely ethical grounds, after learning that what she had consumed had contained a piece of veal. She accused Chef Roulard of having disguised the meal's true nature with a clever French name, thereby forcing her to participate in the slaughter and mistreatment of adorable baby calves.

Chessie had not been so orthodox, however, not to have noticed the baby calf's fine, tender flavor. Months later, she had found a way to morph her moral qualms so as to permit exclusions for veal sampling, at least on a limited basis.

While the promos and announcements peppered the din

around them, Brad and Chessie chattered on and played with the Trojan horse cocktail napkins. The crowd pressed tight. Brad was encouraged to pose for a few photographs into which Chessie graciously inserted herself after first making sure she was showing sufficient navel.

"You're such a slut!"

"I know," Chessie said, pleased with herself. It was obviously a good-body-image day.

Brad smiled, but the grin left his face like a one-night stand.

"Whatcha lookin' at?" Chessie crowed. "Why aren't you looking at me?"

Brad slugged down his drink. "It's that guy. Aria. The graphic designer."

Her face flushed red. "Where?!" She looked this way and that.

Brad pointed.

Chessie set down her drink and turned to the hunt.

Brad snatched her wrist. "Don't embarrass me, darling. He's allowed here. It's public space; can't hope to clear it of all the assholes."

She jerked her arm free and looked as if she might defy him.

"Really," Brad said. "I mean it. Don't fuck this up for Troy by making a big scene. He's harmless."

Chessie narrowed her eyes. "You sure?"

"I'm sure."

"'Cause I'd kill him for you. You know I would, right?"

Brad smiled. Aria would never know what hit him.

"I know."

After nearly two more hours of the din, and a few dozen dances with Chessie, Brad looked up to find Troy's gaze on him from across the room. The crowds melted away and it was like they were alone in this vast warehouse of a room.

Troy's glance was solicitous and kind and full of concern, as if he had been watching Brad for some time now. Troy's eyebrow raised the slightest question, and his head inclined toward the door. Brad smiled. And shrugged. He could last a little while longer. But he was glad Troy had asked. Troy was always watching out for his ass, having his back.

Chessie noted the exchange. Again, she scowled. Like any fag-hag worth the name, she was gratuitously critical of all of Brad's boyfriends and particularly critical—and jealous—of the pretty ones.

"Hey!" she said. "You going to spend all night ogling your boyfriend or are you going to help me out? Huh?" She reminded Brad that when he had been single she was the first one to hook him up with the hotties, picking them out for him, starting conversations, introducing Brad, and pressing for digits.

"OK," Brad said. "Who do you have in mind?"

She was torn between the broad-shouldered gray suit with the black-tie-on-black-shirt look and the scrubby artiste with the mostly unbuttoned DKNY shirt.

"That guy's not gay, is he?" she asked, settling on the artiste.

"Nah, definitely not."

Chessie was not convinced. "Maybe he's just not your type, Brad," she fretted. "You go for that girlie type."

"Troy's hardly girlie, Chessie. Trust me, sister, go get the artiste. I promise. He's a straight boy. Just look at his argyle socks."

"Not all straight guys are bad . . ."

"Dressers," Brad finished for her. "Of course they're not. Just ninety-nine percent. And the other one percent are closeted."

Chessie raised her hand to smack him in mock outrage, but he caught her wrist in the air.

"Go get him, girl. He's yours."

Chessie fortified herself with a slug from Brad's drink, wiped away the look of skepticism, and replaced it with a coquettish hunger and pursed lips. She then slunk toward the other end of the bar, where her artistic soon-to-be friend stood exposing a naturally flat little belly that Brad would have killed for. What good was it on a straight guy? Women didn't have very high standards.

"Attagirl!" a voice shouted after Chessie, nearly blowing out Brad's ear. It was Troy, who had slipped up beside Brad unnoticed, and used every bit of his powerful lungs.

She gave him the finger behind her back.

They watched as Chessie casually slipped in next to the artiste, pulled out a cigarette, and then looked around helplessly as if she did not know what to do. The artiste gracefully offered her a light, and she cupped her hand over his as she took the first puff.

"Lemme guess," Troy said. "She's got a half dozen lighters in her purse, right?"

Brad shrugged. "Sure, of course. But whatever. Nothing wrong with a few tricks in pursuit of love, right?"

Troy grinned as if he had been caught in a game himself.

"See, you thought I wasn't on to you."

"*Moi?*" Troy squealed.

"Yes, you. But you know I love it."

"I don't know *what* you're talking about," Troy said with a wounded Scarlett O'Hara air.

"Well, all *I* know," Brad said, "is my work here is done. The gods of Chessie's horniness and loneliness have been appeased. We can officially carry on with our evening."

Troy laughed and kissed his forehead.

Again, he made all the right noises to their hostess as they left, thanking her profusely and complimenting her companion, whom he had not yet seen. Troy was good at this game. He had an eye for the new dress, the new hairstyle, the results of the new diet, the sadness that indicated a missed birthday, and the spark that indicated love.

Women loved to be noticed, and Troy always noticed it all, every fine detail—and was discreet enough to keep some of the detail masked in a simple appreciative look.

They ended the night on the edge of the South End at a hole-in-the-wall called Wally's Café. On the outside, it was a nondescript dive, its basement marked only by an unlit Schlitz sign. Two serious stocking-capped young black men checked IDs out on the sidewalk.

The interior was one long mine shaft reaching away from the door—narrow, brick, slightly sloped. Against the far wall, away from the entrance, was a stage. It was raised no more than six or eight inches off the concrete floor. The musicians were elbow to elbow with the crowd. The place reeked of bourbon and spilled beer.

Brad and Troy ducked between a courtly elderly black man in a gray, open-necked suit and a fedora, smoothly persuading an obdurate middle-aged woman to go home with him. A clot of suburban frat boys bound for business school were forcing down large quantities of bourbon, smoking cigars, and making uproarious nervous jokes that were drowned out by the keyboards and horns that studded the stage.

Despite its size, Wally's was the premier jazz locale in Boston. The bigger acts played at the hotel jazz clubs, but after their gigs, the headliners drifted down to Wally's, where they could jam with one another and with the fresh young talent from the Berklee School who showed up with their horns.

A T-shirted muscle boy and his preppie accountant boyfriend with tiny hip glasses had colonized a couple of bar stools for Brad and Troy early in the evening before the crowds came in. They had steadfastly maintained their places as the Wally's crowd grew, and now beckoned Troy and Brad to press among the stools and find a patch of welcome ground.

The music was deafening. Troy shouldered his way among the crowd, to within spitting distance of the stage. He stalled there, paying homage to musician friends. To Brad, Troy seemed spotlit and perfect. His head bent to people's ears as he passed, as if he were the mayor of the tiny town that was Wally's Café.

It seemed to Brad that all the horns were triumphal. It was their hour, his and Troy's.

"You're so quiet!" the muscle boy shouted in his ear.

But Brad could only muster a shrug and a Cheshire cat smile.

At closing, they were joined out on the sidewalk by the musicians. A froth of sweat was in their hair. Spirits were high. Someone played a rapid-fire bleat on his trumpet that punctured the night.

The musicians steered Brad and Troy up the street with them, demanding that they come party and Brad cook up something mean. Brad's head was like a traffic jam, still full of music and horns. He suspected from his dry tongue and burning eyes that he would have a monster hangover in the morning, just in time for his famed Sunday brunch at Cheval, which all the gay boys attended in their PJs and robes.

He gave Troy a quick pleading look and Troy instantly came to his defense. He managed to wriggle away from the tide and draw Brad with him to the curb. He started on the excuses and parried the arguments and pleas, and his musician friends finally gave up, laughing.

"You two! It's only two-thirty, man! You're worse than married, for God's sake," they mocked. "Where are the two kids and the minivan and when are you moving to the suburbs?"

Brad was exhausted and a little drunk, but Troy had more energy than he had started the night with. He said good night to his friends and musicians with an exotic series of handshakes that was like an itsy-bitsy spider crawling up the web.

At that moment, Aria Shakespeare stumbled out of Wally's, hustled out by one of the bouncers. "Found this one in the men's room," he complained. "Fast asleep." He laughed and locked the door.

Brad and Troy's eyes met. Troy gave a little "what can you do" shrug. Brad hoped he gave a look that said, "Shoot him, that's what you can do."

"You know that guy?" Brad quizzed.

"Which guy?"

"Him." Brad jerked a thumb, but when he looked Aria was gone. "Who?"

"He was right there!" Brad glanced up and down the street. "The guy they kicked out. I swear he's *following* us."

Troy shrugged again. "I wasn't really paying attention."

"Yes, you were. You looked at me."

Troy put his hand under Brad's chin and raised his face into the streetlight. "I like to look at you, baby. It's a hobby of mine." He nuzzled close.

Brad frowned, feeling drunk and stupid, and wishing he was a little less of each. He sighed. "Let's go home."

Troy yammered on, replaying the events of the night, speculating on its consequences from a business perspective. Whether the press would be good, or whether they would get any press at all. What the next steps were that would make Club Troy a success.

He talked them all the way back to Brad's apartment. His talk made the way short. It was a current at Brad's back, and the night's wind was no match at all.

Troy only stopped talking to let Brad discover for himself what was waiting on his pillow—two round-trip tickets for a three-day getaway to Bermuda.

"What's this?"

Troy took the tickets from his hand and set them on the night-stand. He did not say a word as he unbuttoned Brad's shirt. He just smiled.

"But-bu-but . . . what about work? The restaurants . . ."

Troy put a finger to his lips. "Turner's got the restaurants under control. I told him you had other plans."

Troy slid off Brad's shirt as gently as a nurse would draw a dressing from a wound. It dropped like a whisper at Brad's feet.

Goose bumps appeared on Brad's skin, but it wasn't from the cold. A shiver played down his spine that had nothing to do with chill.

Troy lifted Brad's arms and pulled his undershirt over his head. That, too, dropped away. Brad felt Troy's strong hands slide down his arms, his shoulders, beneath his armpits, his ribs, flash over his belly, and fix on his hips. Firmly and suddenly.

It felt as if Troy were creating him, firming up the muscles of his body, toning and tightening them. Under this hand, Brad felt statuesque and beautiful. Troy unbuckled Brad's belt and slipped his pants down to his ankles. Brad stepped out of the pants, and Troy pulled him close. Kisses just brushing Brad's lips, Troy's eyes fixed squarely on Brad's, until Brad thought he would boil over then and there with love and desire for Troy.

"You're good," he whispered.

Troy opened his mouth as if to say something perfect and sweet back. But then he cracked a grin and said, "I know."

Brad poked him in the ribs and shoved him away. Troy laughed and lunged, but Brad dodged the outstretched hands. He leaped onto the bed and then over the other side, and Troy gave chase.

Troy cornered him finally near the closet, closing the last few steps warily, as if he was trying to tame a wild animal in a trap.

Brad jumped him. Although Troy had the advantage of height, Brad was able to wrestle him to the bed. He threw Troy down. His drunkenness left his body, overpowered by the carnal urge.

Brad tore off Troy's pants and socks and straddled him, pinning his arms back and leaning over his head. "I'll show you good, mister."

Troy's eyes had gone moist with hunger. His body was limp and supple, almost suppliant beneath Brad, but he could feel Troy's hard-on through his underwear. It pressed Brad's butt like a poker fresh from the flames.

"Show me good," Troy demanded. As always, he was unapologetic in his desires—unafraid to take what he wanted, or to be taken.

Brad began to shower his face with deep, open-mouthed kisses. Troy's tongue entered his mouth, gently at first, and then, as if it found firm and safe ground, it began to wrestle with Brad's tongue.

Against Brad's face was the slight scruff of Troy's one-day growth, a pleasant sandpaper scratch. He pressed under Troy's chin, on his neck, in the dimple at his throat. His breath was coming hard and fast, and Troy's hips were working against his bottom, insistent, rude, almost frightening. In a flash, Troy slipped out of his underwear.

Brad pressed his butt cheeks against the erect cock, flattening it against Troy's belly; together they tore off Troy's shirt. His own buckle seemed to melt from the heat and the top button to his pants shot against the wall.

He felt the rude pressure of Troy's cock again on his backside, as he threatened to jam it home dry. He felt the desperate ache. The need to take him in. To be penetrated and obliterated by Troy's strength.

Troy's belly flexed beneath him each time he thrust, and Brad rode him, jockey-like, his eyes focused first on the rippling, flexing belly, then on the moist hungry mouth, then on the burning eyes that were eating him up, hot enough to burn off the top layer of skin.

Brad touched himself, masturbating furiously over Troy's chest and belly until he thought he could no longer take it, and yet he needed more.

He flipped Troy onto his belly. Urgently, Brad spread those cheeks and let a thin drool of spit drip into Troy's crack. Brad spread the wetness with his tongue and finger. Troy was flexing his hips, and Brad teased his cock against him, rubbing just on the rim of his ass.

Troy moaned softly. And Brad teased and teased. He was focused on that rising tide inside of him, that earthquake, that surge of pleasure. Trying to contain it. Trying to control it.

Each time it was close, Brad forced himself to pull away. The loss of contact with Troy's ass was almost painful.

When he could stand it no longer, Brad leaned to the side table. He extracted the condoms and lube, and this time there was no teasing. He was forceful, a hand on Troy's hip, a finger and then two inside him. Troy shuddered a brief moment, gasping. And then that sweet ass relaxed and took him in like a hungry mouth.

He balanced himself on Troy's shoulder blade, which was hard as steel. Brad arched his back slightly and pointed his cock at the small, wet asshole. The muscles tensed beneath his palm, and Brad shivered as he watched himself enter Troy.

His slicked cock went in and out. Troy turned his head to the side, his mouth wet and open. Still inside Troy, Brad leaned forward over him so he could look in his eyes and kiss him. He got closer and closer to that sweet, trembly, volatile edge. He willed himself again to control the surge, to master it, even as he knew that the effort was hopeless.

The mound of Troy's ass beneath him, the muscles in his shoulders alternately tensing and releasing, in a close symphony to his own thrusts. The rhythmic flow of words from his mouth, his own name forming on Troy's lips, the ruby rush of blood to his face, pouting, full with pleasure and lust.

He felt Troy's back crack, and just that extra bit of sensation was enough to push them both over the edge. A gush exploded from his cock and he spasmed forward, nearly biting Troy's lip, cracking his head. Brad's hips convulsed twice, and for the longest moment after orgasm, neither of them moved. They were one. Fused.

A tangled destiny like their tangled limbs. Inseparable. Permanent. Forever. He did not know where Troy began, or where he ended. They were one lush, amorphous fever tide of exhausted pleasure.

Brad had hardly taken a breath in the silence, so he made the first move. He gasped. Spasms littered his whole body, one of them so tremendous that his softening cock escaped from Troy with a hard plop. The moment of separation was almost painful in its intensity.

He rolled off Troy, and Troy immediately rolled onto him, so they were face to face, chest to chest, cock to cock. Troy's weight pressed down on Brad's chest, making him breathless.

"I bought those tickets to celebrate," Troy whispered. His breath was cool and delicious, and Brad raised his head to kiss him. Troy let their lips touch, then coyly pulled away.

"Celebrate what?"

"To celebrate your saying yes."

"Yes?"

"Yes," Troy repeated firmly. His gaze was deep, down into Brad's very soul. At first uncomfortable, Brad relaxed into the look, allowed it to happen, without fear, even as his heart raced with excitement.

"Yes, you will share my house. Yes, you will share my life."

"Yes I will put up with your mother?" Brad joked, made nervous by this wonderful dream-come-true.

Troy smiled, but said nothing. There was no jest in him, no joke. No calculation whatsoever. Brad's heart surged so powerfully, he worried its force would toss Troy against the wall, like a tidal wave. It was so much more than he had ever dared ask Troy for. So much that he had been prepared to wait years to hear.

"Do you love me?" Troy asked.

"Yes." Brad kissed him again and again. "Yes. Yes. Yes. Yes. Yes."

9

They slept for three hours, not a moment more. When the alarm went off next to Brad's ear, he thought it was a buzz saw and he wished that it would cut off his head.

Troy reached over and banged it off. A fresh breeze through the open window roused Brad, as Troy forced him to stumble, protesting, into the shower. When he came out, Troy had already packed Brad a bag and was throwing clothes into his own.

"You seen my Troy Toy shirt?" Troy shouted.

The Troy Toy shirt was Troy's latest obsession. He was so proud of the design that he had not even made it part of his collection yet, because he enjoyed being the only one to own one. It was sexy and hip, shimmering and iridescent, and only someone who looked as hot as Troy would ever do it justice.

"I can barely see my face in the mirror."

"I swear I left it out here for this trip. I know I did."

"Well, I haven't seen it."

"Where could it have got to, though?"

"It's only you and me in here," Brad pointed out helpfully.

Troy glared at him.

Brad grinned.

"Besides, you're not going to need much clothing . . . we're going to keep you in your birthday suit."

Troy went back to searching.

"Why don't you pack something else, anything . . . ?"

"Because that goes with . . . Oh, forget it, you're right." He threw the rest of his things together just as the airport taxi honked outside.

In no time they were on the ground in Bermuda. A private car whisked them from the terminal and up into the hills immediately surrounding Hamilton and Paget Harbor. The ocean was visible from the road. It shimmered, gorgeous and blue beneath them, like a perfect future.

An unbroken limestone wall hemmed the road on one side. Riotous nasturtiums spilled over the wall. Behind the wall was a row of hedges, as if they were a second line of defense. Everywhere there were cedars and palmettos and loquat trees weighed down with yellow-orange, pear-shaped fruits.

The car turned into a gravel driveway, passing through an iron gate. The stone pillars that hinged the gate were decked with a profusion of bright orange hibiscus that had blooms as wide as faces, with irreverent pistil tongues sticking straight back at them. The bright yellow trumpets of the allamanda vines scrambled down the walls like a marching band.

The subtropical forest had been tamed into a neat English garden that crowned the top of the semicircular driveway. The car deposited them in front of a pretty and perfectly kept villa. Although it was only two stories, it stretched from side to side for what seemed like a city block. In the dining room window, a reassuring and discreet rainbow sticker was visible in a pane of glass.

The owners, two elderly English gentlemen, one short and fat, the other tall and elegant, tumbled out of the house. Bubbling with queeny enthusiasm, they whisked Brad and Troy through the house, across the slate patio, and down a winding brick path to a charming cottage, separate from the main house.

Between the cottage and house was a manicured rock garden, lush with Easter lilies and tiny purple Bermudianas. The property behind the little cottage dropped off dramatically toward the ocean. Lush, terraced gardens, each one twenty feet beneath the other, formed a series of steps down the steep hillside.

Tucked into one of these hillside terraces, perhaps a hundred yards from the cottage, was a deep blue pool. It was surrounded by a discreet chest-high stone wall that would mask any skinny-dipping.

A fountain trickled at one end of the pool. The deck furniture around it was made of teak, and two brightly colored umbrellas provided the tables with shade. Purple-blue plumbago vines were twisted among honeysuckle and bougainvillea around the pool. Each of the terraces beneath was planted with citrus trees—lemons, limes, oranges, and grapefruits.

"We call them 'golden lamps in a green night,'" one of the proprietors said, looking at them as if falling in love again for the very first time.

"It's paradise," Brad blurted out, and Troy and the owners beamed with equal pleasure at his praise.

The first day, Brad and Troy rented scooters and zipped around the island to the white sand beaches. Their first night, they had a quiet meal at one of the fine restaurants in Hamilton.

Brad ordered ham croquettes, which were bits of smoky ham bound by béchamel and deep fried. They were crisp on the outside and tender inside—"just like you," Brad pointed out to Troy. Troy had a delicious tartare of salmon wrapped in a parcel of smoked salmon tied with chive string, but he gallantly made a point of opining that the restaurant could not hold a candle to Cheval or Jean-Baptiste or Coriander.

In the morning, their hosts bustled breakfast down to them and served it poolside. There was a pot of marmalade, a bowl of oatmeal, a basket of baked goods, and dark coffee. Their two elderly proprietors lingered just long enough to assure them—with a smirk and rolled eyes—that Brad and Troy had not kept them up all night with their "bedtime recreations."

After another day of beachcombing and arguing in antique shops about how they would decorate their house and frolicking among the freesias and pawpaw trees, they took tea with the proprietors up at the main house in the late afternoon. The back side of the house was covered in white, red, and pink oleander.

The house was a museum, packed with Victorian antiques and knickknacks of every description, much more impressive than anything Brad and Troy had seen that day. The walls had literally hundreds of portraits, daguerreotypes and inks and primitive photos in obscenely ornate frames.

Their two hosts were at least as fascinating as their belongings. They had lived together since shortly after the Second World War, taking over the cottage and house in the early 1960s.

The more talkative and rotund of their hosts regaled them with wonderful stories from over the years, and the taller, thin one spoiled them with fat buttered scones, which would take Brad a week of gym workouts to burn off.

The four of them laughed and laughed, and when it was time for Brad and Troy to go out for the evening, it was hard for them to leave the two old lovers, who were just then ruminating and bickering about what kind of cocktail they would take before dinner. It was between a colonial gin and tonic and a blue tropical mood mixed with Curacao. "Or perhaps a tot of loquat liqueur," the fat one proposed, rubbing his palms together and explaining that they had made it themselves by soaking the loquat fruits in gin with rock candy for six months.

For Brad, the men's love was an inspiration and a goal. Once he and Troy were alone, he pointed out the obvious:

Wasn't it wonderful that they were still happy after fifty years together! Wasn't it amazing that there was still a strong sexual spark between the two, palpable and almost pungent in their quick exchanges, and in the flash of their looks at each other! They made love seem so easy!

"I think," Troy said, interrupting Brad's enthusiasm, "that they're the only two homos on the island. What else are they going to do?"

Brad cuffed him so hard Troy nearly tumbled off the slate tiles and into the vines and ground cover on either side.

"You're such a cynical bastard!" Brad accused.

Troy grinned good-naturedly. He liked to pretend that he was not a sentimental old queen. He liked to pretend that he would never fall prey to romantic or sentimental notions.

But the restaurant he brought Brad to that night showed that his cynicism was a façade. It was the most romantic place Brad had ever been.

It was located in a quiet house by the sea, with a stone foundation and a pier that stuck straight into Hamilton Harbor. They were given an upstairs room against the window, where a small fire burned and smelled of peat. The fire's heat took the edge off the breeze from the sea.

Troy had called ahead, and a '97 Barolo had been decanted and set on the sideboard. A candle burned on each table, in a little sculpted hurricane glass, and Brad approved of the menu and wine list, even if it did have an unfounded (in Brad's view) prejudice for the French on both counts.

When they were seated, with knees almost touching, Troy confessed, "This is my favorite restaurant in all of Bermuda, maybe in the whole world." He touched Brad's hand and winked. "Except yours, baby."

For a moment, the romantic mood was broken. It bothered Brad that if this was Troy's favorite, he had probably been there before, with someone else.

It reminded Brad that Troy had had a life before him, a life that did not include him. He imagined Troy dining here, in this same spot, with his true love, Kurt Tamweiler. He imagined them staying at the same guest house, in the same cottage, swimming by the same pool, having the same conversation with and about their hosts.

Brad shivered. It was like a ghost hadn't just passed between them, but had taken a seat at their already crowded table and planned to linger the rest of the night. It was strange how old boyfriends could still raise Brad's hackles, how susceptible he was—despite two years of history and a promise to move in together—to doubt. And suspicion.

"What's the matter?" Troy asked. "You haven't even opened your menu."

"I know what I want."

Brad looked directly across at Troy, with as bullying a glance as he had ever hit anyone with. Troy nodded and looked down at his menu.

Then he looked up again sharply. What Brad had said finally registered with Troy, and he blushed a shade of crimson that was as deep as the decanter of wine on the sideboard. His eyes went liquid.

On both sides of the table any thoughts of prior loves or prior lives disappeared. There was only each other. Only this moment. Everything else was walled outside.

Brad felt a longing inside him as deep as the ocean outside. It was a tide that rose up and lapped against Troy, drawn in toward him by an inexorable moon.

And Troy Boston was speechless. Which never happened. Not to him.

But there Troy was, with a happy, disconcerted look on his face, almost boyish in the candlelight. He slid a hand across the table, and Brad took it in his. If he was ever dangling off the edge of the world, this was the hand he wanted to be holding—strong, dry, firm, supple, with an almost shocking electricity running over the skin.

Troy raised Brad's hand to his lips.

Still not a word had been spoken. They stared at each other with happy contentment, and sipped wine from their glasses. And then Troy, oblivious to the other guests who were in their own little honeymoon worlds in any case, leaned over the table and planted a Barolo-flavored kiss on Brad's full lips.

Fireworks went off in Brad's head and the room was suddenly filled with light. He was dizzy and fumbled for his wineglass or napkin. Then he decided he wanted neither. He was too afraid to wash off the lingering feeling of those lush lips on his.

It was a perfect, velvet moment, with searing heat.

That was when it happened. There was a muted squawk of falsetto surprise from the stairway. Then that grating voice, crying out like a startled crow: "Troy! Troy! Darling, is that you? With this damnable low light, one can't see a thing! It *is* you, you dog!"

There was a rush of windmill fluttering arms and little dance steps, and then a whirlwind of feathers collided with the table. It was like a pigeon had flown into a picture window and broken its scrawny neck.

Aria Shakespeare caught himself on the table's edge.

"Goddamn shoes!" he said, staring pointedly down at the chunky, square-toed boots with a three-inch lift and a half-inch lip all around the sole.

Aria was fabulously overdressed in white Capri pants and a stunning orange velvet jacket that was all plush and tufts, and he had slung a white feathered boa around his neck. He was lilting and fey, coked up and loquacious, prancing about Troy's chair with glitter in his hair and blue powder on his eyelids.

Aria focused entirely on Troy, as if he were sitting alone at the table.

"Darling," he gushed, "isn't it just amazing that we have to travel six hundred miles in order to see one another? What a wonderful surprise! I was just explaining to my faghag"—Aria turned to his companion, a waifish, washed-out twenty-year-old with heroin eyes—"how absolutely desperate this place is! Not a gay man in miles! Unless you count all these Englishmen, but you know how it is with foreigners—the gaydar simply does not work! I am *so* glad you're here. And oh, this is Bambi."

"My name is not Bambi," she said stubbornly.

Aria ignored her. "Bambi, this is Troy Boston. The *real* Troy Boston. Isn't he to die for? Just *look* how handsome he is!"

Aria's hand made a quick series of touches on Troy's face and chin, a too-familiar catalog of his beauty. Troy looked genuinely horrified. His eyes were fixed on Aria's boa, as if it were a serpent that had slithered out of the shadows and come to life and might squeeze them all to death.

But—as he always did—Troy recovered his composure in a matter of seconds. Like a curtain had descended on a stage, his face relaxed. He mustered a smile.

Under the circumstances, Brad thought angrily, even that smile was a betrayal.

"Good to see you, too," Troy said. And then almost as an afterthought, he introduced Brad.

Aria turned his head over his shoulder and looked Brad up and down. Then, slowly, he turned himself and extended a hand.

"We've met. *Enchanté*, again, I'm sure."

"You've met?!" Troy's surprise seemed fearful, nervous, shrill.

"To plan the branding, honey. With *Caroline*. She and I had a *wonderful* lunch together. We had *all* kinds of catching up to do. What an absolute *hoot* Caroline is! I love her to death. We were telling Brad how you and I go *way* back. When we were just horny young boys."

"Wait a minute! Wait just a minute," Bambi crowed, looking as if she had just been woken from a deep, deep sleep. "I know you! You're Brad Drake. I *love* your restaurant. Cheval. I absolutely love it!"

She looked at Aria accusingly. "Or I would love it, if I could afford it. Or if Aria wasn't such a cheap bastard and brought me there more often!"

Aria shot back, "Maybe if you could get a date, sweetheart, you might get in more often."

Bambi ignored him and chattered on. She described various near misses she had experienced at the very door of Cheval, and how it pained her to no end that she had only been there once. "It's, like, my life's goal to eat there again!" she gushed.

Brad ought to have been flattered by the recognition and attention, which caused Aria to pout. But even Aria's unhappiness was not enough to make Brad happy at this moment. Something had been stolen from him. There were vandals at the city gates.

His eyes were fixed on Troy, and judging from Brad's expression, the *amuse-bouche* the waiter had slipped in front of him might as well have been poisoned.

Make him go away, Brad thought, trying telepathically to force this message on his boyfriend.

Troy did not meet Brad's gaze, or acknowledge any telepathy. He was busy maintaining a plastic smile for Bambi's benefit.

Aria, of course, promptly launched into a story to compete with Bambi's, until the both of them were talking at cross-purposes and great volume, and the other guests began to notice.

Make him go away, Brad thought again, staring at Troy even more urgently.

But it was the hostess who finally persuaded Aria to sit at his own table. As she led them away, Bambi protested, "But I'm not even *hungry*!"

And then a cold silence fell between Brad and Troy. The table that before Aria's arrival had seemed cozy and intimate had become like one of those long, hundred-foot tables you find in Gothic castles, with only a flickering candelabra breaking up the open space. Troy and Brad were suddenly miles apart.

Brad disciplined himself. He would not give Aria the satisfaction of seeing him angry. He would not say a goddamn word. To Aria. To Troy. To anyone. He would just make it through this dinner.

He ate without tasting a single morsel. Any glow the wine had provided was dissipated and done, replaced by a razor-sharp clarity and a sense that deep in the bones of this restaurant was a dark rot, like a sea-dampened beam exposed for the first time to air.

Troy toyed with his food, looking up speculatively at Brad from time to time between bites and courses. His manner was as slow and composed as always. The surprise of Aria's appearance had worn off entirely. And he did not seem to have registered the shattered, changed mood at their table.

Brad suggested bluntly that they skip dessert.

As they left, Aria called out to them again. "Where are you staying, Troy? We must get together."

He gave a little scream of delight at Troy's answer. "That's where *we're* staying! What a coincidence! Small world. Aren't those two old queens to die for?! We'll *definitely* be seeing one another. I'm *so* excited!"

Despite the expression of surprise, Aria's tone suggested there were no coincidences. No coincidences at all, not in the whole wide world. It was all some great big plan and conspiracy to ruin Brad's life. And Brad could contain himself no longer.

"Good night!" he said savagely and departed down the stairs, making as much noise as he could. He heard Aria behind him, saying, "What's *his* hurry?" and "Come give me a kiss good night, sweetheart."

But Brad did not stick around long enough to see whether Troy complied. Out in the parking lot, he tore at the straps of his helmet, which were wound into the scooter's handlebars. He could not get them to come loose.

When Troy joined him and reached over to help, Brad stepped back, put his hands on his hips, and demanded bluntly, "How did he know where we were staying?!" The smoldering fury in him burst into a sheet of flame and accusation.

"I don't know that he did know where we were staying; it's not a big island, you know, and . . ."

"Oh, he knew, Troy. If Bermuda was the size of the entire fucking English empire, Aria would still be at the same place as us. Trust me. I know what that kind is like. He tracked us down. I know it." Brad had been pacing back and forth next to the bikes, but now he stopped and set his eyes accusingly on Troy's face. In an ominous tone, he added, "It was almost like he knew we were down here."

"He could not have known we were down here," Troy replied. He succeeded in freeing the knotted strap and handed Brad his helmet. "I didn't tell anyone. Deliberately. So we would not be interrupted. That was the whole point of the trip, to get away."

Troy slipped on his own helmet as if that were the end of the matter. He laid one hand on his scooter as if to mount it and then froze. "Except my mother, of course. I did tell Caroline."

The guilt played out across his face as if he were a child with a hand in the cookie jar.

"And she went and told Aria . . . Goddamnit! God damn her!" Brad yanked on his own helmet, kicked the stand from underneath his scooter, and fired it up. It did not make the satisfying, deep-throat motorcycle roar he had hoped it would. Instead, running, it sounded a bit like a buzzing bee in a garden of English tea roses, even when he turned the throttle to full blast.

"Damn it! Can't the English make a real motorcycle!" He gave the scooter a few more revs and then killed the engine. Turning in the seat, he spat into the sudden silence: "I thought you said you didn't know Aria, Troy? Didn't you tell me that? Didn't you say you had no idea who he was? You specifically said that. I asked you."

"Who— Oh. I never said I didn't know him."

"Yes, you did. After the lunch with your mother, I specifically asked you about him. You said—"

"Oh. Yeah." Brad watched the gears turning in Troy's head. As if he was trying to come up with a reasonable explanation. "Well. That's because you said his name was . . . What was the name you said?"

"Pssh! Don't pretend you don't know his name."

"I don't know that name. I mean, I do know it. His real name. What does he call himself now? Aria? Aria, right? Well, when I knew him, it was Charles Augustus Thorland III. Sometimes Charlie, when he was really young." Troy cracked a smile, but when he saw it did not amuse Brad, he took it back. "How was I supposed to know he changed his name?"

"Come on. I'm supposed to believe that?!"

"Well, Brad, it's the truth. Why the hell would I lie?"

"Exactly. That's my point. Why would you lie, unless there was something funny going on? That's what's got me worried."

His mind ran wild. He could not help thinking that Troy was covering something up, with that reasonable story of his. How could he not have known? His mother knew! And they talked all the time.

This, Brad thought, was how it always began, how the disinte-

102 : scott pomfret & scott whittier

gration of a relationship always happened. The little things began not to add up. The story could not be tied in neat ends. And then you find out that behind your back a whole other world was taking place. Typical. Time and again with gay men.

"What do you mean, 'funny'?"

"What do you think I mean, 'funny'?"

"Enough of the word games, Brad. I'm not as much into drama as you are."

"Which is your way of admitting you have no heart, and making it sound like a virtue!"

Although they stood just two feet from each other, scooter to scooter, Brad felt like they were a thousand miles apart. Two total strangers.

How could Troy not be pissed? How could he tolerate that Aria had stolen that perfect moment from them as if he had lifted their wallets? Did he care at all? Was there a heart inside Troy's body? Was there someone who got pissed and scared and enthused and passionate? Was there someone capable of falling in love? Not just the convenient partnership they always discussed, the fact that they made a great couple, the co-branding, the restaurant in the club. Not all that. But true, unmitigated, soul-to-soul, heart-to-heart, irreplaceable love. Did Troy even believe in that? Did he know what Brad was talking about when Brad talked about love? About devotion?

Brad restarted his scooter angrily. He was so filled with outrage that it was all he could do to keep himself from telling Troy to go in and spend the rest of the evening with Aria Shakespeare. Or Charlie. Or whatever his damn name was.

And Brad would drive around the island all night, in rapid motorized circles, trying to put the world back together. Fuck Aria Shakespeare! What had started out perfect was now a circle of cold embers. Not a spark of romance left in the night.

Troy reached over and switched off Brad's scooter.

"Hey . . . relax." He raised Brad's chin with his hand. "It's not the end of the world, is it? He's just some unfortunate ass who has no sense of propriety."

"But pretty manners! Your mother said so!"

"Come on, Brad, don't be . . ."

"Is your mother *ever* going to be satisfied until she breaks us up?"

At this Troy drew back, and a flash of anger passed over his face. "I wasn't aware Caroline had the power to break us up," he said darkly.

Brad could not help the surge of triumph he felt at Troy's anger. It was like he had finally gotten him to admit to some feelings.

"Well, she's certainly got the power to be a royal pain in the—"

"She never likes anyone."

"She liked Kurt Tamweiler. She never stops talking about *him*."

A funny look trumped the anger in Troy's face. Brad thought first that it was pain, and that he should have trod more lightly on still-sore feelings. But it proved to be a bubble of laughter, which burst around him. Troy laughed until he had to reach out to Brad's shoulder to steady himself.

"What's the matter?"

"Please. Caroline's sudden fondness for Kurt Tamweiler? That's all hindsight. Like saying nice things at a funeral. Caroline and Kurt hated each other. Hated each other. I never told you that?"

"Um, no."

"She couldn't stop putting him down. Too this, too that. Trust me, you've got it easy."

Brad was struck by the bitterness in Troy's tone. It had never occurred to him how difficult Caroline must be for him to deal with. Although he wanted to hold on to it, Brad felt his anger slipping away. He wanted to snatch it back, hold it tight.

"Anyhow. Whatever." Troy glanced at his watch. "It's OK. We

still have some night left. Don't let Char— Aria spoil the whole thing."

"Only the part at the restaurant," Brad could not help adding, but his anger was nearly spent, no matter how hard he tried to revive it.

"Only that part," Troy acknowledged ruefully. It was his first acknowledgment that anything at all had gone wrong. And Brad was satisfied.

Troy leaned over to give him a serious kiss him on the cheek, but the brims of their helmets cracked together. Troy could not help giggling like a little boy. The dimples on his cheeks deepened, and rich humor ran all over his face.

Against his better judgment, Brad thought, Maybe I *am* making too much of this. It's only that this getaway is so important to me . . . only that Troy is so important to me, that the slightest danger of losing him, or even thinking of losing him, rocks my world.

He removed his helmet and allowed himself to be kissed. Troy leaned close and kicked the kickstand of Brad's scooter down. He took Brad's hand and led him around the side of the restaurant to the pier.

A stand of shrubbery marked the end of the pier, and Troy pointed out the night-blooming cereus among the green branches. Its exquisite white flowers were in full bloom.

"They come out one hour after sunset," Troy said. "And they're worth the wait. Smell them."

Brad bent close and his nose filled with the distinct odor of vanilla ice cream.

They walked to the end of the pier. Brad twisted a cereus bloom in his hand, spinning the petals like a top. At the end of the pier, it was just the two of them out in Hamilton Harbor, and the water lapping at the balustrades, and the smell of barnacles. They may as well have been out in the middle of the Atlantic Ocean.

They sat side by side, feet dangling over the edge, swinging back and forth from the knee, heads leaning against each other.

For a time, they were silent, listening. And then Brad said, "And did you *see* that outfit he was wearing? What was up with *that*? Like somebody skinned a dozen baby Muppets for their hides . . ."

10

In the bedroom, Troy undressed Brad. He kneaded his feet when his socks came off. He drove his thumbs deep into the balls of Brad's feet, drawing a line along his soles like a scar. He worked his hands over Brad's ankles and calves, sliding up and under his shorts.

Brad parted his thighs. The hands reached deep, cupped his scrotum, and located his hardening manhood.

They both stood. One by one, the buttons of Brad's shirt came undone. Troy's eyes remained glued to his face until the shirt had parted and fallen open and slid off Brad's shoulders.

Troy could not resist sneaking a look at Brad's hard torso beneath. The thick and hard pecs, the muscled belly, the dimple at the hipbones that hinted at the covered crotch beneath. Troy's hands touched every square inch of Brad's skin, as if it was the first time he had ever touched him, or the last time he would ever touch him.

He brought his lips to Brad's skin, like a man needing water in a desert brings himself to a running stream. He started at the neck, then feathered along the collarbones. Troy brought one of Brad's nipples into his mouth, and then teased it with his tongue until Brad could no longer stand it, and his shorts stretched into a bulging tent.

He pushed Troy away, savagely. Troy was stunned and surprised. Brad took advantage of the moment. He mounted Troy and climbed up him like he was a backyard tree.

Troy came to life, resisting and wrestling him. Back and forth, they struggled across the covers. First one seized the advantage and then the other. They wrestled right over one side of the bed and onto the floor. They knocked over a lamp that flashed blue. A stack of books tipped over and a loose bottle of lube fell to the floor.

It was a contest that Brad was determined not to lose. His muscles were taut and straining. He sought to pin Troy's wrists, to force the weight of his chest on Troy so that Troy could not move.

Troy rolled and spun Brad off. He leaped to his feet and stood, half-crouched, poised in the moonlight. Breathing heavily and sweating, his hands rose in front of him like a boxer's.

And then, as suddenly as it had come on them, the moment of sexual violence gave way. Troy stood taller, and he placed his hands on Brad's hips. His thumbs teased the nerve point along the crease of the hip. It was a live wire, an electric shock, and Brad could barely restrain himself from pulling away.

Brad was richly rewarded for his patience. His belt slid off, the button of his shorts popped open. Troy reached in with both hands to remove Brad's manhood from its cover. Brad's cock twitched in the warm, sandpaper grasp.

In one move, Brad's shorts and underwear fell to his ankles. Troy pressed him back against the bed. Brad's grateful legs collapsed beneath him, and he let Troy lower him slowly to the sheets. When he tried to move again, Troy's embrace tightened.

Brad lay prostrate in that trap of pleasure. He succumbed to it.

His cock had been unbearably hard. The doubt he had felt earlier in the night only added to the forbidden pleasure. Sex after reconciliation was always painful, volatile, explosive. Pent-up energy surged and mushroomed like a nuclear explosion. Relief ran like a countering riptide.

Troy's tongue danced on him. It controlled his hips. It controlled his body. It brought him up and down, heaving and cascading. He was a puppet on a fleshy string, yanked this way and that by the demands of pleasure.

Brad willed himself to be controlled by Troy. He *wanted* to be controlled. He wanted every square inch of his body aflame. To be a sacrifice to delight.

When Troy raised Brad's legs to expose his ass, Brad felt as soft and pliable as tissue. It took hardly a hint of moisture before his ass seemed to flower, to be ready. Troy was patient. Troy stayed outside. Troy held back until Brad's whole crotch was a sinkhole of want and desperation. It was painful for Brad even to touch himself.

And then Troy was inside him, building a slow rhythm. Brad's ankles were on Troy's shoulders. His legs were a pair of jail bars across Troy's chest.

And Troy enjoyed him. Pleasure was written all over his face.

Brad felt Troy taking the pleasure from his body. The sensation increased Brad's own pleasure, until suddenly there was nothing but his own pleasure, the small ring of nerves around Troy's penis, and the obliterating intensity of his love.

The sleep he fell into after orgasm was a dead man's sleep. The sleep of contentment. The sleep of a man who had achieved all he had ever wanted to achieve in life.

When Brad woke, he found Troy's arms still around him, one draped over his chest, the little black hairs stiff from attention, red-gold in the sunlight falling across the bed. He smoothed the hairs with his hand, and Troy purred in his sleep. The heat from

Troy's body was like a warm bath. Gauzy morning light spilled through the window and across their bed.

Rather than wake his lover, Brad disentangled himself gently. He slipped on a bathing suit, loath to drag anything else against his skin that would ruin the warm cuddled embrace he had felt all night.

He watched Troy sleep. The even rise and fall of his chest. It was steady and dependable, as regular as a pulse. He left him with a tender kiss on the forehead that did not wake him.

Brad scratched himself, and wandered, sans bathrobe, down to the pool.

The gardens were sweet this morning. The hibiscus was almost cloying. And just as he entered through the archway to the pool, Brad sneezed in the bright sunlight and cracked three vertebrae.

The noise caused a shape to move in one of the teak deck chairs. It was Aria Shakespeare, moving as if Brad had woken him from sleep.

Aria hoisted himself to his elbows, raised his sunglasses, and cataloged Brad from head to toe with an expression of sour contempt. He was obviously not impressed by what he saw.

"Good morning."

"Good morning," Brad replied. "You sleep there?"

Aria did not deign to answer and Brad dove into the pool, as much to free himself from Aria's contemptuous gaze as to avoid the necessity of further conversation. He plowed underwater from one end to the other, and then burst to the surface, where he drifted, idly treading water, breathless from the contrast between cold water and bedroom warmth.

On the deck of the pool, Aria stretched and yawned. It was still early, and he glanced up at the main house, where the figures of the elderly proprietors were clearly visible in the kitchen windows preparing the breakfast.

"That's the problem with having fags as hosts," Aria commented aloud. "Getting them to get up before noon is like pulling teeth."

The remark was not addressed to Brad in particular. It hung in the air a bit, as Brad considered whether he ought to respond.

Aria stood and stretched again. Unlike his comment, this movement was obviously addressed to Brad. It displayed for him Aria's body at its best, boyish and smooth. His hips were narrow. The natural definition of his arms and torso was flawless. He was like an anatomy model at a medical school. There was something almost unnatural about his tanned, boyish perfection.

But Brad did not dare look away. He did not want Aria to think that he was having any kind of lustful thoughts that he needed to hide. He told himself that Aria's perfection did nothing for him. No doubt most guys would have fallen all over themselves for a piece of that club-kid trash—the angled aristocratic features, washed out blue eyes, and firm body with the all-over tan, oozing raw sexuality with every movement.

But not Brad. It took more than good genes to impress him. And he already had the best, in Troy. The most handsome. The sexiest.

Aria finished his stretch and plopped himself at the side of the pool in front of where Brad was treading water.

"Aren't those old queens a hoot?" he asked.

For once, Aria's manner toward Brad was almost conspiratorial. He had dropped his usual tone of contempt and hostility, and included Brad in his circle with an alluring warmth and charm.

For a few minutes, Aria prattled on casually about their hosts' peculiarities. His morning offhand drivel would have been disarming, if it had not been so clearly calculated to win Brad over.

When he finished, Aria dipped his hand in the pool and scooped a handful of water which he then let run down his chest into his bathing suit. Again, he looked at Brad over the top of his glasses, to be sure Brad was watching him.

Brad looked calmly back, forcing himself to ignore the invitation that Aria's body was offering.

Aria said suddenly, "I hope you're enjoying this."

Brad snorted. "What? Watching you . . ."

"Being with Troy. Bermuda. All of this." Aria waved his hand at the world around them. His gesture had a pride of ownership. It said: this is my world.

Brad noticed a silver bracelet along Aria's wrist. Strangely, the strip of metal made Aria seem twice as naked than if he had not worn it.

"It's a kind of fantasy for you, isn't it?" Aria persisted.

Brad shrugged, dunked his head in the water, and listened for a moment to the soothing underwater sounds. He told himself he wasn't going to let Aria bother him. Why should he? Troy had already said he did not have the slightest interest in him.

When Brad came up, a few quick strokes brought him to the pool's edge. He hauled himself out dripping, right next to Aria, so that they were nearly touching.

Aria kicked his toes on the surface of the water, making little tinkling noises. He wasn't looking at Brad, but rather at the ocean beyond the terraced gardens.

Dreamily, he murmured, "He's a fantastic lover, isn't he?"

Brad froze, with his towel over his chest. His heart had stopped beating.

Aria turned and drew his knees up to his chest. "Isn't he?"

Brad did not answer. It was like he was looking down the wrong end of a pair of binoculars at Aria. He seemed small and far away. And again Brad's ears were filled with the rushing sound of the sea, the hollow of underwater.

"What *I* like best," Aria added, "is when Troy puts his tongue way up my ass. That's my favorite!" He glanced up at Brad. "Does he do that to you? What do *you* like best?"

Brad was stung. He let the towel drop to the stone at his feet.

Aria pouted. "Oh, for goodness' sake, don't act so surprised, sweetheart. You *must* have known, right? You didn't fool yourself into believing that someone like you was enough for him. I mean, your kind . . . Troy has a weakness for that kind of thing.

"But, you know, it's a question of fit. We grew up together, we know all the same people. People like you, on the other hand, well, they come and they go when Troy summons them. But I'll be around long after you're history. You know that, right?"

Brad was so angry that he thought the drops of water still on his skin would burn off in a hissing steam. He did not believe it. Not for a second.

But the way this tramp lay there unconcerned, an arm around his knees, lazily spooning water as if he was talking about something of no importance at all—it drove Brad crazy! Made his blood boil. It was all he could do not to hold the queen's head beneath the water until he turned blue. Watch him play Mr. Worldy then, when he was scratching at Brad for air!

"You don't know a goddamn thing about a goddamn thing," he snapped.

"How eloquent . . . I didn't know Troy chose you for your wit."

"You prissy little spoiled brat!" Brad took a step closer to him, a step closer in a haze of red, on the verge of living out his fantasy. The towel was knotted in his fists and twisted tight. "You . . . !"

"Ladies, ladies, ladies!"

The two queens who were their hosts interrupted them. One of them carried a tray of food and the other carried an antique Victorian coffee urn.

"Let's save the catfighting for the afternoon hour, when we all will have a chance to really enjoy it and get a ringside seat."

Brad glared at Aria, who smirked back at him. Then Aria raised himself from the concrete and set his attention on flaunting his body in front of the queens. He flirted as easily with their hosts as he had with Brad just moments before, as naturally charming and to the manner born as any rich kid who had wintered in Aspen and summered in the Vineyard all his life.

Brad hated him. Hated them. All of them. All of them who had had it so easy. Who did not have to work. Or work out. Or do anything at all to make people love them. And who did not care about stepping on other people's dreams.

And what killed him, put the nail in the coffin, was that he hated Aria all the more because Aria had talent on top of it all. That damn Trojan horse he had designed for the Club—it was brilliant. It was what everyone would remember.

It might be what Troy remembered. So if Troy had fallen for Aria, that would be no surprise. It made more sense—objectively—than Troy's falling for Brad. Brad knew that now. It was as clear as the Bermuda ocean below him.

He had been fooling himself all along. Thinking somehow that his own innate virtue and talent at a stove would be enough to fight off disaster. No, people strayed in the best of circumstances. People probably often strayed for Aria.

Why not? By comparison, Brad hadn't been born with a silver spoon in his mouth. He didn't have the effortless knack for conversation or the right clothes for the occasion. He did not know all the right people.

Brad looked up and watched Troy shuffle down the path through the terraces, bathrobed and with sunglasses on. He was a god— clean, lithe, and powerful. Around the pool, conversation stopped cold as all eyes focused on him.

Brad's heart sank as he realized that people fell in love with Troy all the time, every day.

Brad felt helpless, hurt, and confused.

Troy's eyes sought Brad out. Troy removed his sunglasses, and a quick smile passed over his face. The look touched Brad to the bone. If this was not something special, why did that smile melt him? Why did Troy bother?

Troy came poolside and kissed him. Brad, desperate to touch him suddenly, let the towel drop again. He slid a hand up Troy's robe, up his thigh, letting it rest against his pelvic bone.

He turned to look at Aria, who was looking at him. He felt his nostrils flare, as if he were a warrior who had defeated Aria and won some great prize.

Aria looked back over his shoulder at his two hosts. He was unconcerned, undefeated, and so calm it unnerved Brad.

Aria has seen this before, Brad thought. Maybe at this same pool, this same dawn light. Anyone that cool and confident must know what he's doing.

"Look at our garden of beauties," one of the fags said and shivered. "At the height of their prime."

Aria invited, "Troy, why don't you and your friend come sit over here with us?"

"Thank you, no," Troy said. "You know I am not much company before I have my coffee. I am better left alone, for your sake. I'm likely to bite you."

"Well, that wouldn't be the first time, would it?" The dismissive wave of his hand was like the snap of a towel in a locker room.

Troy forced a smile, but he and Brad sat at their own table. The breeze smelled of honeysuckle and wisteria, and the bees were busy in the blossoms, buzzing as if they were telling rumors.

Brad could not bring himself to remain silent.

"Troy," Brad asked in a low voice, so that Aria could not hear, "how come we never talk about your past?"

His own voice against the pacific calm of the garden sounded like the grating hiss of a needle on a turntable when it continued to go around at the inside edge of an album. He hated himself for having to ask.

Troy studied Brad over the rim of his coffee cup. It was as if Brad had asked him a question with an obvious answer, and Troy was trying to figure out if he meant something other than the obvious.

"You know my past."

"Yeah, but . . ."

"And besides, what possible relevance . . . What could it possibly have to do with what's happening now? I live in the present."

It was clear that Troy was annoyed. Indeed, he looked as if he really wished for this conversation to stop, at least until he had had his breakfast.

But Brad could not leave it alone.

"Aria seems to think your past is relevant. In fact, we were just talking about it this morning before you came down."

"Really?"

"He said you were lovers."

Troy reached for the pitcher of milk. "Aria has a very active imagination." He sorted among the baked goods and found a scone he liked.

"So you haven't slept with him?"

Troy banged down his coffee cup, which drew the attention of the other men.

His voice low, controlled, and emphatic, Troy said, "I would never sleep with Aria. Never. The men I have slept with are men that I care about. Aria is not one of those men. Now, would you please drop it, Bradley, and try to enjoy this vacation?"

Troy spread marmalade on his scone. Brad watched him apply the thick, coarse jelly with quick, angry strokes.

"Are you going to eat?"

Brad shook his head. He glanced at Aria. "I've lost my appetite."

Brad wanted to enjoy the vacation. He really wanted to believe Troy. He wanted what Troy said to be true.

But Aria was beautiful. And convincing. And Brad had heard all the gossip about Troy, about his phase of slutting around, hopping from man to man, bed to bed, whenever he crooked a finger.

The threads of these stories did not tie together cleanly. Something was missing. Somebody was not telling the truth.

Brad knew that he owed Troy the benefit of the doubt. But Troy owed *him* the truth. And some instinct deep inside Brad— maybe it was just native unfounded suspicion—said that he was not getting the truth. Not the complete truth, anyhow.

Aria Shakespeare laughed loudly at some witticism of their hosts, but Brad felt certain Aria was laughing at him. Brad's face burned. His neck was sore with tension.

He was determined not to let Aria think he had won. He forced a smile and wolfed down a blueberry muffin just to demonstrate his hearty and hale appetite.

One of their hosts strayed to their table. He apologized, "Going to be cloudy today. Sorry we could not send you off with more seasonable weather on your last day."

"That's all right," Brad replied savagely, and loud enough for Aria's benefit. "We can always just spend the day in bed."

11

They had not been back in Boston for more than an hour when Caroline Treadwell called Troy's apartment. She announced that she had booked the Carlyle again for a party she was throwing just for a few of their closest friends. Nothing fancy. A party in honor of Troy. And Brad, of course. Since they were moving in together.

"You told her," Brad said accusingly, as soon as Troy set the phone back in its cradle.

"Yes." Sensing Brad's annoyance at the prospect of their relationship being hijacked again, Troy added, "Maybe it's some kind of apology."

"Fat chance. I get the sense Caroline does not often conclude that she is in the wrong."

"Amen. But look on the bright side: if it gets in the papers, it'll be just before Club Troy opens. We could use the press."

Brad sighed. With Troy it was all about the angle, the spin, the buzz. Sometimes he worried that Troy lost sight of the things that mattered.

"Don't you think we should talk to Caroline about . . . ?"

"About what?"

"What happened in Bermuda."

Troy gave him a funny look, and held Brad's face in his hands. His eyes were penetrating and reassuring. "Trust me, Bradley. I will take care of it, don't you worry. This'll be fine. It'll be fun."

"I don't want him coming to that party," Brad said.

Troy looked pained. "I'll do my best," he promised.

But even Brad knew he was asking the impossible. They could not go around avoiding Aria forever. At these parties thrown by Caroline's set, it was always the same people again and again. Troy could not demand that everyone scratch Aria off their guest lists for the benefit of Brad. These were family ties that went back generations. Brad would have to learn to put up with Aria, one way or another.

This fact made him blame Troy for the whole predicament, as if Troy were responsible for Aria's bitchiness, for Aria's beauty, for the closed circle of Caroline's friends.

And Brad could not understand for the life of him why Aria took such a keen interest in trying to torture him. Or why he let Aria get under his skin so much.

"Aria is just another two-bit, too-young, too-thin, spike-haired, bleach-blond, dime-a-dozen fluttering queen," Brad concluded aloud. "He's plastic and pretentious and utterly without true character."

"That's right," Troy said approvingly. "You just need to keep telling yourself that. You'll see you have nothing to be afraid of."

And you, Brad thought, need to tell that raging queen to back off and take some responsibility for this whole situation. But Brad managed to keep this thought to himself. It ate at him, though, because Brad was not used to keeping his feelings inside.

Caroline's party, which took place three weeks later, proved to be a massive, carefully orchestrated affair at the Carlyle, overlooking Boston Common. Hired cars were double-parked up and down Boylston Street, and there was a cop whose job consisted solely of directing the limousine traffic. Black tie was strictly required, although Troy's friends from the fashion world put their own spin on the theme, with quirky, colorful variations.

The festivities began right at dusk with cocktails and champagne flowing like water. A swing band played in the ballroom and a massive banner bearing the Trojan horse loomed overhead. Club Troy matchbooks littered the tables.

All it needs, Brad thought sourly, is a set of go-go boys outfitted like Trojan warriors and a basket of Club Troy condoms for the guests.

Brad was cynical about this effort of Caroline's. Sure, the invitations had read "Congratulations, Troy and Brad, Two Years and Going Strong!" And it was true that her manner had changed since they had returned from Bermuda.

Caroline had become exceedingly polite with Brad. She had encouraged him to invite his own friends to the party. She had even solicited his advice on the food and wine to be served. Caroline professed to be supremely aware that no matter how hard she tried, she could not best Brad's taste when it came to food and wine.

And this was why Brad had grudgingly agreed to go along with this "little impromptu affair," as Caroline described it, without getting some resolution on the Bermuda issue. Her newfound respect for his cooking was the trump card Brad hoped would eventually get him in Caroline's good graces. Brad hoped that it would crystallize over time into a more substantial regard, the kind of family feeling a mother-in-law ought to have for her son's lover. Brad knew how rich people could be; if you had enough talent, eventually they would have to let you in the circle.

But however much Caroline sweetened her manner, Brad remained a touch suspicious. The wild card in it all was Caroline's love for her son. If it had just been a question of Brad's talent in the abstract, Caroline might eventually have approved of him. But Caroline wanted nothing but the best for her son.

And Brad was not the best. Not in Caroline's eyes. He kept himself in tiptop shape. He had a great career and a relatively stable personality.

But he was not Mr. Smooth. He hadn't gone to great schools. Or the great horseback-riding camps like Drovers. No silver spoons had ever been found in his mouth.

Brad had made his own way. And so, among the crowd of socialites and politicians that showed up at the Carlyle to pay them (and Caroline) homage, it was the politicians Brad felt closest to. At least some of them—the ones who hadn't inherited or bought their votes—had come up from humble beginnings. He could respect that.

For the first hour of the party, Brad did his best to perform to Caroline's specifications. He remained near the front entrance of the ballroom, flanking Caroline and Troy as the guests streamed in. He tried to be friendly with everyone who came through the door—to say the right thing, and be witty and charming and make Caroline see that he was no threat to her son.

By the end of an hour in the receiving line, Brad was so exhausted from being so goddamn charming that all he really wanted was a stiff cocktail. Or a stiff cock. One or the other, please, served up on a platter.

Caroline noticed his flagging spirits.

"Perhaps," she suggested in a break between guests, "Brad would like to take a break."

Brad was about to nod eagerly, but Troy seized him before he could wander off.

"Nonsense."

"It's just . . . he looks tired," Caroline said, with a false, sugary air, laced with contempt and pity. "Maybe we could have somebody up here who is more, um, used to these kind of affairs. Which *can* be quite taxing, you know. Maybe one of your old friends. Aria, perhaps?"

"Aria??!!" Brad blurted.

Troy shot Caroline a hard, furious look.

"Brad is *fine*, Mother. And there's people I want him to meet. We don't need *Aria*."

Brad leaned his head close to Troy's ear and whispered fiercely, "I thought Aria wasn't being invited. You promised."

"He's not invited," Troy whispered back. "She's just being a bitch." Troy mustered a smile and a wave for the mayor and his wife, who had just come in the door. After they had passed, Troy hissed, "Can't you tell when she does something just to get a reaction out of you? She doesn't give a damn about Aria."

"You could fool me," Brad said glumly.

They went back to welcoming guests. As if to make up for Caroline's evident contempt for Brad, Troy went to the opposite extreme. He acted proud of Brad to a fault. He heaped praise on Brad's accomplishments until Brad blushed. He pointed out to all the ladies and half the men how hot Brad looked in the tuxedo Troy had designed for him specially for this occasion.

Although Brad could concede, looking in the gilt mirrors at the ends of the ballroom, that he did look hot, he still felt like a fraud at these fancy parties. He longed for the days of crowded apartments and potluck dinner parties, which seemed more authentic.

So he was thrilled when a voice like a crashing cymbal interrupted his strained conversation with the Republican Party chairman's wife.

"Mister, you look good enough to eat!"

There followed an explosive flash of sequins, an expensive earthy scent, and a swish of coarse brown beautiful hair.

It was Jacqueline, Turner's wife, looking exquisite, buoyant, excited. Jewelry glittered all over her body. And her fine tattoo, drawn down over one shoulder blade, was exposed beneath the spaghetti strap of her dress.

Jacqueline swept down on him like a tropical storm. The woman moved on four-inch heels as if she had been born in them and could run a track meet in them if necessary.

Brad kissed Jacqueline's cheek, and then embraced Turner, who followed a step behind his wife, a gentleman in every way. Turner was dressed with an eye to detail, a scrap of silk at his breast, a top hat he had not yet checked.

"Hey, Mr. Monopoly-man," Brad crowed. He did not think he had ever seen Turner in anything but his grubby workday baggy trousers and white apron for at least a year. "*Now* we can get this party *started!*"

Just as Brad was about to abandon his position at the door—Troy had long since been dragged off into another room for some exclusive, hushed conversation about finances—Caroline approached them. Her attention was like a bucket of ice water. Despite her new manners, she chided him for neglecting his duties.

"Remember, Bradley, you are the guest of honor today." Caroline managed to emphasize the word "today," as if there was no tomorrow. "You have responsibilities you must see to."

Carelessly, Caroline looked at Turner. Mistaking him for a member of the waitstaff, she ordered another glass of champagne.

There was a moment of icy, cringing silence. Brad's mouth dropped open. He wished he could disappear. Jacqueline's skin turned a dusky hue, the likes of which Brad had not seen since he lived through hailstorms in the Midwest.

But Caroline was too quick for the storm to break. Realizing her error, she stroked Turner's forearm and said to Brad, as if he had been included in the drink order, "When you gentlemen get back from the bar, you can introduce me to your friend. For now, I'd like to get this lovely lady to let me in on the secret."

"Secret?" Jacqueline asked icily.

"This lovely dress you're wearing." Caroline unleashed a barrage of compliments so effusive that Brad knew she hated every stitch of it.

Turner roughly corralled Brad and shoved him toward the bar.

Brad started to apologize, started to turn back to rescue the situation, but Turner was ice. As calm as ever. He cut Brad off, saying, "Never apologize for someone else's behavior, my friend. Each of us commits enough of his own wrongs without going around taking responsibility for others'."

Turner gave a throaty laugh and then added, "Besides, trust me, Jacqueline can take care of herself."

Brad hoped Turner was not underestimating Caroline's bitchiness, but he surrendered to the pull of the bar.

As they waited for the drinks, Brad recognized a piercing voice that made the hair on his neck stand on end. Although he had not seen him since Bermuda, Brad knew it was Aria.

He was perched on a high stool at the corner of the bar, at a profile to Brad, holding forth to a small coterie of nasty old queens. Aria's Bermuda tan had only made him more striking. He held a cigarette aloft in a limp wrist, and his legs were crossed at the knee. The glass of champagne he was waving around was obviously not his first.

From time to time, Aria broke off from his chatter to flirt with one of the old queens, who fawned like a puppy at his attention, running off intermittently to fetch him a refill.

"You know Troy," Aria was saying. "He always has had somewhat . . . pedestrian tastes."

For a moment, Brad actually believed the reference was to the bad window treatments of the Carlyle Hotel or the quality of the champagne in Aria's glass.

But then Aria made a little face that delighted his audience, smirked, and added in a stage whisper, "Pedestrian is French for white trash, by the way, for those of you who don't speak the lingo." He put giant air quotes with his fingers around the word "pedestrian." Then he sighed. "White trash has always been Troy's weakness."

Brad shouldered through the other drinkers, intent on yanking the bitch down from her throne. About three feet from his goal, he felt powerful arms wrap around him in a bear hug he could not escape. Turner growled, "He ain't worth it, man."

Brad struggled. But the baritone in his ear was forceful and full of common sense. He had been listening to it for a decade and he could not unlisten now.

"They've got you pegged for white trash and me for a waiter . . . so what? All the better when we show them up!"

Turner released him. They looked at each other and laughed.

Aria peered down from the bar stool as if he were looking into a dirty gutter.

"Oh. Brad," he said in a voice as deep as Kathleen Turner's. "*There* you are."

"Here I am."

Aria smiled stiffly. Then turned back to his crowd and whispered something. A few glances shot their way. Someone laughed. One of the old queens said audibly, "Troy's really brought it to new levels of outrageousness, hasn't he? Poor Caroline."

"Poor Caroline nothing," Aria insisted. "That woman has more cunning than Cleopatra herself. You wait, there's some devious plan behind this, trust me. What Caroline wants, Caroline gets."

Aria winked, as if Caroline had already confided in him but he was not at liberty to say.

"Poor Caroline," Turner echoed with a sneer. He yanked Brad's elbow. "Let's go rescue my wife."

"Oh, Brad?" Aria called out behind them.

Brad turned.

"I seem to have forgotten my purse. Do you think I could persuade you to freshen my drink?"

Aria slid off his stool and broke a heel on the floor. He was caught by some of the queens and returned safely to his throne. They showered him with drink offers, but Aria was focused on Brad alone.

"You *owe* me anyhow, sweetheart. I'm the only one being honest with you."

Disgusted, Brad threw a bill on the bar and turned away.

"That guy's got some cojones," Turner said.

"I can't believe Caroline invited that son of a bitch. I *knew* all her politeness was bullshit."

"I think she was playing your vanity, man—you know, all that about you taking care of the wine and food. Sounds like you're pissed because you fell for it."

Brad nodded grimly. "But the day I don't get pissed at that queen is the day I die."

When they again located Caroline, Troy had beaten them to the punch. He had already swept in to spare Jacqueline from a full dose of Caroline Treadwell, up close and personal. He was engaging Jacqueline in some colorful repartee that left Caroline speechless.

Turner supplied her with the champagne she'd requested, and Caroline fingered the stem of the glass as if she wanted to drink it down in one fell swoop.

"Thank you," she said. "Now, Mr. Turner . . ."

"It's just Turner."

"Turner, then," she said. "What is it you do? How do you know my Troy?"

Troy, who was still in conversation with Jacqueline, glanced at Brad and rolled his eyes.

"Mother . . ."

Caroline turned on him with ferocity. "Troy, would you mind much, dear, if I had a chance to mingle with my guests. I think it's time that I met some of Bradley's friends. Don't you?"

Troy was about to argue, when Turner signaled that he could stand up for himself. As he explained his role in Brad's restaurants, Caroline's interest visibly faded away. She stifled a yawn.

"How nice. Another cook."

"Well, not exactly . . ."

Caroline turned to Troy and Brad and bragged that she had been talking to Jacqueline and learned that she was a housewife.

"Isn't that wonderful," she said. "So many families today don't have a mother to take care of the children . . ."

Caroline looked at her own son with ferociously proud, shining eyes.

Brad could not help but add, "And the next thing you know, the kids grow up gay and motherless."

Jacqueline and Troy barely stifled their laughs. Turner, of course, was deadpan as always.

Caroline sniffed, "Really, Bradley. I meant nothing of the kind." She then excused herself with pointed grace.

"Winning friends and influencing people as always," Turner scolded.

"Sorry, Troy, I couldn't help myself. Do you know what she did?"

Troy shrugged. He looked like he was used to hearing tales of his mother's outrages, and did not need them from his boyfriend as well.

"She invited goddamned Aria. *Aria* is here."

Troy frowned. "That's impossible. I checked the guest list."

"*Aria is here,*" Brad repeated. He glanced over at the bar, but could not see Aria anywhere. He hoped that Aria had fallen again from his stool and cracked open his pretty little skull.

Then he looked back at Troy. He wanted it to be clear that he expected Troy to do something about it. Or else he would take matters into his own hands.

"I'm sure it's just that he was here to hang up the banners . . . ," Troy stuttered.

"Troy . . . ," Brad warned.

"OK, OK, I'll take care of it."

After Troy disappeared, Jacqueline asked, "Who's Aria?"

Brad launched into a blistering account of Aria that had Jacqueline looking as if the heat had singed her eyelashes.

"Meee-ow!" said a sassy voice behind them.

Chessie plopped down in their midst.

"Tell me everything!" she demanded, as she offered Turner and Jacqueline the requisite kisses. "I just love it when Brad gets all in a snit."

They all laughed, and over an hour passed before Troy returned to them. They were just getting around to discussing Caroline's heaping of praise on Jacqueline's dress.

"Caroline does not like it when she is outdone by one of her guests," Troy apologized. "She likes to be the belle of the ball."

"Now that's a compliment I can accept," Jacqueline said. "How come you never say nice things like that, Turner?"

Turner backed off, proclaiming he was staying out of that conversation, thank you very much. After twelve years of marriage, he knew better.

Troy drew Brad off by the arm, apologizing to the rest. He was obviously agitated.

"What's the matter?" Brad asked.

"I'm brilliant."

"Of course you are, honey. Is that what you came over to tell me?"

"No, really. Check this out. Are you listening?"

"I'm all ears."

Brad glanced over his shoulder, back at his friends.

"No, you're not." Troy crossed his arms and pouted as if he would withhold the secret until Brad showed the proper respect.

Brad laughed. "You're like a little kid!" He sighed and stroked Troy and gave him a patronizing kiss on the cheek. "OK," he promised, "now I'm listening."

There was a small battle on Troy's face as he weighed whether to hold out for a more sincere expression of interest, but then his excitement carried the day. Troy blurted, "I've got a great idea on how to spin this thing to get the most press."

"What thing?"

"You know. Our commitment, of course. Our moving in together."

"Press? What are you talking about?"

Brad's eyes went wide with horror, but Troy's enthusiasm steamrolled any objections. He was almost dancing on his toes as he breathlessly described his idea.

"We'll have a wedding. My fall collection will be a pro-gay-marriage photo shoot! We've got the whole thing: mother-in-law dresses, groomsmen's suits, maybe a roaring twenties or Gatsby theme, I don't know. I've got so many ideas—I just *have* to get into the studio. And, of course, Cheval or Jean-Baptiste can supply the food and wedding cake. It's brilliant. And we're much too handsome to waste our model potential—we'll be the central figures. It's a perfect chance to launch our new brand. Aria says—"

"You talked about our wedding with Aria before you even proposed it to me?"

"We can get this all set up, have some New York media buy in . . ."

Troy went on and on, spouting the details, flattening Brad's objections, but Brad had stopped listening. He knew that he should have been excited. Thrilled. Overwhelmed. What had started as their moving in together had grown into a full-fledged marriage.

But it killed him that Troy saw their marriage as a convenient excuse to break out the fall line with maximum media coverage. He saw every aspect of his life as part of a bigger marketing plan. Even the part that was their personal business. Their privacy. Their love.

And besides, where was the bent knee, the ring, the roses?

Brad hadn't even had the chance to accept. Troy just assumed he would—knew he would. Brad wondered suddenly if that unspoken decision was the right one after all.

Disappointment weighed on him like a ton of bricks as he watched Troy wax poetic and not even realize that he had left Brad behind. We want such different things, Brad thought. How can we ever hope to stay together, to get married, to spend forever together?

If Brad had ever hoped for more from Troy, he needed to put those hopes aside now. He needed to see their relationship for what it was: a convenient partnership. A business plan.

The thought depressed him. He watched Troy's gorgeous face jawing away in excitement, apparently unaware that Brad was suddenly stricken by a fit of doom and sadness.

Brad told himself: it's not that bad. Most guys would kill for the chance to be with a guy like Troy Boston. What difference did it make if their union was more business than love? Was that the worst thing in the world? They had fun together. They had great sex. They both liked food and wine.

Brad only needed to reconcile himself to what he had. He needed to stop acting like a child and believing in fairy tales. Like a grown-up, he had to recognize that things were never perfect, and live with what he had—conveniently ever after.

By the time Troy was done explaining his idea, Brad was somewhat closer to this goal. He almost succeeded in persuading himself. For a long time he had been holding out for more, but now he had to face the music. And understand it was not the end of the world.

Still, he thought fiercely, the one thing I won't reconcile myself to is fucking around. Troy may not love me, but he is not going to cheat on me either. With Aria Shakespeare or anyone.

Fidelity was a bare minimum in any relationship of Brad's. It was the bottom line, whether in love or a business partnership. He wouldn't take less. That was his new line in the sand.

Another guest stumbled against him, and the wine spattered all over his shirtsleeve like blood. At the same time, Troy was seized by one of his business advisers, who led him off with a promise of somebody he wanted him to meet.

Brad excused himself to the men's room, where he took a leak and doused his shirt and then examined himself in the mirror, tweaking his bow tie, which would just not sit right. Everything on the whole planet was annoying him.

He took a deep breath, glad for this moment alone. This moment of quiet to think about what he had just heard.

Everything had two sides, a good and a bad. The good side was that Troy wanted to marry him. He had to stay focused on that. That was what mattered.

He gave his bow tie another tweak.

"It's not supposed to be perfect," a now-familiar feline voice said. Aria had come out of the stalls and draped himself on the wall adjacent to the sinks to insure his balance. His voice was ugly with drink. "That's the genius of bow ties. They have lots of character. Like me."

"What are you still doing here?"

Aria ignored him. "I bet where you come from they don't often throw parties like this. Where do you come from again?"

"Iowa."

"Oh. Right. Of course. Well, enjoy Boston while it lasts."

"What do you mean?"

"Well, I mean, we both know this is just for convenience, right?"

The words struck Brad to the quick. He was furious that Aria had figured this out before him. Furious and ashamed.

If there was anything worse than his disillusionment, it was the fact that it was no secret. Maybe, Brad thought, he was the last one to see things. Maybe everyone knew already. Maybe that's what all the old queens at the bar had been laughing about.

"I mean, every once in a while he needs to do something to provoke his mother. Show his independence. You're perfect for that. It keeps her nose out of joint, and Troy can go on thinking he's not some Momma's boy.

"But even Troy doesn't believe it. He knows, as much as the rest of us . . . you're just a tool in the ongoing struggle of Troy and Caroline. Nothing more. When he thinks he's won the latest battle, he'll lose you. Or find some other boy who's even more inappropriate. He has a knack for it."

"That's bullshit."

For a moment, a flame burned in Aria's eye, and then burned to a cold cinder. With great effort, he flounced up from his reclining position. Stumbling a bit, he caught himself on the drying vent.

A hint of pity rose in Brad's breast, but he restrained the urge to put out a helping hand.

When Aria had finally found his balance, he snorted bitterly, "Well, God knows, it's not the sex that's keeping Troy around."

Brad's pity instantly hardened. "What are you talking about?"

"Well, Troy would hardly be coming to me if he were satisfied that way, would he?"

The question lingered a long time in the air, like a foul stench from one of the stalls.

"Oh, please, honey, it's nothing to worry about. Just another convenience thing. I'm available. We're drawn to one another. He's a man. There's plenty of Troy to go around. If you know what I mean."

Aria hiccuped and excused himself. "I don't mean to say he doesn't like you. He definitely has a soft spot for you. The same way that he has a soft spot for all the boys who keep him amused."

"You're a liar."

Aria shrugged. "You just keep telling yourself that if you need to."

"Troy told me you guys have never had sex."

"Of course he did, honey. And he's absolutely right. Absolutely. We never did it. Never ever."

Brad was tired of playing games and made a move to go.

Aria winked like a lewd clown. "Course, I've got proof. The camera never lies."

Brad was breathless. And then, like a balloon around the room, the tension snapped.

"He didn't mention that, did he?"

"You're full of shit. You just want to see people as unhappy and lonely as you are. I see right through you, Aria. Or whatever you're name is. You're just washed up and bored and loveless and pathetic, and you blame everyone else for it."

He went on and on, but Aria merely laughed at him, softly, into the palm of his hand. A drunken, superior titter that would never give Brad the satisfaction of admitting he was right.

Brad emerged from the bathroom with less confidence than he had shown Aria. Why would Aria make that claim about photographs unless he had something to back it up? Why would he not even bother to argue with Brad's diatribe, unless he had an irrefutable argument: Troy's infidelity.

Brad's eyes swept the ballroom. He located Troy telling a story under the massive chandelier in the center of the room. Some acoustical magic of the room made Troy's voice audible even over this distance and din. Brad strained to pick out the words.

But none was clear. From this far away, it was as if Troy were speaking a different language, one Brad had never learned.

But his listeners appeared rapt by Troy's discourse. And others seemed to want to elbow into his circle, like paparazzi. People were helpless to keep from falling under Troy's sway.

As if he felt the touch of Brad's gaze, Troy looked up as he spoke. Their eyes locked. Troy smiled.

In Brad, a raw nerve jumped. As if a ghost had passed, he shivered and found his skin covered with goose bumps.

And then a red curtain of rage descended on him. He was furious with himself for being susceptible to that look. Brad looked away. He consulted a drink at the bar. And counted to ten.

He needed to sort out his feelings before he exposed them to Troy's gaze. He knew Troy would see right through him. And he was not prepared for that. Not yet. There were too many questions, too much hurt and doubt.

He could not pretend to himself anymore that nothing was wrong.

Turner ambled up beside him and occupied the bar stool next to his. He ordered a Scotch. When it arrived, he swirled the glass, swallowed a bit, and slid his eyes sideways.

"Somebody kick your puppy?" he asked.

Brad looked at him gratefully. His body was tired, he thought. As if he had spent a sleepless night.

"I'm feeling suspicious," he confessed. "And it's killing me."

"Don't blame yourself for suspicion. Might be, you got good reason for it. Might be, on the other hand, you're in love. Why don't you try it out on me?"

Brad ordered a caipirinha. Huddled over the drink, mouth soured with lime, he explained the encounters with Aria.

"And it's not like I expect Troy to love me as much as I love him. The world doesn't work that way. It's never balanced. For him, it's all about the business, all about the career, and he manages to fit love into that. Which is fine. Really."

"And for you?"

"There is no career, no business, no nothing when it comes to love." He could not help glancing over his shoulder for a glimpse of Troy. It was a reflex he could not control. "There's only Troy."

Turner took a long pull at his drink. "Do you think," he asked, "that it's a good idea to go into business with your boyfriend? There's complications enough. Me and Jacqueline . . ."

"It's too late, Turner. We're so far down that road. I mean, what are we gonna do, close down Club Troy?"

"Maybe. Maybe. It's not impossible, my friend. Expensive, but not impossible."

"It would ruin Troy. I can't do that to him. Or ask him to do that. He would never get another investor."

"Priorities, man. If it breaks up your relationship, it's not going to happen anyway. Salvage what you can."

Brad understood what Turner was saying. But the stubborn, defiant streak in him made him believe that he and Troy could have it all. Whatever they wanted. They could be business partners and also lovers and friends, sharing lives and a home. When it came to love, Brad was as ambitious as anyone on earth.

Turner smiled. "I can see from your face you ain't gonna take my advice."

Brad blushed. "I like to think that I might take a modified version, after I have some chance to think it over."

Turner gave him a skeptical grin. "No, you won't," he said cheerfully, finishing the last of his Scotch. "You got too big a heart. Good for you, my friend."

"Keep believing in fairy tales, right?"

Turner shrugged. "If there's pieces to be picked up, my friend, you know where I'll be."

"Thanks, Turner."

"No prob, bro."

Again Brad glanced over the ballroom, but the familiar leonine head was now nowhere to be found. He searched high and low, in every corner, but there was no sign of Troy, who usually stood out so clearly in a crowd. A surge of momentary panic seized him.

Leaving Turner behind, Brad scooted from cluster to cluster of guests, and from bar to bar in the great ballroom. He exhausted every square inch of the floor. And the area behind the band. And the men's room.

Troy had disappeared. Brad frowned. Mere annoyance was displaced by a feeling of profound gloom. Don't make me have to guess where you are, Troy. Not tonight. Not when I am thinking . . . He did not know what he was thinking. *Except the worst.*

A few more minutes of searching and Brad gave it up, now genuinely angry that Troy had left him here without a word. Letting his rage get the best of him, he made a beeline for the door. If Troy could, he decided, then he, too, could leave.

Caroline swooped out of nowhere to intercept him.

"Brad, dear, are you saying good night?"

"I'm looking for Troy."

"He just stepped out for a minute. Come now, there's someone I want to introduce you to."

At first Brad succumbed to the invitation. He did not really want to leave in a huff. So he allowed himself to be deflected from the door, led by the wrist.

But something in Caroline's sudden interest in his social life made him wary and suspicious. He planted his feet firmly on the parquet floor. Like a petulant child he refused to be led any farther.

Caroline looked back at him darkly. Her eyes were smoky. For a moment, there was a battle of wills. She refused to give up his wrist.

"Caroline, let go."

"Bradley, don't be such a child."

"Caroline, I need to find Troy."

"Troy will be back in a moment." She spoke each word through gritted teeth as if each one were separate and not part of a longer sentence.

"I need to see him now."

Caroline held his wrist one moment longer. Then, as if some momentous decision had been made in her mind, some surrender to fate, she released him.

"You can lead a horse to water," she said, "but you cannot make him drink."

Brad did not try to solve this cryptic cliché. He turned and made his way back through the crowd toward the door. Out in the hall of the Carlyle, he looked left and right and then through instinct selected a small door to the side, where there was no bellman and no bright entrance lights, and a quick passage onto Dartmouth Street.

He found Troy huddled in a nook of the building created by its balustrades, out of the wind. Aria was draped on one of Troy's shoulders. His hand was around the back of Troy's neck. He was whispering insistently in his ear.

Troy did not look happy, as his eyes found Brad on the sidewalk. He forcefully removed Aria from him, as he would strip off a piece of wet or sweaty clothing.

Leaving Aria behind, Troy approached. Aria stayed where he was, with a crooked, triumphant smile.

Troy scooped Brad's elbow and steered him back inside, toward the party.

Brad refused to be moved.

"I don't want to interrupt anything . . ."

"Don't play games, Brad. There's nothing to interrupt."

Speaking in his best Scarlett O'Hara tone, Brad said, "Well, then my eyes surely deceive . . ."

"Hey!" Troy jerked Brad's arm and bullied him up against the wall of the Carlyle. Troy was impatient, angry, breathing hard, almost frightening in his intensity. "There was nothing to interrupt. Period."

For a moment, they stood belt buckle to belt buckle, Troy's hands on Brad's chest, twitching, as if he wanted to pound him from frustration. His body was arched and angry, his aggravating calm absent, his face twisted and mottled.

And then, that hardness in his body and in his voice broke. Troy pleaded, "Whatever happens, you need to believe in me."

Brad wavered. It was this moment of intensity he had been searching for, this piercing look that skewered him. He had always believed that someday he could get Troy to break. He had always thought that moment would come in bed, in the throes of ultimate passion.

But here was Troy, outside the lobby of the Carlyle Hotel, pushing Brad up against a cold stone wall beneath a streetlight. With a sign that said "No Parking—Loading Zone" above his head.

Have I reached him? Brad wondered. Have I actually gotten to the soul of the man?

But as he watched, Troy visibly recovered his calm. The blood drained again from his face. The pressure of his body on Brad's and the tightness of his clenched fists became a degree less.

Brad slipped away, retracing his steps into the lobby. Again, Troy gave chase. But he was calmer now.

When he caught up to Brad, and again blocked his way, his eyes were searching out the lobby. Calculating, glittering. Checking whether they would make a scene. Whether this stretch of carpet, visible from the front desk, between a potted fern and a

Waterford wall sconce, was a place he really wanted to play out his drama.

Troy became as unruffled as ever, as purely reasonable in tone as he always was. It was like watching a shirt being pressed under a hot iron.

He said, "Aria and I were just talking about the campaign, the branding campaign. The wedding. Aria's a little lit. Well, drunk. He needed some air. But his ideas are good, you know."

Even at this range, Brad tasted Troy's breath. It reeked of smoke, but Troy never smoked. Not since Brad had known him. Not for years.

And although Brad himself had smoked in his day, at that moment he found the stink of it toxic and oppressive. He felt it in the lines of his face, the folds of his skin, the pleats of his shirt, enveloping him, souring him. It tasted to Brad like the worst kind of deceit.

12

In the morning, as Brad expected, the phone rang.
The caller ID showed that it was Troy on his cell phone. Brad let it ring a long time. One after another, the shrill chimes peeled through his otherwise silent apartment.

Brad was standing with his back to the mirror. He was looking at the empty bed. He was trying to get used to it. He was telling himself this was not so bad. That the expanse of white sheets was not some form of global ice cap. Or a new ice age.

Then he reached out for the portable and clicked the "talk" button.

Troy pretended nothing had happened, even though they had never before spent an evening together but the night apart. Not once. Troy acted as if Brad's snagging a taxi home in the middle of the party was something they had planned.

"How was the rest of the party?" Brad asked. He tried to make his tone as icy as possible, to match Troy's affected nonchalance.

"Fine. I think Caroline was pleased that you left, because she did not have to pretend the party was about anyone but her anymore."

Brad managed to bite his tongue. And he found he had nothing more to say. The phrase that went through his head came straight from his grandmother: "If you don't have anything nice to say about someone, don't say anything at all."

An awkward silence froze the line. It was like getting caught with a distant acquaintance in a checkout line or an elevator. He would have welcomed an "I miss you" or an apology, but both seemed out of reach. Something palpable and thick cast a pall over their conversation.

Troy would never admit he was wrong, Brad thought. Troy might never even *think* he was wrong. Troy was too used to pleasing people and getting his own way.

As if to confirm it, Troy said, "Well, I guess I'll let you go now."

Brad snorted.

"You do that," he said. And when he put down the portable, he waved his extended fingers at it like a pair of magic wands.

"Jerk," he snarled. The word felt awkward and insincere in his mouth. Dirty and inappropriate. He said it again to see if it felt better. It didn't. It was not the word he wanted to use for Troy. Not the tender sounds that came out of him without bidding, without thought, for the man he most loved in the world.

Pulled this way and that by anger and hurt, his stomach rebelled. It was a tight, empty knot.

"You didn't fight it out with him?" Chessie demanded.

She had grudgingly agreed to meet Brad for coffee, but was still cranky because Brad had left her behind at Caroline's party without saying good-bye. And because she had ended up going home with some tipsy financial type who had fallen asleep in the midst of their foreplay and had committed the unpardonable offense of neglecting to ask for her number in the morning.

She was outraged and incredulous, hungover and sunglassed,

and dressed in a peasant smock that revealed excessive cleavage, a silk scarf that hung to her knees, and a pair of flared, artfully torn jeans that were the height of shabby chic and casual fabulousness.

As they walked along the street nursing their coffees, Chessie unleashed a fifteen-minute-long sidewalk diatribe against men in general and Troy Boston in particular, and the whole stinking world, from top to bottom, left to right. As far as she was concerned it had all gone down the shitter.

As she spoke, she punctuated her commentary with waving arms and punching gestures that made passersby shy away and splashed hot coffee on the unsuspecting like holy water from a priest. Chessie was supremely oblivious. A queen passing in a motorcade, for all the notice she took of the havoc she wrought.

"Are you done?"

"Maybe," she allowed grudgingly. She pretended to adjust her sunglasses, and acted surprised that her coffee was now three-quarters empty.

"OK. So you think I should fight it out."

"Yes."

"What's to fight about?"

"That bitch Aria, of course."

"Aria's not worth fighting about," Brad said firmly, even though the mere mention of Aria's name made his blood boil. "What's between me and Aria is strictly between us. With Troy, Aria could be just anyone. Troy could have his pick of boys just as beautiful as Aria."

"And as talented. And not white trash. And loved by his mother."

"Um, hello! You're supposed to be on *my* side, remember?"

"I am, Brad, but . . ."

"No buts. I know Troy. He may not get passionate about me either, but he sure as hell has nothing for Aria."

"How do you know, Brad? People are different when they're alone. They . . ."

"I know. Trust me. I know."

Brad knew the problem with Troy was not Aria, but all future Arias. All little twinks with hot bodies who thought they could take him for a fling, who had no understanding of the value of loyalty, and no respect for relationships.

And Brad could not win against them—did not want to win against them—unless Troy was willing to guard against it by pledging himself entirely to Brad.

Chessie broke into his thoughts, saying gently, "People go back to their own kind."

Brad stopped where he was in the middle of the sidewalk. "I am Troy's kind!"

Chessie looked back at him as if she did not quite believe it. And maybe didn't even believe Brad believed it himself.

"Maybe *I* should talk to Troy," she proposed.

"No!"

Chessie was the last person Brad wanted talking to Troy. She was like a bull in a china shop when it came to delicate feelings.

There were some tasks Chessie was particularly good for. Despite her lack of success with men, she was a never-ending font of relationship advice. When Brad had been single, she had also been an excellent source of introductions. He would bring her to the clubs and let her pick out and chat up the guys whose phone numbers he hoped to get.

But subtlety and diplomacy . . . no. These were not Chessie's forte. He would not trust her to solve the crisis in the Middle East. He would not rely on her to mend a broken relationship. Hell, he would not rely on her to mend a torn shirt.

They turned into City Steam Café for lunch. Chessie got a salad to nibble on. Brad ordered only a diet Coke. Chessie rumi-

nated under her breath about the ingratitude of friends who refused an offer of help.

Brad tried to deflect the anger by asking her about her own life,
but she pointed the fork at him and snapped, "Don't you go trying
to change the subject, mister. There's plenty of time to talk about
my own pathetic excuse for a love life."

She repeated the phrase, making quotes in the air to go with
the word "love." And then she proceeded to rattle on for an hour
about the latest escapade she was having with a married man who
had demanded that she crush herself down to the floor of his car
so he could drive by the school where his kids were playing soccer.

"If you're going to have an affair, at least have the balls to come
out and own up to your mistress, be proud of her. Especially when
she is as hot as me!"

Chessie had meant to be funny. But Brad only reflected softly:
"Yes, it would be nice if people told the truth."

After lunch, they strolled up Newbury Street together, arms
linked like newlyweds. Chessie tried to cheer Brad up by pointing
at all the must-haves in DKNY and dissing all the designs in Sola,
where a salesgirl had treated her badly the week before, guessing
that she weighed 120 pounds when in fact she was a size 4 and
not an ounce over 117.

They stopped outside the Troy Boston boutique. Its windows
stretched nearly two stories from the sidewalk. Each held a long,
thin banner photograph of a beautiful, dark, impossibly handsome
young man. These thirty-foot men stretched from floor to ceiling.

Chessie accused Brad of drooling. She poked him in the ribs.
She joked, "Imagine the size of the dick on that guy!"

An older, well-dressed woman on the sidewalk behind them,
stooped like a question mark but with remarkably clear eyes,
emitted an audible *harrumph*! Lips curled with distaste, she looked
Chessie up and down.

Then she turned up her nose and continued along the sidewalk, muttering, "Harlot!"

"Harlot?!! Hey!" Chessie yelled after the stooped departing back. She turned to give chase to the tottering woman, but Brad snatched her arm. He dragged her away, half-running, digging in his heels when she reached some new level of fury. "I'll show you harlot!"

The old woman had again turned and planted herself on the sidewalk like a defiant, righteous colossus, complete with a bag from Lord and Taylor.

"You can't let that bitch get away . . . . Hey!"

"You are not going to terrorize an old woman."

"Hey!"

He dragged Chessie farther away, until she finally stopped struggling.

"No, really," she insisted. "Stop."

"Why?"

She pointed.

Troy was headed toward them, almost running. Brad fought off the urge to flee like a hunted animal.

Chessie rolled up her sleeves. "While you deal with him," she proposed, "I'll go find that old bitch and finish her off. When we're done, we can both drag the bodies back to our caves and eat them, OK?"

As Troy approached them, Chessie turned and gave him the double middle finger and stuck out her tongue. Then she flounced off.

Brad could not suppress a smile, and he even let Troy give him a kiss on the cheek. Troy did not smell of smoke anymore, he noticed. Instead, the same seductive smell that had won him over the first night filled Brad's nostrils, and his heart beat faster in his chest. He had to remind himself how much he hated Troy, and how important it was not to give him the time of day.

"Hey," Troy said. "You running away from me?"

He put a hand on Brad's neck and pulled him in, and the next kiss was full on the lips. Brad tried to mumble an answer, but his crushed lips made it unintelligible. Troy put his index finger over Brad's lips for a moment, said, as softly as the air, "Shh," and then kissed him again. Kissed him good. Right down to the toes.

It took Brad a moment or two to remember that he was not supposed to be kissing Troy. He pushed Troy away. Troy pretended not to notice.

"You eat lunch?"

"Yeah, you?"

"No, I was going up to meet Caroline. You're welcome to come. She's in a sparkling good mood."

"How come she always gets in a good mood when we're having a fight?"

Troy's face clouded over. "Are we having a fight?"

Brad smiled tightly, with no humor at all. "I'm kidding."

Troy stared at him, not saying a word. He was trying to bully Brad to finish his thought. To communicate.

But the silence only made Brad defiant. More determined not to be the one to say the first word. Brad looked right back into Troy's Ray-Ban eyes.

It felt almost daring to do it. As if they were crossing swords. And Brad vowed he would not be the first to fall.

"I'm kidding," he repeated. His voice was stilted.

A look of disappointment and then resignation passed over Troy's handsome face, as he realized that Brad would not be bullied. Brad felt a weird sense of guilt, as if he had just destroyed a ceramic vase or some other invaluable work of art, because disappointment was the only look that could make Troy Boston's face look un-handsome. Brad got no satisfaction from having won this duel.

"I am," Brad said. "I'm kidding."

Troy let a stubborn, pregnant pause elapse to show his skepticism.

Brad suddenly wanted to talk about anything at all other than their fight. Or their problems. Just this moment, he would rather have had his skin peeled off in layers and the resulting wounds salted than get into a deep discussion about Aria Shakespeare and Brad's lack of trust and what exactly was wrong. He wanted things to go back to the way they were supposed to be.

"Why's Caroline happy?" Brad coaxed.

"She's been in touch with her lawyer."

"Uh-oh."

"The lawyer told her he was confident that no other state would recognize a Massachusetts gay marriage, so if things did not work out between us, any assets outside Massachusetts would be safe from you. You see, Caroline fears you're after me for my money."

Troy chuckled ruefully. Brad did not.

"What did you tell her?"

"That you had plenty of your own."

"That's it?"

He yanked Brad close so that they were again hip to hip. "I told her that it was my body you were after, not my money."

From close range, Troy grinned the mischievous grin that Brad had fallen in love with. A grin he had not seen in the weeks since Bermuda, weeks during which they had been walking around each other on eggshells and not having enough sex and being deliberately busy at work.

Brad wanted to raise a hand to shield himself from Troy's grin.

It was like being in bright sunlight with a sunburn. It only exacerbated the wound.

He reminded himself how pissed he was at Troy. How much he hated him. But it was hard to keep focused on that with Troy playfully unbuckling his belt in public. Hard to keep focused on anything but the growing, growling lust and the hardness in his crotch.

Brad broke loose.

"So what are we doing tomorrow night?" he asked. "I think we should get together and talk."

"Tomorrow night? Oh, damn!" Troy clapped himself on the forehead. "I'm sorry, got to skip tomorrow night. I've got to go down to New York. Didn't I tell you? I've got to pitch the gay marriage photo shoot."

The topic made Troy visibly buzz with excitement. All else was forgotten. Most notably, the fact that a marriage required a couple that really wasn't fighting, that actually wanted to get married.

"I think," he said excitedly, "we're going to have a 'bad guys' line of clothing—you know, hicks and bigots, out to disturb the peace and overthrow the wedding, you know what I mean? A darker shot to contrast the white and washed-out blue of the wedding. You like?"

"Who's going to model the bad guy outfits? Aria?"

For a brief moment, Troy had nothing to say. But the comment had certainly let the air out of his balloon, exactly as Brad intended. Which wasn't, Brad thought, the nicest thing to do to one's boyfriend. But justified in this case. In his personal opinion.

As if he was deciding whether to respond to Brad's bitchiness, Troy remained silent. Then he said evenly, "Actually, it *was* Aria who proposed the idea."

Brad bit his lip, and Troy seemed pleased that he had in turn taken Brad by surprise. They stood eye to eye, as if each was considering whether he wanted to continue on in this petty vein.

Then Troy stifled the pleasure on his face and reached for Brad's hand. He took it in his own, turned it over, and ran his fingers across the palm, massaging and kneading the knuckles.

"You know, Bradley, I was not—am not—lying. He really is talented, you know. I'm not saying he is not a bitch to you. But his ideas are . . . inspired, for lack of a better term. That's the only reason I have bothered to speak to him. That's it. Beyond his talent, Aria means nothing to me. I don't mean to sound like an ass or like I am using him . . . but the fact is, you're all that matters to me."

Brad was grateful for the words. They almost choked him up. They were almost enough.

But he was not sure he was ready to believe them. He was not a trusting soul by nature. There were good reasons he did not have a hundred friends, only two that he could trust to the ends of the earth. And he wanted to trust Troy.

Brad wanted the moment to last longer, as if its duration was a measure of its sincerity, but Troy was again off on his animated, high-speed, high-energy romp.

Brad excused himself pleading a need to go to Jean-Baptiste and work. He just was not up to facing Caroline for lunch today. He had vowed to himself that the next time he saw her, he would set her straight.

But this was not the day for that. He needed a day when he was on top of his game—and on his own turf. Then, he vowed, he would take matters into his own hands and explain to her for once and for all how lucky Caroline should consider herself that Troy had landed a man who loved him as much as Brad loved him.

That night, when he got back to his apartment after work at Jean-Baptiste, Brad sensed something wrong the moment he stepped foot inside. Something off-center and disturbed. He looked around, but he could not put his finger on what was amiss, what little detail awry had destroyed the integrity of the place.

The only thing he could think of was that he was home earlier than usual. He had left one of the sous-chefs to close up. Maybe that subtle change was making the apartment seem strange.

Brad took to the kitchen, where he had recently begun experimenting with a soup so light that he called it foam. He had a foam that suggested in an intense but ephemeral way each of the major vegetable soups: tomato, carrot, cucumber, celery. They whispered around the tongue like gossip. Brad's only problem was how to make them into a mass production item suitable for restaurant use.

He did not know what made him suddenly look up toward the hallway. Some shadow, or change in the light, or perhaps some breath of human presence. He saw nothing, and yet he was drawn away from his work and drifted in slow motion into the foyer.

The front door was wide open.

All of a sudden, things started moving again at hyperkinetic speed. Brad heard the tumble of footsteps on the stairs and he hurled himself toward the rail, looking down three floors below. A blond head was just visible, a tanned hand on the railing.

Brad threw himself down the stairs in pursuit, stumbling, nearly falling, snatching at the rail for dear life and then starting again. He covered three steps with each bound. His ladle clattered to the landing, dropped over the edge of the staircase, and fell two stories to the stone foyer.

Someone yelped. The heavy door to the apartment slammed back on its hinges. Brad heard the slap of footsteps on the pavement outside. A flash of color took the corner at the end of the block into the alley just as Brad came out into the street. He started in full pursuit, taking the corner at full speed.

A car emerging from the alley nearly plowed Brad over. There was a flash of headlights and the screech of brakes. The driver shouted and shook a fist, but Brad was already gone, down the alley. At the far end, haloed by lights in the street beyond, Brad could see a slender shape running away from him.

He was headed for the Fens, a park at the far reaches of Brad's neighborhood. The Fens was a notorious cruising ground for married men and diseased hustlers, and the shadow Brad was pursuing seemed drawn to it like a moth to flame.

A streetlight and an iron railing marked the entrance to the Fens. A set of concrete steps dropped from street level to a hollow of the park beneath. Brad did not hesitate. He hurled himself down these steps into the gloom, nearly colliding with a couple coming up from below.

It was as if Brad had entered a netherworld. Large trees overhead blocked out any residual light from the street. On one side was a marshy swampland ringed with rhododendrons and other thick brush into which little paths disappeared. On the other side was a row of community gardens by day, fenced against rabbits and other pests. Bordering the gardens was a steep landscaped hillock that led back to road level.

Brad stopped to let his eyes adjust to the dim light. The ground beneath his feet was muddy. Men were smoking in groups and alone. He heard murmured conversation from the bushes, giggles, a rush of air, a fart. A stoned college kid was leaning back against a tree trunk with his pants unzipped and his dick hanging out. He fingered himself and someone soon took notice and kneeled in front of him. The air smelled of duck shit.

Brad forced himself to walk slowly and languidly, but his heart was skipping inside. A powerfully built forty-five-year-old man with a shaven head was obviously interested. He abruptly stopped and pirouetted around Brad, looking at him from head to foot and back again. There were other men, on either side, in the shadows. Someone reached out and let his hand brush against Brad's crotch.

Brad followed the path that led straight down the middle of this gauntlet to another set of steps on the far end, three hundred yards distant. He had lost his prey, the shadow that had brought him down into the Fens. He did not dare stop to ask whether anyone had seen a skinny blond thief.

Every face was indistinguishable, leering, predatory. The air was thick with sex and desperation. Brad heard the thump of an impatient fist on ribs. He glanced into an open cavity in a bush and found four men waiting in line over a young man on his knees.

The shadow he had been chasing had lost himself in this nocturnal crowd. There was nowhere a sign of hurry. It was all strutting, preening, waiting, fucking. Condoms underfoot slippery as banana peels. Someone asked Brad to borrow some lube.

Then he saw it! Ahead! At the base of the far stairs, just visible in the flash of headlights from a passing car. A face turned back toward him, and platinum hair.

A shout of triumph came from Brad's lips, and he began to run. He tripped over an exposed root, fell, picked himself up, and again gave chase. The figure ahead was on the run again, near the top of the stairs and out of sight.

Brad was only a few yards behind. Up the stairs, back at street level, he looked this way and that. On one side was only parked cars and garbage put out for collection. In the other direction was the green light of the subway stop. Near the token booth, he could see his man fumbling with change.

"Stop! Thief!" Brad shouted. He could think of nothing better to say.

All the help he got was a bunch of quizzical looks and sly remarks about needing to keep your boyfriend in line.

Brad felt the rumble of the train underfoot.

No! he thought and willed himself to extra effort, springing like a madman toward the subway entrance. Ahead of him, the blond figure vaulted the turnstile. The newly arrived train was already getting ready to depart.

It was Aria! Brad thought vindictively. It *had* to be Aria.

He threw himself between two doors that were already closing. The train began to chug away. Brad sprinted to keep up with it, to catch a confirming glimpse through the window, but the blond head became lost inside the crowded car, and the train left the station, and Brad found himself standing there covered in duck shit and mud.

13

Over the next few nights, while Troy was down in New York, Brad tortured himself with a few sets of extra curls and persistent thoughts that, despite all the love, Troy was misbehaving in the big city. His mind would not let a minute pass without a vision of Troy being romanced by some sweet, young, big-dicked, dime-a-dozen Chelsea twink.

The ringing phone promised only bad news, and he could barely bring himself to answer. It was Chessie.

"So how'd it go?" she asked.

"Fine," he replied with a forty-pound grunt. "Did you catch the old lady and beat the snots out of her?"

"No, the wily little bitch got away from me."

"Using her elderly superpowers?"

Chessie sniffed in derision. "That's all right. She's going to die soon and I'm going to be pretty for a long, long time."

Brad grunted again as he hefted the dumbbell.

"You're not laughing," Chessie pointed out. "Why aren't you laughing? Because I'm not only pretty, I'm funny, too. Remember?"

At this remark, he could not help but smile. Her teasing reminded him of the days before Troy came along, when she used to cheer him up by swapping bad boyfriend stories.

Back then, Chessie would never hesitate to take Brad's side, even when he was in the wrong. They would bitch and moan and permit themselves to eat pints of ice cream and watch *Sex and the City* reruns and then blame themselves together for getting fat and pathetic, all in the name of camaraderie.

Chessie evidently had the same memories.

"Enough of this pity party," she declared. "We're going to go out. Like we used to. You and me. Since the cat's away, these two mice are going to do up the town."

Brad succumbed to Chessie's bullying and enthusiasm. He figured it would keep him from thinking about what Troy might be up to in New York. It was a city with too many pretty boys and not enough chaperones, as far as he was concerned.

They went out to the White Swallow, a club down in the theater district with a deceptively lyrical name.

Brad had not been to the Swallow in ages. The bottom floor contained a rectangular bar. Each of the two floors above contained dance floors that filled with sweaty shirtless boys crammed up against one another in a pulsating rhythmic mass. The deep bass of the amplifiers seemed to rain heavy storm clouds of sound down on the first-floor bar.

The volume, coupled with the stench of beer and the scent of sweaty men, was overwhelming. It was a feast for the nose, eyes, and ears. It was as if Brad had been on a diet for years and now had the run of the banquet table. Hard shirtless bodies flowed past in a steady stream, and the air was alive with second glances and sharp looks and longing.

They won a pair of prize bar stools on the first floor. Familiar faces he had not seen in years lined up to give Brad kisses, and for a while he quite enjoyed the special attention. He noticed that his shoulders looked good in the dim overhead light, and his biceps were still pumped from the evening's curls.

Any time Brad's thoughts strayed to Troy, Chessie read it on his face. She set off an explosion of distraction. A joke. A well-timed reach for a convenient man. A fresh drink.

In time, the club heated up and the drinks took hold, and the two of them migrated to the second floor, hand in hand.

Chessie led Brad out on the floor. She was one woman among a hundred beautiful men, dancing with her bare midriff and low-slung jeans. The floor was not yet crowded, and Brad was giddy. He dipped Chessie and marched a sudden tango across half the width of the floor.

With the hypnotic beat of club music in his head, Brad began to feel younger, hotter, safer. Even daring.

Chad, one of Brad's old friends, seized him from the dance floor. The banter went back and forth between them. Chad touched Brad's abs and squealed about how he managed to keep so thin. He brushed a piece of Brad's hair back into place and said enthusiastically, "It's good to see you again."

Brad did not close the distance between himself and Chad. But he didn't back away, either. He was conscious of Chad's body and the short distance between them. He let Chad buy him a drink. He lounged with him on one of the purple sofas in the room out back, where men were groping one another shamelessly in various states of semi-undress.

Brad and Chad sniped at the young chickens in the room, with their visors and Day-Glo and glitter. And at the hawks hiding in the low light that masked their age.

And then again they danced.

Brad felt safe in his flirtation. He had a boyfriend, he was off the market, off-limits. And this fact made him desirable to the other men in the room. But it obligated him to nothing. He could accept the flattery and attention for free.

And Brad was not at all tempted. The flirting was gratis, a get-out-of-jail-free card, and much more comfortable than if he had been actually trying to pick someone up.

"Flirting's easy," Brad said aloud. "There are so many beautiful men out there." He surrendered himself to the alcohol's high and the music's pulse and Chad's smile.

"Flirting is easy," Chessie agreed. She went to do some of her own. From across the room, she caught his eye. She winked and gave him the thumbs-up. Then she was enveloped in a convulsing crowd of gay men, with whom she had her own sparring and flirting to do.

A Madonna medley poured from the speakers. The remix was abrupt, garish, punctuated by random samples from a huge range of artists. Laser lights swept the room. A disco ball erupted in a splash of colored light and then went dead.

It's been so long since I flirted, Brad thought.

Chad's face went blurry in front of him. The music seemed to get louder and the crowds swelled. Hands shot up in the air, and pretty college boys on K wheeled in skip-hop moves all around the room. They embraced and melted one into the other, an indistinguishable mélange of firm flesh.

Brad shook his head. He wiped sweat from his eyes.

It was two years since he had flirted with anyone but Troy, he calculated. Two long years. And the task of flirting, which had at first seemed effortless, had now exhausted him completely. Exhausted him to the point where he felt drugged.

His limbs felt heavy. Grace got away from him, and did not return. His moves were all awkward motions, hardly really a dance at all.

Suddenly sad and empty, Brad longed for the press of Troy's body up against him. For his smile across the room.

He scanned the faces in the crowd. Some danced with eyes

closed. Some were wary. Some were predatory. None was familiar. None was capable of sending a lightning bolt to Brad's core.

Brad thought: Maybe I do not know how good I have it. Isn't what Troy and I have on our worst day more than most people get? He had found someone he loved. Really, really loved. He loved every inch of Troy . . . every particle. His smile, his hair, his cock, his soul.

When he looked at it this way, Brad asked himself, wasn't being loved back asking too much? Asking for the moon?

Like being hit by a two-by-four, he was felled by a sudden conviction that Troy would be with him forever. Physically next to him. This was a given, a guarantee.

The thought put energy back into his body. His heart jumped. But again, doubt took its toll: Would they ever truly be one? How would Brad ever know? Would Troy confess to him, tell Brad the truth? Could Brad forgive him if the truth was ugly?

Drifting, flailing on the dance floor, in a sweaty anonymity of heat and groping hands, Brad cataloged his own behavior. Tonight's behavior. Last night's behavior. All he had done over the two years that he and Troy had been together. He asked himself: Do I have something to confess, too?

The club beat was like a racing pulse. Hands soared in front of him. Chad—bored by Brad's distance—had disappeared in pursuit of some more likely prey. Club kids skipped in place with windmill arms, and the shirt came off another beautiful young man. He was lithe, with a muscular build and a pair of fantastically swiveling hips, like a Spanish dancer's. A bead of perspiration spilled from the nook at the base of his neck and ran down between his pecs, toward his belly. A light sweat on his forehead reflected the flashing light.

The boy gave Brad a knowing, full look. Then he looked away, then back again. He sidled closer when he saw he was still drawing Brad's gaze.

Brad stared at the boy and thought: Am I tempted by this? He ached to tell himself the truth. To be true.

The boy leaned close to talk. The other dancers forced him to jostle up against Brad, and the boy's lips brushed his ear.

Brad shouted back, "I have a boyfriend."

And the boy smiled wolfishly and said, "So do I. So what?" He reached out to play with the buckle on Brad's pants and encouraged him to lift his shirt.

Brad drew away as if he had been struck. He knew for sure that he was not tempted. Not even a little bit by this pretty, lost boy. He had better things to do, and a true man's love to secure. He knew now, buoyed by vodka grapefruits, exactly what he had to do.

Are you going to regret it in ten years and find you did not do everything you could do to keep him? Discover you could have tried harder and never know whether—if you had given the extra effort—you might have won him over? No. No. He would not live that hell of doubt. That hell of regret. He would win Troy or die trying.

Brad broke away from the dance floor. He lowered his shoulders and bulled his way through the crowd. He said his good-byes to Chessie.

Chessie was about to upbraid him for party pooping, but the serious look on his face and the set of his shoulders made her stop.

"Where are you going?" she shouted.

He shrugged. It was not a shrug of indecision. Instead, he simply had no time to waste arguing or explaining.

Near the coat check, Brad found a bank of payphones and a phone book. He paged through the directory for Aria Shakespeare. Finding nothing, he called information and could not find a single listing in the whole greater Boston area.

It was like Aria did not exist. And maybe had never existed.

Brad tried to recall Aria's real name, but it eluded him. Failing that, he described Aria to bartenders at the Swallow, mentioned his name. But most of them did not know him, or rolled their eyes at a description that could have fit any one of a hundred identical clones, club trash.

But one lone clubber, perched dangerously on a bar stool in the corner, overheard his request.

"Trust me," he said. "You don't want to go there."

Brad nearly pinned him to the wall in his eagerness. "You know him?"

"I know him. He's a goddamn piece of trash. Whore. K-head. Not afraid to pass on whatever disease he's got."

"You know where he lives?"

"You crazy, man, didn't you hear what I said?"

"Tell me."

Shaking his head, he said, "No skin off my ass." And he described a section of Jamaica Plain Brad was unfamiliar with, and gave him an address to try. "That's where he lived when I knew him. Good luck to you."

The chill air outside the White Swallow only buoyed his determination. A steady flow of traffic moved by at an even pace, bound for destinations he could not imagine. The thin air reeked of Chinese food and the gutter.

He hailed a cab and gave the address. The cabbie made him pay up front.

The long ride lulled him, and he dozed. Only when the cabbie barked at him did he jerk awake again. They were in Jamaica Plain, before a triple-decker with vinyl siding and a rusted washing machine on its sagging porch.

Brad examined the names under the doorbells. None was familiar. He prowled around, down the long driveway to the fence out back, then came back to the front door and started ringing bells and knocking on the door.

"Aria! Aria!"

He shouted until a neighbor's window opened and someone yelled at him to shut up. Then he just pounded the door, without shouting, determined to wake someone.

After ten minutes, a window above opened, and someone cursed him out in a slurred, ugly tone.

Brad stepped back to the sidewalk, looked up, and said, "Aria?"

"No, you asshole, he doesn't live here anymore. I kicked his ass out. Exactly because of this crap, people like you showing up in the middle of the night. Get your ass out of here or I'll call the cops!"

"Where did he go?"

"Fuck if I know. Now, get outta here!"

The window slammed.

Brad slumped against a light pole, discouraged and exhausted. What had seemed like a good idea now seemed foolish. He looked at his watch. 2:30 A.M. And not a cab in sight. It was a long walk back to Brad's apartment in the South End.

When he finally arrived, Chessie was waiting. She had let herself in and curled up on the couch beneath one of Troy's overcoats.

Brad shook her awake. It was all he could do to keep from lifting the coat off her body and inhaling deeply the smells in its fibers.

"I've been looking for you everywhere," she complained.

Brad put a finger to her lips to silence her. "Let's go to your place," he proposed. "I don't need any reminders to keep me awake."

But when Brad was in Chessie's bed and she snored softly beside him, he suddenly wanted more than anything else in the world a piece of Troy's clothing to slip into, so he could feel close to him, feel as if the cloth were Troy's arms wrapped tightly around him.

In the morning, Brad woke with only two hours of sleep under his belt. He felt pathetic, furious with himself for his shenanigans the night before. He ran through the events in his head to see if anyone in Jamaica Plain was likely to be able to pick him out of a police lineup.

His stomach a little unsettled from the drinking and his hands shaky, Brad returned to his apartment. He forced himself through his morning routine in the fog of a hangover, which was a leaden weight attached to his limbs and soul.

After enduring that punishment, he stood in front of the bedroom mirror, looking at the haggard form staring back at him. He felt pumped up now, fully recovered.

I am strong, he told his reflection. I am invincible. He struck an aggressive pose that flexed his powerful biceps to the maximum degree. His veins bulged and his muscles responded. But the face looking back at him was skeptical.

Maybe not strong enough, that face said to him. But at least you know what you want. So don't take less.

A bitter taste filled his mouth, and he cursed Troy for not working harder to make sure it worked out between them. It felt to Brad now like he was the one pulling all the weight in the relationship. He was making all the sacrifices. If Troy were to make the slightest effort, there would be magic.

But first, Brad reasoned, Troy had to realize how special it was, what they had. He had to see that before it was too late and he made a mistake for which Brad could not forgive him.

But I cannot do that for him, Brad realized, looking in the mirror, which seemed to reveal the precariousness of his strength. I can only love him. I can only not give up. I can only hope that will be enough.

14

A few nights later, while Troy was still in New York, the phone rattled Brad out of a dream of Troy that involved licking every syrup he had ever cooked with from every inch of Troy's body. In the dream, it had been hard work, but Brad imagined that someone had to do it.

Turner was short and to the point. There had been a break-in down at Cheval in the dead of night. There did not appear to be any damage to the safe, and the night's earnings had been safely deposited in any case.

"The problem was . . ." Turner began.

"The recipes!"

"Yes," he confirmed.

Brad clapped a hand to his forehead. Someone had gotten away with the recipes he had been planning for months for Club Troy. His little black book.

Brad rushed down to Cheval. A couple of Boston PD cars were parked at odd angles out front. The cops were joking around inside. Turner, of course, had brought in one of the sous-chefs and prepared the police a feast.

There were a few clues, but—given that nothing of monetary

value had been stolen—the cops were not optimistic that their lieutenants would think the case was worth pursuing.

"This isn't the first break-in," Brad said, and then wished he hadn't.

The cops were interested. Turner was interested. Brad explained the blond stranger in his apartment who had escaped by subway.

They brought out their pads to take notes, but Brad could offer no other description but blond hair. And maybe smoker's lungs, since it had been so easy to catch up to him.

"Do you have any ideas?"

Brad and Turner exchanged a glance.

"N-n-no," Brad said. "It's not important."

When Troy got back from New York, he came straight from the airport to Cheval, where Brad had been working feverishly to try to reconstruct his notes for the Club Troy menu. Troy did not give Brad a chance to explain. He simply dropped his bombshell: *Glam!*, the magazine that was underwriting the cost of the gay wedding photo shoot, wanted to feature it in its June issue.

"It's supposed to be the anti-bridal magazine," Troy enthused. "This placement's going to guarantee maximum exposure and dish, as a contrast to the height of the hetero wedding season."

"June is pretty soon," Brad said doubtfully. They were sitting together at the bar in the early afternoon, while the staff hustled around them making preparations for dinner. Troy was nursing a vodka on the rocks.

"You're not kidding," Troy said. "It means we have to do the shoot by the middle of next month, to give them time to get the production done for the June issue."

"Wait . . . Next *month*?!"

"Yeah, babe. I can't do anything about it. Otherwise, it gets booted to next year. And who knows where we'll all be then!"

"I don't know about you. *I'll* be here!"

"That's not what I mean. I mean, where we'll be in our *careers*. You know I'll be wherever you are, right by your side, sweetheart."

Troy poked Brad playfully. He was dressed in pencil-slim pants and a snug turtleneck that clung to his hips and pecs. He looked a little haggard in the blue light, in the sort of handsome, unshaved heroin chic way that made Brad have instantaneous fantasies about playing hooky.

But he managed to redirect his attention to the matter at hand. He did not like having his romantic life—and the biggest commitment he would ever make to another human being—dictated by a magazine's production schedule.

"So we're going to do all this in a month?! Is that what you're saying, boy?"

"Yes. Why? Don't you want to?" Troy asked archly.

"Well . . ."

"I thought you loved me." Troy pouted, but the teasing glint in his eye was unmistakable. "I thought you said you would have done it yesterday if I had asked."

Brad both loved and hated this confident teasing that Troy was using to smooth over their obvious disagreement. It might have been OK had it not been so calculating. Troy knew just the right buttons to push.

Yet Brad wanted Troy to seem a little more afraid of losing him. He did not want to be taken for granted. Troy seemed unaffected by the maelstrom around him. Unaffected by the opening of Club Troy. Unaffected by the hurried ceremony. Unaffected by the break-ins at Cheval. Unaffected by Caroline's machinations. Unaffected by having been caught in a compromising position with Aria outside the Carlyle Hotel.

Brad was not nearly so good at covering up his nerves. Just once he would have liked to see Troy break down, show he was human, and address Brad's discomfort with rushing things along. Even if Brad wasn't sure himself why he gave a damn whether the ceremony happened sooner or later.

Brad sighed. Maybe, he thought, he was having his period.

Troy's calm certainty ought to have been reassuring. It meant Troy had no doubts about the road he was going to take. And that he had confidence in the strength of their relationship. He wasn't worried about their ability to withstand the pressures of work and family and preparation for the Big Day.

That was a good thing.

They pawed through the stack of brochures for old country inns that might serve as a proper setting for the reception. They needed a white clapboard ambiance, with six-foot hearths and horses in the barn, but they also needed a front lawn large enough to accommodate the six hundred guests Caroline and Troy proposed inviting.

This, too, was a bone of contention. Brad would have been satisfied with a guest list composed of Turner and Jacqueline, Chessie and Troy's family. And no one else.

Caroline had rolled her eyes at this proposal, and Troy had patiently explained that he had certain social obligations.

"These obligations," Brad observed gloomily, "seem to extend to half the city of Boston."

Glumly, he had watched the list of guests grow and grow. It seemed like they disagreed on a lot of the details. Each time, Troy got his way, soothing Brad and assuring him he totally agreed with his reasoning, but they had to think of how it would look in a photograph.

After some bickering, they had narrowed the possible selection of inns to three, when Troy suddenly turned to Brad and said bluntly, "So when are we going to have sex?"

Brad nearly fell off his bar stool. "What?"

"I've been back from New York for two whole hours. And no action."

These words were enough to give Brad a powerful erection that, he told himself, he needed to fight. Physical urges were not supposed to control his life.

"Hmm . . . ?" Troy persisted. He put a hand on Brad's knee. Brad shifted uncomfortably.

Troy leaned forward and whispered something naughty in Brad's ear. Brad felt his face light up like a Christmas tree.

He pushed Troy away. "Hey, I'm working, you know."

"I'm good friends with the boss," Troy said. "I'm sure he'll give you the night off." Troy licked his lips. Which were wet, full, and moist. He let his hand play at his belt buckle.

Brad swallowed hard.

At that moment, Troy's beeper chirped and the moment shattered.

"Sorry, babe," Troy apologized. "This will just take a minute."

Brad watched him chattering into his cell phone, putting out some Club Troy fire. With just a month until the opening, these interruptions came fast and furious. A DJ fell through. The flatware was mistakenly shipped to Sydney. Some other civic group wanted to challenge the license City Hall had granted.

And Troy insisted on becoming involved in each and every one of these details, because he was such a perfectionist and could not bear for Club Troy to be anything but a success.

If only, Brad thought, he realized that I need the same attention.

As the argument lengthened and became more animated, Troy paced away from the bar. He seemed to have entirely forgotten the flirting he had seemed so deeply moved by. To have switched it off.

Brad began to fold cloth napkins into an arrangement suitable for the tables. His erection was gone. And he was glad he had not given in to temptation.

Brad had always had a good instinct for knowing when things

weren't right in his relationships. He had gotten hurt more than once by ignoring the alarm bells in his head. He felt as though there was something unresolved between them that Troy was trying to smooth over with sex and humor. Aria hovered near them, like the prancing, proverbial elephant in the room.

Brad decided Troy's page had been the best thing that could have happened. Now he was glad he had not succumbed to Troy's invitation. They needed to deal with the trust issue before they were distracted from it in a haze of lust.

They needed to deal with Aria, because he would not just go away. And Troy had done fuck-all to fix the problem thus far.

Brad could not help reading the worst into it: that Troy had *wanted* him to catch Troy and Aria embraced on the curb outside the hotel during Caroline's party, that he had wanted it to force *Brad* to be the bad guy. And break them up. He did not know why he hadn't thought of this before.

When Troy returned from answering the page, Brad sent him away. Troy left with a disappointed look on his face, like a kid who did not understand what he had done wrong but was nevertheless being sent to bed without supper.

Brad nursed his anger the rest of the night. He felt taken for granted, used, unsure as to whether he was any different from a hundred boys Troy could have had. He cooked badly and antagonized his staff and skipped his usual experimentation after-hours in the contemplative silence of Cheval's cavernous kitchen.

"Am I wrong?" he asked Chessie at lunch the next day. "Am I wrong to complain that the biggest event of my life is being dictated by the whims of fat old French editors and nasty anorexic fashion waifs?"

"You're right. It *is* a little quick." She pretended to look down the barrel of a shotgun. "Are you pregnant, honey? Come on, you can tell me."

"Very funny," Brad moped. "Nobody takes me seriously."

"Of course we do. It's just that you're easy to get a rise out of."

"It's not how soon it is," Brad complained. "I'm ready to do this tomorrow. As long as I know Troy's doing it for the right reasons. And not just as a wise career move."

"Look on the bright side: maybe it's a good career move for you, too."

"Of course it is! That's what the problem is. It shouldn't even be part of it at all. I would rather it sucked for my career. Then I could trust it more."

"Oh, Christ, what a drama queen you are! You won't be happy unless you're miserable."

"That's not true!" He just did not want to make a mistake. And yet he was unable to talk about it with the only person it mattered to. He just could not get himself to confront Troy. He genuinely felt that it was Troy's job to bring it up.

But even though Brad could not confront Troy, he could not let him go free either.

So he did the obvious: Brad decided to stalk him.

Dressed in a nondescript sweatshirt and baseball cap, Brad loitered on the hood of his Civic outside Troy's apartment until he saw the cobalt-blue Beamer emerge from the underground garage. Then he leaped behind the wheel and followed at a distance he hoped would not arouse Troy's attention.

With a mixture of disappointment and relief, Brad was pleased to see Troy drive straight to the garage underneath the Franklin Street Tower, which housed the offices of Troy Boston, Inc.

Brad waited a moment in the street and then followed into the parking lot. He took the elevator to the twelfth floor, which Troy's office shared with a public relations firm.

Brad took up a strategic spot in the waiting room of the PR firm, brushing off the inquiries of the intern behind the reception desk.

When Troy emerged from his office three hours later and entered the elevator, Brad raced down twelve flights of stairs, two at a time, and burst out onto Newbury Street. Brad looked left and right. He spotted Troy already almost a block away to the north.

Ducking behind convenient clumps of pedestrians, he jogged until he was within twenty feet of Troy. What was he doing? Where was he going? He darted from sidewalk tree to sidewalk tree, store entrance to store entrance, peering up the street at Troy's back until the coast was clear and then moving on to the next hiding place.

Troy dropped by his flagship retail store. He lingered only a moment and then emerged with a suddenness that caught Brad napping. Impossibly, Troy walked right by Brad, within three feet of him, as Brad cowered in the door frame at Newbury Comics.

Troy did not see him.

Brad sighed. It was so much easier to follow someone on an episode of *Charlie's Angels*. Brad resumed his pursuit, this time allowing much more space between him and his prey, so he would not be caught off guard by Troy's impulses.

Several times he thought he'd lost Troy in the lunchtime crowd. But then he would spot his quarry's distinctive profile and resume the chase.

Troy stopped in at Tsunami for a box of sushi. Then he went to the bank, and Brad took the precaution of ducking into the vestibule of the Banana Republic across the street.

When Troy came out, however, he did not head back up the street toward the office as Brad had expected. Instead, he looked both ways, crossed the street, and lugged his sushi box straight toward the door where Brad was standing.

Brad was aghast. What was Troy doing? He never wore Banana Republic clothes. Never ever. Anything other than Troy Boston wear was strictly off-limits.

And the sushi! Troy *knew* that the sushi should be eaten immediately and not lugged all over the city as if he was taking it on an Ol' Bostonian Tour on a hot summer afternoon.

But Troy, oblivious to the thoughts racing through Brad's skull, headed straight for the door where Brad stood with his jaw hanging open. Not a moment too late, Brad had the presence of mind to hide himself in a rack of brand-new must-have stretch wear in bright citrus colors. Troy came in the door and began nosing around among men's shoes, slowly closing the distance between him and Brad's hiding place.

He's on to me, Brad thought desperately. He's just toying with me now to see what I do. The best thing would be for me to confront him.

But at that moment, when he was about to noisily burst from hiding, one of the impossibly thin young salespeople approached Troy.

"I love your pants," the salesperson lisped. He was one of those mass-production retail twits Brad hated, so thin he himself could have been folded and stored on the shelves.

Troy flashed him that million-dollar smile. "Thanks."

"Can I help you?" The boy's eyes raked Troy up and down.

What a slut, Brad thought. Was it possible that Troy got these come-ons a hundred times a day? How could Brad expect him to resist every time? Troy was human, after all.

"Just looking," Troy said, the wattage of his smile undiminished.

"Well, if you need anything, anything at all . . ." The salesboy left the sentence deliciously and suggestively unfinished, and slunk back behind whatever rock he had crawled out from.

Brad was torn between the desire to flee and the desire to explode. While Troy was inspecting an apparently appealing set of square-toed shoes, Brad dashed for the second story. He took the stairs two at a time, nearly upending a muscle boy in a bucket hat on the way down.

At the landing, Brad looked this way and that. The open structure of the second floor did not offer any hiding places.

That was when the sales queen from the first floor pounced.

"May I help you?" he asked belligerently. He was like a cat at a scratching post. He was determined to feel better about having been turned down by Troy by trying to belittle Brad, who was obviously not his type.

"No. You can't help me, little boy," Brad said. He had no time to waste sparring with him. Troy would soon come up from below, he was sure of it. He was as sure as he knew his name. Brad glanced around desperately and blindly snatched a pair of women's underwear from a pile next to him.

"Sorry, I mean, yes. Yes, you *can* help me. Where can I try these on?"

"You want to try on a camisole?!"

"C'mon, squirt, don't mess around. Where's the changing room?"

The salesboy pointed and Brad dove into one of the open cubbies. His mind was racing and his breaths came in painful rasps. His ears were as alert as a dog's for any sound that might signal Troy had found him.

Five minutes passed. Then ten minutes. And Brad was too paranoid to reemerge. How could he be sure that Troy had gone? Cursing, he vowed never to stalk anyone ever again. It wasn't worth it.

Brad remained hidden for another full twenty minutes, sadly contemplating the unkind overhead light in the changing room. There was only so much eye cream and sit-ups he could do. Soon, Brad thought, he was going to have to break out the pec implants and haul out the cutting knife, pin back the ears and pluck the back, tuck the chin, lipo the ribs, and offer a prayer of thanks to God Almighty that Troy was nearsighted.

Brad only moved when a gratingly familiar voice sounded on the other side of the wall.

"Do you ever intend to come out of there, sweetheart? He's gone now."

Brad opened the door to find Aria Shakespeare on the other side admiring himself in one of the mirrors.

"My, but you are coy."

"I just needed a place to think."

"Let me guess . . . you were masturbating, right? Being around Troy *is* a constant hard-on, isn't it?" Aria turned and hiked up his shirt. "What do you think of my butt in these pants?"

"I don't think of your butt at all."

Aria flashed him a lofty, superior smile. "Why is it that you're never happy to see me, Brad? We could be friends, you know. We have so much in common."

"We have nothing in common."

"Except Troy."

Brad took a deep breath. He vowed to remain calm and reasonable.

"You know, there's only so many times you can go down that road, Aria. I stopped believing you a long time ago."

"Is that why you're chasing your boyfriend around town and hiding in the dressing room when he catches on to you?"

"That's not what I'm doing."

"Oh. Well, sor-r-r-r-ry. Don't get your panties all in a bunch."

"That's not what I'm doing," Brad repeated. "And my panties are *not* in a bunch."

"Aren't they? Well, excuse me for drawing the obvious conclusion from . . ."

"Aria, you think you can treat me like shit because you go to Drovers and ride horses? You think that makes you somehow better than me?"

"Oh, pull-LEASE. The closest I've been to a horse since Drovers was to take horse tranquilizers in the back room of the

Roxy last week. And that's not the reason I'm better than you. There's a whole *host* of reasons I'm better than you. Let me count the ways."

"The Roxy? In New York?"

"Sure. I love New York. We had a good old time. City that never sleeps, you know, because they're too busy fucking." He yawned. "So it really wasn't my fault. When you're in Rome, do like the Romans. Or Trojans, as the case may be."

Aria laughed at his own acid joke.

"You were in New York?"

"Oh, yes, didn't your boyfriend tell you?"

Brad was impressed with his own self-control. "Of course he told me. I forgot."

"You forgot."

"Yes."

Aria studied him intently.

"He tells me everything," Brad said.

This comment made Aria grin. "Not everything, I'd guess, or you would not be standing here, with your jaw caught in your hands."

"I'm not going to discuss this with you any longer, Aria. You don't matter. You're nothing." Summoning as much dignity as he could manage, Brad descended the stairs like a queen at the prom.

Behind him he heard Aria comment blandly, "I don't care what he says. I think my butt looks damn good in these."

And Brad heard the ubiquitous sales twit fawningly agree.

Slumping and beaten, Brad walked back to the Franklin Street Tower. He repeated over and over to himself that he did not and should not believe a word that Aria said.

Nevertheless, since he was in the building, he decided that he should drop by and see Troy. Not to check up on him, just to see him. It would be rude not to.

The receptionist told him that Troy was gone for the day. In fact, she said, he had not even come back from lunch. She offered to reach him by pager, but Brad declined. He wanted the element of surprise.

It was late afternoon, four solid hours later, by the time Brad made his way to Troy's studio. For a long time, Brad just stood outside and listened. He heard not a sound from inside. Finally, he mustered the courage to knock. But his knock went unanswered.

Giving up on the element of surprise, he knocked again in a trademark pattern they had worked out. At this, Troy came to the door.

He had shed his business clothes and was dressed only in a pair of silk cargo pants. There was a pencil behind his ear and an intent look on his face. The floor by his drawing table was littered with sketches. His face was smudged endearingly with pencil lead.

"It's good you came over. I had dozed off. I can't afford to sleep. Four weeks to go." He kissed Brad hello.

"I can't sleep either," Brad said. "Maybe for a different reason."

The remark went over Troy's head. "I know," he said sympathetically. "There's so much to do."

Brad suddenly could not remember why he had come over and what he had planned to say. Perhaps he wanted Troy spontaneously to sense his doubts and fix them. They talked about the wedding in a desultory sort of way. Troy did not seem to doubt that the wedding would take place as scheduled. He contented himself with reciting the frustrations of planning the party. His hands twitched like a pair of bored toddlers kept from the playground. It was obvious that he was entering one of his periods of creative frenzy. He could not wait to get back to the drawing board.

During these lockdowns, which happened once or twice a year,

Brad usually maintained a healthy distance. Troy's only visitors would be a succession of his assistants. They would drop by at all hours, take instructions, hunt out fabrics at his suppliers in the Haymarket and Chinatown, and collect and discard Troy's stale pizza boxes. That is, if he remembered to eat anything at all.

"I'll let you get back to work," Brad said, "Just wanted to drop by."

"Sorry I'm so distracted."

"Nah, no problem." Brad mustered up a casual air. "Hey, was Aria down in NYC with you?"

"No," Troy said quickly. His air of distraction had sharpened, but it might easily have been annoyance that Brad was not yet gone. "Why would he be?"

"Don't know, something he said."

"He might have been down there, I don't know. Just not with me." Troy seemed to mentally review his answer. Then he added, "We're beyond where Aria is much help. I mean, with the wedding. He's more of an 'idea guy,' if you know what I mean. Execution of those ideas is not his forte." Troy put a hand on the door so that Brad could not open it fully. "He's not bothering you, is he, Brad?"

"No, I just ran into him at Bana— downtown."

Troy gave him a strange look. "Let me know if Aria bothers you. I'll take care of him."

Brad looked at Troy with a rush of confusion, gratitude, pity, and indignation. He yearned for Troy to recognize that Brad could take care of himself. As long as Troy made clear once and for all that he loved Brad alone and had no interest whatsoever in Aria. Or any would-be Aria.

If Troy simply made this declaration—and meant it—then Aria would lose the ability to get under Brad's skin.

"Hey, by the way," Troy said, "we haven't even gotten a chance to talk about a honeymoon."

"No, but I'm glad you brought it up. I was thinking . . ."

"We're probably going to have to put it off, of course, what with Club Troy's opening and needing to be available for reshoots. And I need to be where I can keep tabs on what the staff at *Glam!* is up to. I didn't negotiate that veto clause for nothing."

Brad was crestfallen.

"We'll do the honeymoon later," Troy promised. Then he relented. "Maybe," he suggested, "we can get away for a day or two."

"Don't do me any favors."

A day or two was not the sun-drenched three-week orgy in Greece that Brad had imagined. He had trouble believing that Troy would toss away his cell phone and pager and Palm Pilot and wear nothing but bathing suits and flip-flops and linen shirts (unbuttoned) for days on end, what with all that was going on.

He suggested to Troy that they should also be looking at houses together. After all, that was the plan: to move in together once they were hitched. For days, Troy had shrugged off the suggestion, pleading that he was busy.

Finally, Brad had confronted him with an open house advertisement in the newspaper. Troy had reluctantly agreed to attend, but the morning of the open house, he had again pleaded himself too busy on account of Club Troy.

Where was the burning desire to move in? Where was the anticipation? Where was the love?

Brad could not understand why Troy did not want to participate. A house meant a future, after all. Maybe Troy did not see them with a future beyond the promo wedding. Maybe they had different ideas about love.

Maybe today was the day Brad should start trusting his instincts. Back at Cheval, Brad cornered Turner, who was checking the inventory behind the bar.

"Turner," he demanded, "Were you excited on the day of your wedding?"

"Happiest day of my life," Turner said solemnly. A wineglass chimed in his hand. "And to the very last minute, I didn't know if Jacqueline would show up, because I could not figure out how a girl that beautiful would end up with a bastard like me."

"Happiest day of your life? For real?"

Turner nodded. "The woman ain't around to hear me, is she? God's honest truth, happiest day of my life."

Brad thought about this. Why wasn't the wedding feeling like it was going to be the happiest day of *his* life?

He felt he was going through the motions. The proposed menus he had prepared for the wedding—and even those for Club Troy, which he had painstakingly reconstructed from memory after the break-in—seemed dull to him. The wines he chose did not sparkle and dance. They were not "inspired," as Troy would say.

The truth was, *Brad* did not feel inspired.

"You seem disappointed," Turner said. "Was that the wrong answer?"

"No," Brad said carefully, not sure what he felt. "It's just that I had hoped everyone went through . . . well, had problems just before . . . I don't know what I thought."

Not *everything* could be Troy's fault, after all. Brad was afraid, he realized, that he did not know if the right Troy was actually going to show up. He was not even sure he would be marrying the right Troy. Or whether Troy thought it was a marriage. A *real* marriage, with absolute commitment.

"What's the matter?" Turner asked. "You look like a lightbulb just went on over your head."

"I'm just suddenly wondering who's afraid of commitment. I used to think it was him. Now I wonder whether it's me. Maybe I'm making this whole thing up."

All this time, he had thought Troy was pushing him away. But maybe, Brad thought, he was pushing Troy away. Maybe he did not really want to believe Troy was the real thing. That took a leap of faith—it meant that Brad had to give Troy his trust.

That Friday night, after five days holed up in the studio, Troy met up with Brad at Wally's after Cheval had closed. It had been days since they had seen each other, and Troy's pleasure at seeing Brad was unmistakable.

This threw Brad off guard. He had been prepared to be mature and to talk to Troy about fear and commitment and put this thing to bed for once and all.

But when Troy's mood was so good and he was so obviously glad to be there, Brad did not want to spoil the moment with a lot of serious talk.

The band broke into a *muy rapide* Latin jazz tune that made the room seem to roll and shake. Blue cigarette smoke filled the air, and the room grew tighter until it was hardly possible to talk above the din. The band took no breaks.

Brad had his arm around Troy's waist, and he felt the Latin pulse moving Troy's liquid hips. The thump of congas in his belly was a warm thunder.

He matched his hips to Troy's and let his feet move in the small space the crowd allowed him. Troy's body gave off a powerful, nasty, alluring odor from two days without a shower. The stank was hot.

Hours later, the band lapsed into a sultry, almost New Orleans–style melody. They played raunchy horns and sang guttural, off-key, obscene lyrics that made everybody laugh.

Brad's eyes burned from the smoke and his eyelids grew heavy. He felt Troy's body flowing against him like water from a river.

"Hello, stranger," Troy whispered. "Hey, sleepyhead."

A tiny trumpet made a shrill warning bleat that pierced the lazy room like a car alarm. A couple of other musicians crowded onto the stage, and a more muscular beat took possession of the room.

A voice in Brad's head that was clear as day said: *Careful, Bradley. Do not get lulled to sleep. You came here for a reason.*

A beautiful black man with a shaved head and a tattered vest took the stage. The other musicians gave him room.

He had no shirt beneath the vest. His barrel chest showed under his saxophone, and it was wet with sweat. The sax sang out a sorrowful, sad-but-true sort of tune.

Brad glanced toward Troy to see if he had heard the music the way Brad had heard it, but Troy was talking to the person next to him about Club Troy.

Brad slipped away, gravitating toward the stage and the Nubian prince. As crowded as the stage was, the man was alone there, just him and his horn.

No one was really listening for miles. Except Brad, who was listening close. The man's eyes were closed. His attention was ferocious. His hands ran over the stops in a purely sexual way.

Then, suddenly, as if he sensed Brad's focus, the man's eyes popped open. The sudden whiteness in the glare from the stage lights was like a strike of lightning. It stopped Brad short, struck him frozen, and for a brief riff, it was as if the man were playing for him alone.

That man knows something about me, Brad thought. He knows more than anyone else knows.

As if he sensed this connection, the man began to wail through his sax, a trembly, warbling crescendo that made Brad sweat.

He yearned to know what the man could tell him of his future.

Abruptly, Brad shook himself. He realized he had gotten quite drunk at some point in the night.

He shouldered his way back through the crowd and announced to Troy that he had to go. He had a busy couple of days ahead.

Troy snagged his arm. "Go? Go home? Your home?"

"Yes." Brad felt as if his eyes hardly focused.

"Are you boycotting my bed, Brad?"

"What do you mean?" Brad asked warily.

"You know what I mean. It's been, what, five days since we slept together and . . ."

". . . but who's counting . . ."

" . . . and you've been so . . . cautious, lately. You don't seem . . . excited."

Troy was choosing his words carefully, but what he did next was not careful. He drew Brad close. Touched him. Kissed him. His kiss was so deep that even in a place as free as Wally's, the other patrons yelled at them to get a room.

The Nubian prince played a siren soundtrack that seemed now to be playing on Troy's side, trying to lull Brad to let down his guard. A friend pressed a drink into his hand. A woman, feeling him muscle by, turned and started to dance, flirting, trying to draw him in.

They were all trying to betray him.

Brad insisted, "No, I really have to . . ."

Troy caught him at the door. His eyes were on fire. His face was flushed. He flagged a taxi, shoved Brad firmly into it, and slid in next to him.

"Hey . . ."

"Turner will take care of it, whatever you have to do. We'll call him in the morning. Trust me."

Brad gave the driver his South End address, but Troy overruled it, naming his condominium on Beacon Hill. At home, Troy was a whirlwind in the bedroom. Brad heard him gathering clothes and boots.

From time to time, Troy yelled, "Don't you fall asleep out there, mister. I don't want to have to haul your ass down three flights of stairs!"

Brad slumped fully dressed on the living room couch, his boots up on the glass coffee table. He wished he had the energy to set a fire in the fireplace. Finally, Troy announced he had finished.

He was standing in the hall with two backpacks.

"Go where? It's three in the morning."

"If I told you, I'd have to kill you."

Troy's BMW was already fully loaded. Skis were mounted in a rack on the back bumper and trunk, and packs were crowded into the space behind the front seat. The engine purred seductively.

The lulling rush of tires over concrete put Brad to sleep as if he had been drugged.

15

Three hours later, Brad woke. They were parked at the side of a road in the Berkshires, in a tiny lot etched out of the snowbank by the plows. Miraculously, there was still spring snow clinging to these hill towns. The first streaks of dawn were reaching over the looming hills in front of him. The rich scent of steaming hot chocolate filled the car.

Troy pressed a Styrofoam cup into Brad's hands.

"Thanks."

"Drink that up," Troy instructed, "and then put on these gloves and hat and boots."

Troy hopped out, then leaned in quickly. "And don't even begin to bitch to me about what the hat's going to do to your hair." He smiled savagely.

Brad drank down the mixture of hot chocolate and crème de cacao, while Troy unpacked the skis from the rack. The heady evaporating alcohol filled Brad's sinuses, and the warmth churned his belly. He switched on the radio. Billy Holiday's long wail was the only sound for miles.

When he had finished, Brad braced himself for the arctic air and joined Troy at the back of the car, where he stood among their gear. He was cinching straps and buckling buckles and squeezing free items into unlikely pockets.

Above the four-foot snowbanks behind him, Brad noticed a weathered sign hammered into the tree. It read "Treadwell."

"My mother's place. I don't think she's been here in thirty years. She took it from my father when they divorced. Out of spite, I think."

They strapped on cross-country skis in the dim dawn light, and Troy helped hoist a small pack onto Brad's back. He shouldered a much larger pack himself. They set out into the woods. The only sound now was the whisper of their skis cutting through the inch or two of powder that had dropped in the last night.

Although it was late March, winter had not yet lost its hold on western Massachusetts. The air was cold and did not invite talking. As he skied, puffs of moisture came from Troy's lungs and hung in the air behind him. Following Troy, Brad made a game of trying to breathe in these puffs before they evaporated.

Brad resigned himself to emptying his head of thoughts or guesses or predictions. It was like letting the current take him downstream. All around him, the trees were laden with fresh snow. He relaxed into the delicious disorientation of not knowing where in the world he was.

Every gay boy wants to be spirited off to nowhere and pampered, he told himself.

He let himself be lulled, following Troy, turning himself entirely over to Troy.

This is what it is like to be in his control and care, Brad thought. This is what it is like to trust him. It was a delicious, comforting feeling, like cuddling under warm blankets. His skis whispered softly over new snow.

They came to a wooden bridge suspended over a narrow gorge.

It was no more than fifteen feet across, but the gorge was at least that deep beneath. A river ran through the bottom of the gorge, beneath a thick layer of ice. The ice glowed blue in the dark shadows.

The bridge itself was solid but angled slightly to one side, which made their crossing seem precarious. Since the snow on the bridge was thin, they carried their skis and kept a tight grip on the railing. This delicious sense of danger—that he might slip and slide over the side of the bridge—made Brad follow Troy closely, stepping exactly in his footprints.

On the other side of the bridge, Brad spotted a cabin set back under the shelter of some passive pines. On one side, between the bridge and the house, was a patio near the water. It was protected by a wall of stones that was nearly buried in snow.

"It's quiet now," Troy said. He held a finger to his lips and indicated that Brad should listen. "No more than a trickle. But in the spring, these rapids will be a loud rush, like a freight train, as all the snow melts off the mountains and fills this gorge. A mist rises off the river and hangs here the whole months of April and May."

They set their skis to the side of the door, stamped the snow from their boots, and Troy effortlessly fetched a house key from its hiding place in a knot of wood.

A gas lantern inside the door brought the shadowy room into better view. The entire bottom floor was open. There was a stone hearth big enough to walk into at one end. In the back was a kitchen, separated slightly from the main room. A giant black stove took up much of the space, with a gas griddle covering most of the surface.

A sturdy wooden ladder hewn from logs led from the main room to a loft overhead. Brad could see the edge of a bed. A stack of folded blankets and quilts was at the base of the ladder, ready to be hauled up.

In front of the fireplace was a braided rug that showed burn holes from years' worth of sparks. To one side was a giant barrel that Brad realized was a rustic hot tub.

The cabinetry in the kitchen was sleek and Scandinavian, and showed signs of having been improved recently. But the rest of the cabin featured rough-hewn walls, gray with wood smoke.

Antique farm implements and strange turn-of-the-century devices of every type had been affixed to the walls. A pair of ancient downhill skis were crossed over the fireplace. Dried wood was stacked neatly in a massive rack next to the fireplace.

A fire had been left prepared by whoever had last used the house. Troy opened the flue and set the kindling ablaze. From across the room Brad could soon feel the heat on his wet cheeks.

"We've got gas heat as backup," Troy said, "but this should do the trick."

Troy urged Brad up the ladder to the loft and tossed a mountain of blankets and quilts after him. "There should be pillows up there. This should keep you plenty warm, until the heat kicks in."

Brad watched over the edge as Troy unpacked the contents of the packs and stored them in the cabinets, which contained nothing but pots and pans and canned goods.

"What about you?"

"Don't worry about me."

For a while Brad watched as Troy emptied the packs, lit another lantern, left the house and returned with a big block of ice for the ice chest. Then Brad undressed to his underwear and crawled beneath the dense blankets.

He grew drowsy. The crack and pop of the fire lulled him to sleep. The trickle from the river outside was a lullaby, and Troy's manly movement on the floor beneath him was a great comfort.

When he woke again, there were new sounds—bacon and eggs frying on the grill—and the scent of tomatoes freshly cut, cinnamon and apples from a pot of oatmeal, and coffee—rich, dark puts-hair-on-your-chest coffee.

He peered over the edge of the loft, and what he saw made him laugh. Troy was in the kitchen, wearing snowmobiling boots, wool socks that went to his knees, a pair of woolen knickers with suspenders, and a waffled, long-sleeve underwear shirt tucked into his narrow waistline. Over that mountain-man outfit he had on a flowered apron that he had taken from the condo on Beacon Hill. His sleeves were rolled up and he was juggling two or three cast-iron skillets at once, all the while holding a wooden spoon by its handle in his mouth, so that he could stir the simmering oatmeal from time to time.

"Hey, Paul Bunyan . . . ," Brad called out, swimming from beneath the covers.

"Don't you move from under those blankets, mister," Troy answered, waving his spatula menacingly. "I'm almost done."

Brad lay back, and a few moments later, he heard the ladder creak. Troy's head appeared over the edge. He had dropped the shirt and apron, and his chest was spanned by the leather suspenders, which cut just inside his nipples.

He was now balancing two plates and two bowls in one hand, and two dangling cups and an old-fashioned percolator of coffee in the other, with the utensils clenched in his teeth.

He reached nearly the top step before he had second thoughts. "OK. Now you can help."

After this rousing breakfast, they descended together to sit in front of the fire, wrapped in blankets. Troy snapped the old leather suspenders against his bare chest, where they left light red welts.

The light from outside put a halo around his body, and the light from the fire threw his chest and abdomen into a strange, changing relief. The strong parts of his face stood out, making him even more strikingly handsome.

It was strange to see Troy Boston this way, with his face unshaven and his fine couture clothing exchanged for these rustic lederhosen. But he looked as natural in this setting as he did in a ballroom, equally comfortable in his body and equally at peace with himself.

For the first time in thirty-six hours, Troy slept, and Brad watched over him. Troy's mouth hung slightly open, and the muscles of his face slackened. He looked barely more than a boy.

Brad stroked his face, and Troy muttered agreeably, turned in his sleep and pressed closer, nuzzling his face into Brad's chest. Brad tried not to disturb him, rising only to add new logs to the fire and to punch down the rising of dough he had made for their dinner's bread.

Despite the gorgeous sun, they did not venture out all day. There was a careful tenderness to their lovemaking that had not been there in weeks. Afterward, the wool blankets scratched against Brad's skin, and a film of sweat beaded his forehead. He fell back satiated and content, and watched the flames dance.

In the late afternoon, clouds gathered and darkness fell quickly. They stood naked together, wrapped in one huge old blanket, and watched the snow fall. It was just a dusting—no more than an inch or two was expected. It would not trap them up in the Berkshire hills.

But Brad almost wished they *were* trapped until this was all over. Trapped together in this amber moment of perfect contentment. His eyes wandered to Troy's face. Troy felt his gaze, glanced over, and smiled. He had his arm around Brad's hip, and squeezed him tight.

This is the man I am supposed to be with, Brad thought. This handsome, strong, talented man. Brad could not even seem to remember why he had ever doubted him.

Brad suggested dinner and consulted the ingredients Troy had packed. Using a dozen shallots, mushrooms, and rice, he prepared a soup. They uncorked a bottle of wine, and added some to the broth. They also drank some down.

While the soup simmered and filled the cabin with a pleasant earthy smell to compete with the wood fire, Brad turned to the main course. He enjoyed the challenge of the rudimentary cooking tools: a *mezzaluna* for dicing, big spoons, cast-iron pots. Troy camped out on a bar stool and drank wine, watching him cook. Troy's contentment with this inactivity was like a balm on a wound.

Brad shaped the dough that had been rising all day into *boules*. The tang of yeast filled the kitchen and the julienned carrots cut into the dough provided festive color. On the stove, Brad added hearty potatoes and cream to the soup, and simmered a rousing broth in which he poached a tenderloin. Several sauces simmered to the side as he struggled to control the heat from the wood stove. Last, he fried up several crowns of broccoli laced with orange and sweet peppers.

He extracted the *boules* from the oven and cut them into soup bowls, reserving the excess bread. These he browned again for three minutes in the oven to give them a toasty flavor. Then he poured the soup into the *boules*, garnished it with tenderloin slices and broccoli crowns, and they ate heartily and drank like medieval knights after a joust.

Afterward, both of them were a little giddy with wine. Troy pulled a hatchet down from the wall and headed out into the cold in just his lederhosen and suspenders. The sky had cleared again and his nipples turned hard in the chilly air.

Brad watched, fascinated, as he wielded the axe and hatchet with equal skill. Every sinew in his shoulders stood out in perfect relief. The two muscular cords on either side of his spine bulged, and his belly clenched and unclenched with each *thwock!* of the blade in the wood.

With these extra logs, they fed the woodstove and brought the flame to a roar. Troy pointed to a pipe that led from the hot tub, passed through the stove, and then doubled back and returned to a spout that hung over the tub. There was a small valve mounted on the pipe and a battery-operated pump. Troy hit a switch on the pump and opened the valve. Water from the tub soon flowed through the pipe, over the fire in the stove, where it gathered heat, and then dumped back into the tub. Soon, the room was steamy and they were naked, submerged in the powerful stream of hot water that poured from the pipe that ran through the stove.

When they had roasted themselves sufficiently, they jumped outside and threw themselves naked in the snow. The cold was a rush like a punch to the belly, and each of them screamed at the tops of his lungs. Their cries bounced off the starlit sky, which seemed so close.

They wriggled around in the snow until they could stand it no longer, and Troy had made snow angels in two or three spots.

Then they jumped again back into the hot tub, dizzy with heat. Brad played with Troy's crotch, which obediently grew in his hand. Troy's breathing went deeper, coming in sheets. He was looking with predatory hunger at Brad's body beneath the water.

All gentleness deserted the night. As Brad rose from the tub, Troy seized him, pressing his manhood against him. It was all Brad could do to get out of the tub without being knocked over and taken then and there.

He darted toward the ladder to the loft and Troy gave chase, catching him as he took the first step. Troy pinned Brad there, pressed against him, whispered in his ear. His tongue feathered down his backside and Troy ate out Brad's ass on the steps of the ladder.

Up in the loft, they tossed and wrestled. Their bodies were locked. Their eyes were locked. They were breathing in time. First one was on top, then the other. Troy managed to pin his arms, but Brad broke free. And each time he moved, he felt the firebrand of Troy's manhood against his skin, and it was all he could do not to give up then and there, take the warmth inside him as he so desperately wished to.

Finally, Troy took him, pinned him on his side. Troy's thrusts were not tender. They were deep and hard, and there was a pulsing of his sphincter as it gave up, and let itself be pierced, followed by a delicious, dull pounding inside. Brad felt he had never been closer to another man, and he loved the sweet rage with which Troy took pleasure from his body.

Troy spasmed. His strokes evened out, in long, hard, even thrusts that seemed to poke to Brad's soul, to a place no one had ever been. Troy's body was as hard as it had been when he chopped wood, with the same tension and release, the same sheen of sweat, and the same hard grunt as he burst deep inside Brad's body.

He lay over Brad for a moment, breathing heavily, as if he did not quite believe what had come over him and was only now getting his conscious self back. Then he rolled off and Brad squirmed away like a wounded man, oddly content in the scratch of wool blankets on his bare skin.

Every sense was more alive than it had been, and when Troy reached over for him, those two strong hands against his cock were all that he could bear. He exploded all over Troy, falling into and against his body with a soft shudder, a sigh, a groan. Soon he was fast asleep.

At dawn, brandy and coffee seemed like the perfect antidote to the heavy, contented sleep of the night before. They filled a Thermos with the mixture and then set out on skis for a trek deeper into the woods than they had been before.

Brad had never felt further removed from the rest of the world, and this remoteness seemed to drive them together. They stopped in open glades to share from the Thermos and catch their breath and then raced off again through the tracks and the even, unbroken bed of pure white snow.

Troy knew all the trails and landmarks. He remembered summers he had spent here as a child, and told Brad about collecting brake greens and mushrooms, and the first boy he had ever kissed.

"How come you've been keeping this secret hideout from me?"

"I wasn't sure you would like it."

"I like it."

"I know."

They skied on, Brad oblivious to the details of the trail. He was mesmerized by Troy's butt beneath the woolen knickers, its rise and flattening, the hardness unbroken by pockets and cloth.

He was surprised when they were suddenly at the cabin again, where they had begun an hour before. They had traversed a giant four-mile loop without Brad's even noticing the gradual curve.

For breakfast, they popped the cork on a late-harvest Riesling, chilled to thirty-eight degrees in the snow outside. Brad cooked up a vegetable frittata with a side of andouille sausage and fried plantains. A blood-red streak of chipotle pepper sauce stained the egg-yellow surface of the frittata.

A satisfied Troy grinned after he polished off his plate.

"Something's not right about this," he said.

"What?" Brad stared down at the meal as if he had forgotten some essential ingredient.

"I always get the best of everything. The best eggs, the hottest boyfriend, the best family. I don't deserve it."

Brad snuggled up to him. "You do all right," he murmured. He spooned Troy and wrapped his arms around his chest. He brushed his nipple and ran his lips on the nape of Troy's neck. He felt molded to Troy's form, like a second skin.

With contentment came perfect sleep, counted off on the beats of Troy's heart.

They spent three more days that followed the same pattern.

On the last night, they slept off the wine in front of the fire until it was time to go. They talked quietly in the car on the way home. From time to time, they fell into a pleasant silence and Troy reached out and stroked Brad's thigh.

"What are you thinking about?"

"This is how we should always be. This is perfect. No one can touch us here."

Troy stole a kiss on the open highway, and the car lurched from lane to lane, making them laugh.

16

Troy dropped Brad at his place in the South End. Their kiss was long, but there was no desperation in it. It was the perfect cap to the long weekend: the rasp of stubble, the full lips, the insistent pressure.

Brad watched Troy drive off to his own place to unload the gear, watched the receding red lights, and remembered with pleasure that soon he would not have to watch this sight. They would have their own home, their own place, forever.

As he turned to climb the stairs of his condo, Brad nearly tripped over a manila envelope on the stairs. It was marked with Brad's address in red ink, but Troy's was the name on the envelope. A strip of tape said "Photos—Do Not Bend." By hand, some-one had added, "Do not open" and "Confidential." Inexplicably, Brad shivered. His heart beat faster. He experienced an instinc-tive sense of dread. Somehow he knew this envelope was bad news, like a phone call in the middle of night, a howling winter wind. A chill cut through his body.

It was all Brad could do to keep from hurling the package in the trash and pretending it had never happened. Whatever it might be. He wanted to hold on to just a few more moments of the per-fect contentment that he had brought back to his apartment.

"Get ahold of yourself!" he commanded himself. "There's nothing, absolutely nothing, that should make you lose it."

But he did not believe himself. He knew the package was poison as surely as he knew his own name.

Brad left the package on the stairs and climbed up to his penthouse apartment. He poured himself an inch of Scotch from the liquor cabinet. He swirled the amber liquid around in the glass, and then drank down half of it in a sudden swoop. It barely warmed him at all.

Then, decisively, he scooted back down to the landing, seized the envelope, and ran back up to the apartment like a thief.

Brad set the package on the table in front of him, next to the empty tumbler. He examined and shook it. There was no hint as to what it contained. Other than photos. Other than, Brad suspected, his fate.

Brad knew he was not supposed to snoop. He left the envelope and went to the phone to call Troy to see if he wanted the package. He did not let the phone ring long enough to be answered before he hung up and returned to the living room and the package.

He could not help himself. He put a finger under the flap and the tape came unstuck. He glanced around the room as if there were a witness to this subterfuge. Then he pushed the package aside one more time and pretended to read.

All at once, it was too much. Brad seized the package and tore it open and then waited, as if the contents would spill out by themselves. It took two more strong drinks before he finally spread the photographs out on the table in front of him.

What he saw sickened and outraged him. There were ten photographs. Six of the ten showed Troy in the embrace of Aria Shakespeare. One showed the inside of a hotel room, with Troy's unmistakable Troy Boston bag on the bed. One showed a used condom on the floor.

A couple showed a dark-haired figure in the unmistakable Troy Toy shirt lying on the bed, his upper body turned to the side, and Aria Shakespeare's head in his crotch. There were another half dozen photographs of the same dark-haired figure in the Troy Toy shirt inside Brad's bedroom!

It was a documentary of betrayal, and Brad felt the tears on his face before he felt the ache in his heart. He flipped a second time through the photos. His hands were numb. His rage was cold. The hot tears spilled over the prints.

He sat frozen at the table for what seemed like a lifetime. His eyes were on the photographs, but he was seeing nothing.

Gradually, he woke from the shock, or at least his body did. Calmly, he inserted the photos back in the envelope, placing it neatly aside. He unpacked his clothes, tidied his already spotless kitchen, and sat again at the table with another glass of Scotch that he did not drink.

He waited out the night. It was the longest night of his life. In the hours around midnight, he decided never to speak to Troy again. But as the night wore on, and pity and pride warred inside him, he wanted nothing more than to confront Troy with his own shit—to see his reaction, to make him pay.

Four times in the night he reached for the phone. Once he reached for his keys. Each time he stopped himself. He could not trust his own body. His own feelings. He did not want to kill him. And he did not want to cry. He just wanted to be icy and ferocious and filled with contempt. He was not yet sure he was ready to carry that off.

His knees wobbled beneath him. He took a photograph of the two of them from its frame. For a long time he stared at it, but he could not bring himself to tear it in half.

Everything was lies. All men were shit. He would never believe another man.

He sat at the table all morning and all day long. He did not answer the phone or the bell, and barely got up to use the bathroom. It seemed like more betrayal to give in to these needs, when he wanted to focus all his energy on Troy's betrayal.

At seven, he finally moved, gathering up his keys and the offending package of photographs and taking the familiar route to Cheval. Troy had a seven o'clock reservation. At the best table, as befitted the cook's boyfriend. Or ex-boyfriend.

When Brad arrived, he barely nodded at his maître d' or any of the servers who said hello. He made a beeline instead for the table where Troy presided over a small group of retail clients.

Troy felt his presence before he saw him. He stood abruptly.

"Brad, what're you . . . ?"

"Can I talk to you?"

"Um, sure, hold on." Troy excused himself and dropped his napkin on the chair behind him. His dinner guests looked curiously at Brad and whispered to one another.

Finally, recognizing Brad, one said, "Hey, aren't you the chef? I *love* what you've—"

Brad sniffed, but before a rude comment could escape, Troy yanked him out of earshot.

"What's up, Brad? You look like shit." Troy glanced back at his dinner guests as if he would protect Brad from their seeing him at anything but his best.

This protective gesture cut Brad to the core. He shouted, "How can you be such a liar?!"

Troy's alarm deepened and he gently steered Brad over to the bar, where they might not draw as much attention. "What's the matter with you?"

By this time, Brad had collected himself again and he did not raise his voice. He did not look at Troy, but slid the package across the bar until it rested in front of them.

Troy looked down at the package. Brad looked at Troy.

For a moment, Troy said nothing. His lip trembled. His face flushed, and then yellowed. But he made no move toward the envelope.

"Open it up," Brad commanded.

"No."

"Open it up," Brad repeated. He was surprised by the even, unflinching anger of his own voice. He had not thought he would handle this so well.

Troy pushed the envelope back toward Brad and said, "I know what's in there."

Brad's eyes blazed. "Well, I didn't think it would be a surprise to you . . ."

"No, the photographs were a surprise—the first time I saw them."

Brad was thrown off by this admission. For a moment, he felt unsure of his footing.

"You knew about them?"

Troy nodded. Then he added, "And it's certainly a surprise to see you have them—but not that much of a surprise. Aria . . ."

Troy's jaw set and an angry pulse beat in his forehead.

Brad held out his hand. "Don't even mention that name around me."

They fell into silence. And in that space, Troy finally met Brad's eyes. Troy seemed to flinch a little. His eyes turned liquid. His mouth opened to say something but nothing came out.

"So." Brad gathered himself on the bar stool like a panther preparing to pounce. "You admit it?"

"Admit what?"

"Admit *what*? That you lied to me. That you've been cheating on me. And with *Aria,* of all people. And who knows who else."

As if Brad, by accusing him, had given him hard ground to

stand on, Troy changed. His posture became straighter and his chin a little higher. Only the tension in his muscles and the pulse at his temple betrayed any nerves at all.

He said, "I have never, ever betrayed you, Bradley."

Brad gave a little hiccup laugh. He was incredulous. "How can you say that, Troy? That's despicable . . . It's all right here." Brad seized the envelope and brandished it. The photographs spilled out all over the bar.

One of the busboys swooped in to retrieve the fallen items. Brad barked at him, sending him scurrying off with apologies.

"Is this really a conversation you want to be having here? In public? At your restaurant?"

"Why not here?! You've already humiliated me in every way possible!"

"Nothing happened."

"Look at the picture—you're kissing him!"

"He's kissing me."

"Forgive me if the difference escapes me," Brad said acidly. He tried to put as much of the bitterness and sarcasm that filled his soul into his voice, but it came out shaking.

Don't you dare cry, he admonished himself. You are too angry to cry.

Shaking with fury, Brad pushed away from the bar and marched out into the night. Troy chased him. He dragged Brad into the alley beside the restaurant and pinned him against the brick wall next to a filthy Dumpster. Rats scuttled in the shadows.

"I didn't know Aria was going to be there. He showed up at my hotel. I had no idea. He was stalking me, outside my room, in the lobby." There was an edge of desperation in Troy's voice. "You need to believe me."

"Oh, come on . . . You're so full of it! How can you expect me to believe you?"

"Because I'm telling you the truth. Why would I have it photographed? Why would I allow it?"

"Because you didn't know."

"No I didn't know. That's just the point. Aria set it up. I pushed him away and that was the end of it."

"What about the ones in your hotel room?"

"I swear to you, he was never in my room." Here, Troy hesitated, as if he was not as sure of his answer. "At least, *I* never let him in. And he wasn't ever there when I was there."

Each of the painful images was emblazoned in Brad's memory as if it had been seared with a red-hot iron. He could not stop thinking of them, recalling each hurt one by one, an exponential expansion of his pain.

"For once in your life," Brad begged, "tell the truth, Troy! Don't put some special spin on it for your audience. Tell me the truth. I deserve at least that."

Brad desperately wanted him to admit it. He wanted to hear the painful words of betrayal from Troy's mouth. Then he could move on. It was torture for Troy not to admit it.

Troy leaned close. His body seemed to swell. His voice was hoarse and husky.

"Bradley," Troy said.

Brad closed his eyes. Brad loved it when Troy called him Bradley. But he hardened himself again. Of course Troy knew that. Troy was just pushing all his buttons. It was that damn calculated irresistible charm.

"Bradley," Troy said again, "you must believe me!"

Brad shoved him away. "No, Troy, I mustn't. I must *not* believe you. I can't believe you. I don't believe you."

Troy pressed close again. "Please."

"No! People cheat on one another all the time, Troy."

"I don't. I never have."

"Ha! What about all those guys . . . ?"

"What guys?"

"You must have fucked hundreds of guys before you met me."

Troy shook his head. "No. No, I never did. I could have. I never wanted to."

Brad had not slept and his exhaustion bred a horrible confusion. Everything was lies, he said to himself. The restaurant lights bathed half of Troy's face, but the other was covered in darkness. I will never know if he's telling the truth, Brad thought.

"How can I believe you?" And Brad found, in spite of it all, that he wanted to believe Troy. He wanted it to all go back to the way it had been over the weekend.

Brad had too much pride to let himself believe Troy in the face of the damning evidence. He had too much skepticism, and had met too many liars in the past. He couldn't afford to believe Troy, no matter how much he wanted to.

With a Herculean effort, Brad pushed Troy away and stalked off.

Troy again pursued him, wrapped him in a bear hug, arms around his chest. His mouth was near Brad's ear, and now more than ever, with that hot breath on him, Brad wanted to give in.

"You need to have faith in me, Brad. I want to be with you. Always. I would never betray you."

Troy rocked him gently back and forth. Brad was holding himself taut and still as a pencil.

Troy whispered, "If you are afraid, I can convince you. The lawyers say I'm crazy but . . . I'll give you everything."

And Brad then broke the bear hold. He had to at that moment, or he knew he was going to give in. And he would not give in.

"It's not the money part that'll convince me. How could you know me so little?!"

"It's not that I know you so little," Troy said. "It's that I don't know what else to do, and I'm crazy about you."

"You've never said you love me, did you know that?"

There was a long silence. The two of them were poised one against the other, as if they were doing battle.

"I'm sorry," Troy said finally. "It's just . . . I just can't find myself whispering 'I love you' into empty space again. Like after Kurt died."

Brad looked at him and could not forgive him. It was not enough.

"Why would you do this to me? To us?" His voice was filled with desolate wonder.

And suddenly, Brad was detached from feeling anything. It was as if he stood at a great distance, watching this drama, but not knowing either of the players.

This is it, Brad thought. This is the night we break up. He had thought he could not face it, but now he was calm. The realization would come later, he thought. That would come when his soul was shredded and every square inch of his skin was crying out for Troy's touch.

Now he mustered his energy. He tried to keep the bitterness from his voice, and any blame.

He said, "You are not ready, Troy. You are not in love with me. I am a stopping place along the way. I could deal with your not loving me, but this—cheating—is too much to ask. If I am going to be humiliated, at least let it be in the confines of our relationship, and not in front of everyone you know who can pity me and say, 'That's the guy that gets cheated on and he doesn't even have a clue.'"

They stood in silence. Troy's chest heaved. There were wet spots of sweat at his neck and underarms.

We may not say it tonight, Brad thought to himself, but this is the night it all changes. This is the night that breaks us apart.

17

That night, Brad did not sleep. He entered his apartment like an automaton. He was waiting for the crushing blow,
the tidal wave of hurt and heartache. The longer it held back, he
knew, the harder it would come down on him.

One by one, he dragged himself up the stairs of his condominium. He turned the lock, let himself in, and shut the door behind him. Every little movement seemed to require supreme new
effort.

His apartment seemed strange to him, different from the place
he had left that morning. There was not a single thing amiss he
could point to—not a stick of furniture out of place, not a picture
moved or a dust mote stirred.

And yet everything had changed.

Without thinking, he found himself in the kitchen. He ran his
hand over the granite countertops, the stainless steel stovetop,
the breakfast bar, and the backs of the bar stools.

Absently, he pulled down a pot from its hook on the wall. He
studied it as if there might be an answer in its depth. Then he
took down another. The first he filled with water and lit a flame
underneath it on the stove.

Then, as if some clear decision had been made in his head, he began to draw things from the cupboard. He did not have much—just staples: flour, maple syrup, cornmeal. He was out of eggs, so he ran down the street to the convenience store.

At this time of night, the traffic was light, but it seemed angry to him, piercing flashes of headlights, sharp horns, the squeal of brakes, and muffled curses. The straight-edge kid at the corner glared at him malevolently and snatched up his skateboard, as if Brad had ruined his whole night. The entire city seemed to bristle against him.

Back at the apartment, he cooked. It was all he could think to do, hiding out in the privacy of his kitchen, where no one could touch him.

He froze and laughed out loud, paring knife poised in his hand. Except Aria Shakespeare, who had *already* touched him. Aria Shakespeare had managed to get behind the locked doors and into Brad's heart.

Brad cinched himself into an apron as if he were three sizes smaller. He banged the pots and turned up the heat. He browned onions in a hot skillet. Bread rose in a round bowl. He sweat root vegetables by wrapping them in parchment and cooking them slowly in a small amount of fat. He expertly julienned a carrot, cutting a thin wafer, then drawing long, perfectly uniform strips from the wafer's edge.

Brad was glad to be out of the limelight, alone with his agony. Troy knew him as well as he knew himself: he did not want to suffer in public. He didn't want commiseration or consolation or pity.

He wanted to cook, alone, with predictable techniques and flavors he could trust—that wouldn't sour, or go bad, or prove other than what they were supposed to be.

The menu he chose was somber, serious, full of earthy flavors with an edge of heat. Nothing light, nothing playful, crusts seared to a hard, crackled edge.

He cooked throughout the night. Hours passed. His heart raced. He extracted concentrations of flavors from the food that he had not believed were possible.

By dawn, he was done. Pots and pans were stacked high in the sink. Dishes covered the breakfast bar. He surveyed the little feast he had made, and the loneliness, which had been at bay while he worked, now found its way into him, in trickles and starts.

He collapsed on one of the bar stools in front of his feast. And eventually the sadness was all through him, marbled like the fat in a fine piece of beef.

He ached miserably. It seemed so sad to have this giant feast with no one there to eat it. No one in the world.

What had he done? How had this happened?

From habit, he dialed Troy's number, but hung up before Troy picked up. He did not want to know what Troy was doing this particular dawn. Or *whom* he might be doing.

"Sorry to wake you," he apologized, when Chessie answered the phone.

"You didn't wake me. I've been up all night trying to clean up the yack this guy left in my bed. Prick!"

In what seemed like minutes, he heard her storming up the stairs of his condo. He heard her keys jangle and the lock give. And then she was there, sitting like a tomboy on the edge of a seat at his breakfast bar, hands on her thighs, looking back at him with a profound, angry look.

She looked over his feast and gave a low whistle. "You really *are* upset."

He nodded, but was too pained to speak yet. He began to load the food onto two plates, and she did not stop him. She listened instead at length, in uncharacteristic silence.

She picked indifferently at her food, shoving it around on the plate with her fork. Chessie was utterly indifferent to food, even food like Brad's.

"You got any tequila to go with all this?" she asked. It was the only thing she said until he finished.

Then she reached over the breakfast bar and cupped his chin in her hand. She shrugged and looked at him as if he were a child.

"Brad, baby. Gay men are dogs. They cheat. Is this news to you?"

"No, but . . ."

"So what? The big thing is that you've got one. He cares about you, doesn't he?"

"Well, yeah, he's *fond* of me," Brad snapped bitterly. "As Caroline says. But what's that worth? He's too much of a catch to love me back?"

"Too much of a catch to keep to yourself, maybe. People make mistakes."

"Chessie! Whose side are you on?"

Brad felt betrayed. Never in his life would he have imagined Chessie siding with Troy on this one. She hated Troy. She had been urging Brad to dump him since day one. That was why he had called her.

Chessie caught the look on his crestfallen face, and put a hand on him. "Look, Brad, I'm sympathetic. I'm on your side. Who else's side would I be on? I'm your best friend."

She allowed these words to sink in, and then added gently, "But we all make compromises. No one ever finds Mr. Right. Or Mr. Perfect. Just Mr. Good Enough. Or, in my case, Mr. Good Enough for the Night, and cross your fingers and hope he does not mess up your silk sheets."

"I would rather have less of a catch who was loyal to me. Because you know what—that's more of a man, as far as I'm concerned."

Chessie sat back on her stool, swiveling back and forth, and biting her lip.

"You're a sweetheart, Brad," she said.

"Yeah, well, being a sweetheart and twenty-five cents will get me fuck-all."

For a long moment, he said nothing. Then he looked up.

"I want him," he confessed. He was so ashamed to admit this that the tears poured down his face.

Chessie came around to his side of the bar and drew him against her bony shoulder. "I know you do, sweetheart," Chessie said.

"Every hour, it gets worse and worse. I want him more and more. I tell myself I've just got to forgive him, that's all. It would be so easy."

"So forgive him."

Brad dried his eyes with a dish towel. His gaze was fixed on the floor.

"I can't. I would never forgive myself if I forgave him. If he cheated on me, I mean. Which I guess he did. I can't do it."

The stubbornness leaked out of him like air from a cheap balloon.

"What *do* you want?" Chessie asked.

"I want this—*all of this*—never to have happened."

"You don't want Troy to have happened?"

Brad wanted to say yes out of stubbornness, but he could not. He would not have exchanged his time with Troy for the world.

"Do you love him?"

"Yes."

"Do you believe him?"

"No. I don't know."

"That's not a good sign."

"Maybe it doesn't even matter, Chessie. People put up with it all the time."

Chessie studied him for a long time. Then she said quietly, "Hey, I'm a slut, I could probably get over it. But it matters to you. I know it does. I know you."

"I just don't want to give Aria the satisfaction of having broken us up."

Chessie leaned back and set her jaw. "Don't worry about Aria.

I'll take that little nancy queen's balls off and string them around his throat. The question is, What do *you* want?"

The question seemed absurd. Even to ask it. Wasn't it obvious that Brad wanted love? Desperately? And not just anybody's love—he wanted Troy's.

But if he did not—could not—get that, what would he settle for? He thought about this a long moment. And then decided he would settle for fidelity. Companionship and fidelity, if he couldn't have Troy's love.

Was that so bad to settle for? Lots of gay guys drifted from relationship to relationship, cheated on one another, or got lonely in old age. Wasn't it very mature of Brad not to have excessive expectations? Wasn't it mature to settle for someone he respected and who respected what Brad had to offer?

This argument played out in his head for days. The days turned to weeks. But in the end, it did not satisfy him. It would never satisfy him. He couldn't settle. He needed to be needed. He needed to be loved.

"Don't be hasty," Turner advised, when Brad called him one afternoon to tell him he wouldn't be in. "No need to make a decision today, one way or the other. You got all the time in the world."

"What if he calls me?" Brad asked, secretly hoping Troy would call him.

"Tell him you need time. Tell him you won't see him. The man will respect you," Turner said. "Trust me."

"Maybe I don't want respect," Brad snapped nonsensically. "Maybe I just want a fuck."

Turner's voice was glacial and patient and slow. "You can get that anywhere, my friend."

Brad was embarrassed he had spoken that way in front of Turner, but he knew Turner did not think less of him. In fact, Turner did not even believe it. Turner knew Brad better than that.

And Turner would not countenance self-pity. He refused to

permit Brad to stay home. "You have a job," he said. "You're going to do it."

"What?"

"You heard me."

"Turner, I can't. I can't cook. I can't even think."

"You can. Get your ass in here."

Brad refused again, and Turner said simply, "Well, I'm not going to be there either. So don't be expecting me to take your place. You'll have to shut it down."

"What are you talking about?"

"I've got to go away for a few days, down to New York City."

"Now?! I need you. The restaurants—"

"The restaurants need all your attention. And you need to keep busy to keep your mind off of this. Like I said. So get your ass in here and get to work. I'll see you in a few days. There's some business I've got to take care of."

18

Turner was gone for five days, and each one of them felt endless. Brad terrorized the kitchen staff at each of his restaurants. He made the rounds and bullied the waiters. He could not remain in one place for any length of time.

And then, after closing, he would stay until 4 A.M. every night at Cheval. He would not leave until he had personally assured himself that every corner and every square inch of the place had been scrubbed and that each and every piece of flatware gleamed like a diamond.

Brad's energy was manic, because each time he slowed down, his thoughts gravitated to Troy. He was determined to work in a high-speed blur in order to forget all his problems.

He was sorely disappointed. Instead, it was like half of him had been cloven away. In bed, his whole body was a raw wound. He could not restrain himself from going through the items in the closet he'd given Troy, smelling his belongings one by one. The odors outraged and teased and comforted and betrayed him.

He succumbed to instant nostalgia. He thought of the different forms of paradise they had had—in the bedroom, in Bermuda, in the cabin in the Berkshires. All with one common element—Troy Boston.

Sometimes he woke after having imagined that none of this had happened. Sometimes he awoke at the cabin deep in the Berkshires at the peak of happiness. Sometimes he woke from a dream in which Troy had a perfectly good explanation.

And each time he remembered the truth, it was more painful than the last. The prospect of getting over Troy seemed as daunting as building the Great Wall of China.

"I'm dog-tired," he complained to Chessie at a weak moment. "But I've got to start again. Start dating. Start fucking. Putting it all behind me, whatever the consequences."

Chessie looked concerned. "I don't think that's a very good—"

"No, I've got to," Brad insisted. "Don't try to tell me not to. I've *got* to put Troy behind me. The sooner the better."

"You're just trying to convince yourself—"

"I've got to do something, Chessie. I'm all ears for solutions. Temporary fixes, whatever. I can't just stand here working myself to death and torturing myself and hoping one of you guys will tell me what you've heard about Troy, so I don't have to humiliate myself and ask you. It's been, what? Three weeks? Four weeks? And it's not getting any better."

Chessie looked wounded. A shadow passed over her face. "I'm sorry," she said. "I would have said something right away. I wasn't sure you wanted to hear . . ."

"I don't. I don't want to hear a thing. I'm fine."

"OK. I won't tell you."

Brad stared at her. "I'm kidding, bitch. Tell me everything. Now."

Reluctantly, Chessie told him that she had heard Aria was on a three-day sleepless bender in Boston's nightclubs. That Paul Jenkins at the Carlyle—Brad's chief competitor—was now serving one of the stolen secret recipes that Brad had devised for Club Troy.

That she had heard Troy had passed papers on a new million-dollar town house.

Well, that was final then, Brad thought. Troy had gone and bought his dream house without him. So it was over. His demeanor deflated like a fallen soufflé.

He kicked himself.

I decided it was over, he said. *I* made the choice. Not him.

But it still felt like a kick in the groin. Castles made of sand washed into the sea.

And, amazingly, Troy had gone and built a new castle, without Brad. Within a week of their breakup, as if Troy had never even known him. As if he had already found someone new to step in and fill the breach.

The thought nearly made Brad retch.

"Club Troy's supposed to open next Friday," Chessie said gingerly, like somebody testing the ice before she put her full weight on it.

"I know. With a now-redundant menu. Or maybe he decided to replace me with a new cook, too, to add to his new boyfriend."

"I heard the restaurant piece had been delayed."

"Exactly."

"You going to the opening?"

"I'd rather pierce my testicles with knitting needles."

"You're going to let him go through with it, though?"

"What else am I supposed to do?"

"I don't know. Screw him. Make him pay."

"How will that help? My money's in it, too."

She nodded. "Do you want me to come over that night? We can eat popcorn and watch bad movies or something."

Brad struggled for some dignity. "I'll be OK. I'm not going to off myself or something."

212 : scott pomfret & scott whittier

But as the days counted down, Brad grew more agitated and miserable. The night of Club Troy's opening, Brad lit a candle in the window, played Enya on the stereo, and tried to be spiritual and philosophical about it. He even tried to meditate.

But after 10 P.M., he could not help but think of the Club. In his mind, he walked through the old theater, now empty of its seats. He remembered the fabrics and furnishings in their various shades of purple, pink, and fuchsia.

"The colors of love," Troy had once said proudly.

The colors of love, Brad thought bitterly. What bullshit. What total bullshit!

At eleven, Brad imagined that he could hear the sounds of the pulsing music.

It was all he could do not to dress himself and go. To show up undercover. To go in drag. Anything to see what was going on.

When he could bear it no longer, he called Chessie.

"I was just thinking of you!" she exclaimed.

"I need you after all. I need you to go to Club Troy."

"Brad, I'm in the middle of . . . uh . . . something."

"Send him home. I need you to do this."

Chessie gave a long, hard sigh. A petulant voice in the background demanded her attention.

"If you don't go, I'll have to," Brad threatened.

"Don't you even think about it! I don't want you backsliding. And I don't want you hurt." There was a long, considerate pause. "OK, I'll go."

"Thank you, Chessie. Turner will get you tickets."

"Turner's in New York."

"He's back."

When she had hung up, Brad turned out the lights. The candle in the window burned down and flickered out. The wick smoldered a minute and then thin smoke rose from the ashes.

Much later, the buzzer startled him. He was surprised that he had slept, and it took him a moment to recognize what had woken him.

Again, the buzzer rang. Insistent.

Brad roused himself. He could hardly breathe. He was terrified. Could it be Troy? Could it be Troy coming to make it all right?

"Hello?" he said in the intercom.

"Lemme in, wouldja, I'm freezing my tits off!"

It was Chessie. She flounced up the stairs and found a place on his couch. She was breathing hard and obviously drunk.

She demanded a vodka even before she sat.

"So what happened?" he demanded. "Tell me everything."

She shrugged. "Nothing much. It's pretty cool. They have this great design of this fiery Trojan—"

"Horse, I know. Do we have to talk about that, for God's sake?" Brad found himself shouting.

"No." Chessie lit a cigarette. Her face had gone blank as stone. "What would you like to talk about, Bradley?"

He bit his lip and remained silent. He thought he would cry.

Chessie looked disappointed. She blew a long, thin column of smoke toward the ceiling.

Then she said, grudgingly, "OK, we'll talk about Troy. He was there, of course."

"How did he look? What did he say?"

"Same as always. Perfect. He didn't say anything at first. He seemed surprised to see me. Scared even." Chessie obviously relished this thought.

"But give him a few seconds to recover, and then he was all over me. I told him to fuck off, but he wouldn't leave me alone.

"You should have seen it. The mayor's wife tapped him on the shoulder while he was talking to me, and he turns and tells her to

214 : scott pomfret & scott whittier

leave him the hell alone. This was Troy. Political Superman. Can you believe it? I don't think I've ever seen that guy angry. Except at me," she added proudly.

"He was like a king who had lost his queen," she said with some satisfaction.

"I am *not* a queen," Brad snapped. He was trying to imagine what would cause Troy Boston to lose his cool. And at the mayor's wife, no less. It was unheard of, unthinkable. Maybe, just maybe, he had realized all he had lost. It gave Brad almost no consolation, though he had hoped it would.

"Of course you're not a queen," Chessie said, with a twinkle in her eye. "Just a . . ."

"Come on, come on! What else?"

She shrugged. "Nothing much. Standard club and all. It was pretty fun."

"What else about . . . Troy?" Brad could hardly bring himself to say the name aloud.

"Nothing. He just stood there watching me the whole time, like I was suddenly going to turn into you at the stroke of midnight. And of course, people kept asking him where you were . . . And he'd just fake that smile, look around the room, and change the subject. There was definitely something—someone—missing."

"Oh." Brad tried to sound malicious or vengeful, but hurt and disappointment won out.

"And by the way, they wouldn't let Aria in."

"That's the first good news I've heard all night," Brad grumbled.

"I guess he ran out of tricks for getting in where he wasn't wanted. Security was pretty tight."

"I don't want to talk about him."

"No," she agreed. "It doesn't matter."

They lapsed into uncomfortable silence, as if there was nothing more to say.

Brad looked at his watch. It was only 1 A.M. "So why are you here so early? Why aren't you picking up men?"

"Well, actually," she said, "I've got a guy downstairs waiting for me."

"He's waiting in the car?!"

She shrugged. "Yeah."

"Let me get this straight. You picked somebody up and made him wait in the car for you?" He went to the window and looked down. There was a Boxster double-parked at the curb.

"Um, yeah?" She bristled. "Are you trying to say I'm not worth it?"

He shook his head in complete admiration. "What a piece of work you are!" Then he soothed her ruffled feathers. And assured her she was worth every second of waiting.

"I thought so," she said primly.

"You should go, babe. Don't torture him."

"Pshaw. Whatever. He can wait."

"No, go. I mean it. I'll be all right."

"Really?" She looked at him wistfully. Her normally taut face was a mask of concern.

"Really," he assured her.

"You got groceries?"

"Groceries?"

"I know you'll want to cook."

Brad smiled sadly. "I've got groceries."

She kissed him on the forehead.

"I promise," she said. "Soon as I'm done here with this guy, I'll kill him for you. I promise."

"Who?"

"Troy. Aria. Whoever."

Brad opened the door for her. "Thanks, Chess."

"*De nada,*" she said. "Probably more fun for me than this guy waiting downstairs is going to be."

The door shut. Brad leaned his head on it. He heard Chessie traipse downstairs, and then a car door slam. Then he dragged himself back to the kitchen and began to cook. And cook. And cook.

He thought he would just keep cooking until things made sense again. Until he was fat and old and died of a chub-induced heart attack.

19

By morning, Brad had created a four-course meal for all the ghosts in his head. But he had also reached a firm resolution.

He called Chessie and bullied her into setting him up on a date.

"Come on," he urged, "you must know dozens of men. Just get me one of them. I don't care who it is."

Brad was determined to go on a date with someone else. Determined to sleep with him, if necessary, to get it over with, now and for all. If he slept with someone else, it would mark the end, make it impossible ever to go back to Troy. Troy could buy his town house. And open his club. And cancel the Club Troy restaurant. That was fine.

Brad was glad he had learned now rather than later. So he could move on and stop wasting his time.

If he cheated on Troy, that would make them almost even. Even if it was not really cheating anymore, since he and Troy were broken up. Free agents.

Chessie was reluctant to help out. "Maybe we should talk a bit, take it easy."

"No, I need to do this now, or I'll think I can go back to him. If I do this, it'll really and truly signal the end. No crawling back."

Chessie grunted skeptically. Her doubt was as thick as tomato paste.

"I've got a better idea. Let's dismember Aria," she proposed. "That would make you much happier."

"No, it wouldn't."

"Well, it would make *me* much happier. Do you know where he lives?"

Brad remembered the night he had stalked Aria over to Jamaica Plain.

Reading the blush from Brad's face, Chessie exclaimed, "You do, don't you? Tell me!"

After some embarrassed explanation, Brad admitted what he had done. Chessie insisted they go back to the house in Jamaica Plain and get some further intelligence. She made Brad hide in the bush while she went to the door.

The homeowner who had been so rude to Brad in the middle of the night when Brad was pounding on his door was more forthcoming to Chessie, especially when she flashed a fake press pass and claimed to be an investigative reporter from the *Globe*. The owner said that Chessie was ten times more beautiful than Lois Lane, and a few minutes later she had a lead in her hands.

For the next six hours, they planted themselves outside an address in Dorchester. According to the guy in Jamaica Plain, this was the apartment of a friend of Aria's, where he sometimes stayed. Brad thought he recognized the name of the friend—it was the woman Aria had brought to Bermuda with him. The woman he had called Bambi. Chessie thought the lead was hot.

For the first three hours, Chessie talked incessantly. Afterward, she lapsed into sullen silence. The CD in her disc player went round and round, and they began to get a little chilly in the April cold as the sun went down.

Just as Brad was going to suggest they give it a rest, their prey emerged from the building. Chessie and Brad sank into an alley until he passed. Despite the dusk, Aria was shaded in sunglasses.

"I can't believe he stole your fucking recipes," Chessie said.

"I can't believe he stole my boyfriend."

They followed him onto the subway, where he got off downtown near Beacon Hill. Brad and Chessie followed.

As Aria got closer to his destination, Brad's heart began to harden. His anger throbbed in his temple.

"He's going to meet Troy."

Aria pressed the buzzer outside Troy's condo door. For a moment, there was no response, and then a short staccato bark.

Aria immediately adopted a playful pose, as if he thought there might be a video camera watching him from above.

Chessie and Brad strained to hear the exchange, but they could not get close enough without giving themselves away.

As they watched, Aria's pose hardened. His hand went to his hip and he stood like a teapot ready to boil. There was an argument back and forth over the intercom, and then, after a while, radio silence from the condo.

Aria backed away from the door. He scanned the upper windows as if he might pick the one behind which Troy was hiding.

All of a sudden, the door in front of Aria burst open and Troy confronted Aria on the sidewalk. Brad gasped at the sight of Troy. He had not seen him in over a month, and Troy was still the most beautiful man in the world.

In an instant, Brad wanted Troy so badly he would ignore everything, all that had been done to him. He had to fight every impulse not to hurl himself at the man he wanted to love.

"What do you want from me?" Troy shouted at Aria.

Aria's response was inaudible. He sashayed up next to Troy and brushed his hands over Troy's lapels. He moved as if to kiss him on the lips.

Troy thrust Aria away from him.

A brief shouting match ensued, and then Aria stalked away, yelling over his shoulder that Troy would be sorry. He sounded, Brad thought, like a six-year-old.

After Troy had again closed the condo door, Brad and Chessie emerged from hiding.

"That doesn't look like there's much love lost there," Chessie said. Her voice was full of doubt.

Brad tried to play brave. "Well, duh. Now that he got caught. He realizes what he lost."

Down the street, Aria stumbled. They watched him withdraw a hip flask from his pocket, drain it, and throw it in the gutter.

"Should we run him over?" Chessie proposed.

"We don't have a car."

"Push him in front of a trolley?"

"No."

"How about stringing him up by those pretty mascaraed eyelids and poking him with fondue forks?"

"Now, there's an idea . . ."

"See, I knew you could laugh."

Brad forced a grim smile. He looked back wistfully over his shoulder at the condo he had known so well. He said, "I can't believe I am going to have to go out on the market after all these years. I don't even know how to date anymore."

"It's like riding a bike," she promised. "It'll be like the old days, when we used to hook each other up and raise hell and . . . OK, so the old days weren't that good."

They walked in silence and then Chessie proposed, "Look, you're right. Why don't you let me set you up on a date? I've got just the man."

Brad wasn't sure he could go through with it. His whole body was one long bruised nerve. He didn't even know if he could find another man attractive at this point. His feelings were still raw and his physical need for Troy too strong.

"Trust me," Chessie said, when he confided his fears, "if this is what you want, you'll go through with it. At least you will when you see this guy I am setting you up with. He's hot."

She arranged for him to meet her friend at the K-Bar. It was a small place near Kenmore, where they wouldn't have to worry about missing each other in a big after-work crowd.

Brad was nervous as he got ready. He sweated. His hands shook as he buttoned his shirt. His reflection in the mirror looked like a hunted dog. Every bone in his body told him to cancel.

Chessie was waiting in his living room. She would not hear of it.

"You need to get out of your comfort zone. This will be the best thing you ever did for yourself."

She smoothed out his shirt and tucked the tag at his neck back under the collar, just the way Troy used to do.

"Yesterday you were telling me . . ."

"Today's a new day, sweetheart."

Chessie took the taxi with him all the way to the door of the K-Bar to be sure he did not change his mind or back out.

"I don't want to do this," he said, with the taxi idling at the curb and the neon K-Bar sign blinking overhead.

Chessie pushed him out onto the sidewalk and yanked the door shut. Through a crack in the window, she said, "You can thank me later."

And then the taxi roared off into the stream of traffic headed home.

Stranded, Brad swallowed hard. He straightened his shoulders, said a little prayer, and walked into the bar.

The first face he saw belonged to Troy Boston. Brad gasped. He thought he was imagining things, a horrible hallucination born of stress and loneliness and wishful thinking.

Troy raised his drink in a manner that said cheers. He wore a big, smug, shit-eating grin. He seemed to be enjoying Brad's discomfort.

Brad glanced around to see if his date had shown up. How awkward would that be! How humiliating! To run into Troy on his first blind date. Troy must have gotten laid a hundred times since they broke up.

He and Troy had the place to themselves. No blind date was anywhere to be seen.

Troy beckoned Brad to his side. He had a leather messenger bag looped over his shoulder and the little Troy Boston logo hanging from the zipper was going back and forth like a metronome. Brad could not keep his eyes off it.

"You're getting sleepy," Brad mumbled to himself as he approached Troy. Each of his steps seemed hypnotically slow and unreal.

"Sit down," Troy said. "Have a drink. Take off your coat. Stay awhile."

Brad remained standing. "I can't."

"Why not?"

"I just can't." Again Brad glanced at the door, desperately hoping his date would show up and at the same time desperately hoping he would not. "I'm meeting someone," he confessed.

Troy seemed entirely unsurprised. "Yeah? Who is it?"

"Just someone. No one important."

Brad expected Troy to be the least bit jealous, but instead he smiled.

"A date?"

"Maybe. It's really none—"

"Is he cute?"

"Um . . . yeah." Brad was emboldened by Troy's teasing manner. "Sure. He's fucking hot. Of course, he's fucking hot." Brad could not believe that Troy was so ready to surrender him. What an asshole. To think it could all go up in smoke so quickly. Goddamnit, love was bullshit.

Or maybe it just wasn't love, from Troy's perspective.

"Look, I've got to go," Brad pleaded.

Troy snatched at his wrist. Hard. And Brad suffered that feeling again, that steel grip, the one he would liked to have felt if ever he was dangling from the edge of the world.

It made him want to cry. Anything for Troy to release him. And yet he did not ever want to be released. It was agony. His heart was tugged this way and that.

Brad's eyes met Troy's, and then quickly sidled away, like a pair of frightened squirrels.

"I was supposed to meet someone here," he mumbled, "but looks like he couldn't make it. So I . . . I need to go."

Troy lifted Brad's chin with his free hand. "Who's the lucky guy?"

There was a smile in Troy's eyes that did not appear on his lips. He's mocking me, Brad thought, but he could not square that idea with the steely grip on his wrist, which was in deadly earnest.

"Some friend of Chessie's." Brad squared his jaw. "He's a really great guy, the best. We have a lot in common."

"Is that right?"

"And he's great in bed."

"I'll bet," Troy said.

"The best."

Troy nodded again, still blissfully undisturbed, his face expressionless.

"Doesn't that bother you at all, Troy?"

Troy nodded his head up and down and then said, "No."

"No?"

"No, I take it as a compliment."

"You take my sleeping with another guy as—"

"I mean, after all, it's me you're talking about. I'm your date."

The world froze. It was a long moment before Brad found occasion to breathe. "What?"

"I'm . . . your . . . date." He spoke the words at the pace you would speak them to a confused child.

And suddenly Brad felt exactly as if he were dangling from the edge of the world. He gave Troy's hand a thankful squeeze, and then immediately wished he had not. A hundred thoughts rushed through his head.

"What are you talking about?"

"You came here on a blind date, right?"

"Ummm . . ."

"That's all right. I don't blame you. But . . . I'm the date."

Brad sat down. He did not think his legs would hold him anymore.

"Good," Troy said. Slowly, as if he half-expected Brad to run again, Troy released his wrist. "You're not going to run again, right? Because I have something for you in my bag. If you'll stay long enough for me to get it."

Keeping an eye on Brad as if he expected him to dart away, Troy pulled open the messenger bag.

"Tell me what's going on."

He extracted two brown envelopes. Brad flinched. He did not need to see those pictures again.

Troy touched his arm. "Hey. It's all right."

Brad noticed that the envelopes were smaller and cleaner than those that had held the photographs. OK, he thought. So far, so good. He tried, and failed, to piece together all parts of the story.

"Chessie called me. Can you believe it? Who would have thought Chessie of all people would give me a call?

"Anyway, she teased me for a while. She let on that you were going on this blind date. I was mad, but then she said it was her idea. Anyhow, it's the longest conversation we ever had without going at each other's throat, and . . ."

"Goddamnit, Troy. Get to the point!"

Brad was as surprised as Troy by his outburst. Brad's hands shook, and his fingertips left little dots of moisture on the envelopes. Beneath the table his knees were jittering up and down like pistons.

"All in good time, my friend. Good things come to those who wait."

"I mean it."

Troy squinted, as if he was trying to judge how serious Brad was.

"Don't fuck with me," Brad warned again.

Troy said, "So, Chessie told me I should meet you here. She promised not to tell you. She warned me not to make her regret it or she would personally remove my manhood with the serrated edge of a rusty can and sew it to my forehead with a darning needle. That's the nicest thing she's ever said to me."

Brad was speechless. He wondered whether he was angry, happy, or delirious.

Troy looked coy. He sipped from his drink. "So, do you still think the guy you're meeting is hot?"

"Maybe," Brad allowed. And then he answered truthfully: "Yes."

Suddenly, he needed a drink like nobody's business, and he corralled a passing waiter. The bar had slowly begun to fill up around them, and Brad kept looking about as if he expected this fantasy to come to a crashing end and his blind date to show up.

He shot a fierce look at Troy. "This doesn't change anything!"

Troy looked chagrined, maybe even hurt.

"It's nice you and Chessie played this little game. But nothing has changed."

"You're cute when you act all butch and tough," Troy said.

"Look, I'm . . ."

"Open it."

Troy had gone suddenly serious. The playful tone was gone.

"No," Brad objected. "You tell me what it is."

"Open it."

Brad stared at Troy for a long time, deciding whether he would walk out right then, for pride's sake.

Then he opened the envelope. It was a legal affidavit, signed, sealed, and notarized. Under the laws of the State of New York. It stated that the attached report by a private investigator in New York City was a true copy of the same and that it accurately reported what the investigator had learned in an engagement for Mr. Turner Page of Boston, Massachusetts.

Brad's heart beat faster as he read. According to the document, Mr. Turner Page had hired the investigator to look into an incident that took place in the towers of the Waldorf-Astoria Hotel in New York City.

After a series of interviews pursuant to the engagement with Mr. Page, the investigator was able to report that one Aria Shakespeare (a.k.a. Charles Augustus Thorland III) had bribed his way into a room registered in the name of Troy Boston. Furthermore, he reported that Mr. Shakespeare had hired a private photographer to assist him, and that the subject of the photographs—Mr. Boston—was not aware he was being photographed. Lastly, according to the interview with the photographer, Mr. Boston had reacted by striking Mr. Shakespeare "upside the head," in the words of the photographer.

Finished reading, Brad did not dare look into Troy's face. "Where did you get this?"

"I didn't." Troy sounded very pleased with himself. "Turner did."

"Turner?"

"You know how he knows everyone and his sister. Well, he came across the pictures we left on the floor at Cheval. And he noticed a maid uniform in the far corner of the photograph, almost off the page, a patch of black cloth—it was a maid's dress. She had let Aria into the room and was waiting for him to finish up. So, one thing led to another, and he asked around in New York until he found this investigator."

Troy choked on the last word, and now Bradley looked up. Troy's face was shining. His eyes were wet.

"Open this," he said, referring to the second envelope.

Brad did not think he could stand any more surprises. He turned the envelope over and over in his hands, but he could not bring himself to open it.

"I'm all surprised out," he pleaded. "Tell me."

"That's a legal document. It says that we are joint owners of the town house located at 334 Union Park, Boston. Not to mention joint owners of everything I own or hereafter come into possession of. 'Till death do us part,' as they say."

Troy stood, pulled Brad up from his chair, and cupped his hands on either side of his face, staring deep into Brad's eyes.

"Come with me," he said. And then he amended his command to a plea: "Will you come with me?"

"Where?"

"To our house. Our castle."

"I don't know, Troy . . ."

"It's just a hop, skip, and a jump from here. That's why I chose this place to meet."

"I've been killing myself trying to figure out how to make you happy," Troy said. "To reassure you. And everything I say comes out the wrong way. I am impatient. For you to come around. I love you. There's nothing in this world as important to me as you, Brad."

Still hypnotized, Brad thought, None of this is real. In a moment, I'll snap out of this dream.

They walked around the corner to a quiet side street, with a park running down the median, complete with a fountain and dogwalk. Troy produced a key for the second house in.

From the outside, Number 334 was a stately old Boston brownstone, with bay windows and tiny cupolas on the roof. Massive oaken doors guarded the entrance, each with a mosaic of stained glass mounted in the panel.

The doors opened to a vestibule, which gave way to a second set of doors, which Troy pushed open to reveal a massive, modern sunken living room. In fact, the whole interior of the house contrasted with the stately traditional exterior. It was four stories of pure modern design, with steel beams painted black, railings that looked like suspension bridges, open architecture that gave the sunken living room three stories of ceiling space and skirting balconies that looked down.

Each of the bedrooms had its own private porch, and the kitchen was larger, cleaner, and more beautiful than the one Brad had designed for his own apartment. To top it all off, there was a magnificent roof deck with panoramic 360-degree views of the Boston skyline.

The city lights had begun to go on, and a soft pink halo glowed in the west. The lights winked tantalizingly, seeming to make tempting offers and then withdraw them again.

"What do you think?" Troy asked. He shifted from one foot to the other like an embarrassed teenager, waiting for the verdict to be delivered.

"You know, most guys would just have bought flowers," Brad said.

Troy smiled. "I'm not most guys."

Brad looked him in the eye, and all the fabulous elements of the new house faded next to the luxury of Troy's gaze. Brad turned and looked back to the glow in the sky, which was much less dazzling.

Troy enveloped him from behind, wrapping his powerful arms around Brad's chest and pressing his head against the side of Brad's.

"What do you think?" Troy whispered. "Will you be with me . . . forever?"

Brad struggled. And wriggled. And closed his arms around the arms that enclosed him. He confessed, "I *can't* think! Not when you're touching me."

Troy kissed him.

"And *not* when you're kissing me."

Troy kissed him again.

"Stop," Brad begged. The strength of the arms around his chest made it impossible to breathe.

Troy released him. For a moment, they faced off. Brad straightened his collar, smoothed out his shirt, wiped off his forehead. He took a slow catalog of himself, making sure all was in order. Then he slyly raised his eyes to Troy.

"OK," he declared. "*Now* you can kiss me."

Troy obliged. And kept kissing him. Finally, he released Brad's lips and said, "I'll take that as a yes to my question, Bradley?"

"A maybe. A definite maybe. If you're lucky."

Troy kissed him again.

"I'm not that easy!" Bradley mumbled into the powerful lips, drinking in the taste of his breath, the feel of his skin, the pressure of Troy's body on his, like a man in the desert who finds an oasis.

"No, you're not easy. That's for sure. But you're worth it."

They were leaning against the wall in their empty living room, butts on the floor. Troy's legs were extended and spread wide in front of him, so that Brad could sit in his embrace. The ceiling soared above them.

Brad asked, "How did you know about those pictures, Troy?"

"Well, I found out that Aria added a little extra zero to the check my mother cut him. So I went to fire him, and he pulled those out. He said I could fire him, but it would cost me this. Asked me for money. He said he would give them to you if I did not pay him off."

"So what did you do? You didn't . . ."

"I told him that you would never believe it. That you knew me better than that."

Brad looked up into Troy's face. A touch of guilt and a renewed surge of love filled his chest. And he did know Troy better, now. After all this. And he hoped always to keep knowing Troy better, day after day, discovering, delighting in the secrets of the man he loved.

From Troy, he sensed an animal whiff of excitement under the calm exterior, as if he'd let loose a secret messenger from the walls of the castle keep.

Troy reached back into his messenger bag one more time—like a magician pulling one more rabbit out of his magic top hat—and removed a smaller white envelope.

"What's this?"

"Our travel itinerary."

"Where are we going? No, let me guess. Aruba? Key West? Monaco?"

Troy shook his head.

"Lenox," he said firmly.

"Huh? Where?"

"Lenox. It's in the Berkshires, about a half hour from my mother's cabin. On skis." Troy smiled. "There's a little church there I thought you would like, a liberal, Unitarian place. I thought you and I would take a trip there. Tomorrow."

"Tomorrow?"

"Tomorrow. I don't know about you, but I can't wait another day."

"Are you talking about . . . ?"

"Our wedding."

Brad's eyes shone.

"But what about the photo shoot?"

"We'll do that, too," Troy promised. "In a couple of weeks from now, as scheduled. With all the pomp and circumstance we've been planning. But that's for everyone else. Tomorrow . . . is for us."

20

As Troy promised, the little stone church was nestled in a valley under evergreens. There was a simple sign out front next to a gravel path. The first crocuses were coming up through patches of snow.

The church door stood open. Light streamed through the windows, throwing bright rectangles over the plain wooden pews. Everything about the church was carefully crafted but deliberately plain.

Troy and Brad walked up the aisle a little self-consciously. The minister was standing at the altar with Turner. He was an old friend of the Treadwell family. He shook their hands and turned over the altar to Turner, then slipped off to leave the three of them together.

Turner grinned and clapped his hands together. "Showtime, boys!"

Troy and Brad faced one another. Turner handed them a candle. Brad gripped it and then Troy put his hand around Brad's. It shook just the slightest bit.

"Go ahead, boys," Turner said. "It's your gig. I'm just here as a witness."

Troy cleared his throat. He pulled a sheet of paper from his pocket, but before he could start reading, he had to wipe his eyes with his sleeve. He laughed at himself and looked deep into Brad's eyes. Brad had never seen him so unpoised.

"Brad Drake," Troy read, "I love you with all the strength in my heart. I pledge to stand with you. To put you before everything and everybody. To care for you, to make your struggles mine, to make your triumphs my triumphs. Our triumphs."

Though the words were recited from the page, they were awkward on Troy's tongue. "Whatever might come, we'll face together. We'll climb mountains, sail seas, cross deserts."

In response, Brad did not need a paper. The words he said came straight from the heart.

"Bitch," he said. "If you step out of line from here on out, I'm going to ream your ass. Who's your Daddy?"

Turner and Troy both looked shocked.

Brad grinned.

"I'm joking."

He put his left hand around Troy's hand, which was already wrapped around his.

"Because I love you so much, I promise to speak up when I am confused or the moment I feel hurt. I promise not to let your career or mine carry us away from the most important thing in the world—us. I promise to trust you no matter what, through thick or thin, war or peace. I promise to tell you I love you before we go to bed at night and when we say good-bye in the day. And I promise to make you do the same, and make you mean it when you say it. Because I promise to be sexy and loyal and everything for you, and never take you for granted, and to care for you until the end of time."

Turner lit the candle and again stepped back.

Troy said, "This flame is the symbol of our love. We are no longer two people, but now one in spirit, shining bright."

Troy shielded the candle with his hand, and they walked awkwardly down the aisle toward the daylight streaming through from the great outdoors.

Under the evergreens and the witness of the sun, Turner poured wine into goblets heavy as cinderblocks. The sounds of the spring's first songbirds served as their wedding dance. Troy and Brad drank from the goblets with their arms entwined, gazing at one another like they would never look away, and murmuring simple sweet nothings that only the two of them could truly understand.

A few weeks later, they traded this private simplicity for public sumptuousness. Instead of the simple church, the wedding was set for a grand country estate on a bright Berkshire morning in May. In Chessie's room, sunlight streamed over the bridesmaid's dress, which had been arrayed on a Victorian clotheshorse in the center of the room.

The dress was a fantastical creation fashioned from hammered silver discs strung like beads on nylon fishline. The metal glinted like chain mail in the sun.

In the shadow of the room, where the morning sun had not yet reached, Chessie was smoking a forbidden cigarette. She had pulled a chair in front of the clotheshorse and was lounging deep in its upholstery. Her eyes were fixed on the dress. She was wearing a plush terry robe, and both arms and legs were crossed in a defensive posture of extreme disapproval.

"What do you think?" Brad asked nervously. He was already dressed in his wedding outfit, a marvelous Portuguese peasant-inspired version of the traditional tuxedo, with flowing sleeves and a narrowed waistline. "Isn't it fabulous?"

"No," she said bluntly. "After I saved you guys' asses, this piece of junkyard refuse is the thanks I get?! You expect me to put this scrap yard on?"

"What do you mean?"

"This dress is completely unwearable. No one will buy it."

Troy had been waiting impatiently in the doorway in a state of half-dress. His shirt was open and his tie hung loose and his powerful chest was visible. "You just don't understand, Francesca," Troy said. "Why should I give a damn if someone buys it? That dress is a statement, not just some piece of random cloth."

"There's not a whole lot of cloth going on there at all," Chessie shot back. "It looks like its made of tinfoil and floss."

But despite her bad-mouthing, Brad could see Chessie was intrigued. She would never admit it in front of Troy, but she wanted to be the first to wear the dress and to be seen wearing it. She just needed someone to coax her into trying it on.

After plying Chessie with a second mimosa and sending Troy on an errand, Brad was able to twist her arm. She practically jumped into the dress, although it weighed nearly forty pounds.

Chessie turned this way and that in the old Victorian mirror hanging on the wall of the cozy little room at the inn. She kept trying to see over her shoulder what impression the hammered discs made on her butt. The surprise and delight on Chessie's face were unmistakable.

"It's kind of heavy at first . . . but . . ." Chessie strolled around the room so that Brad could admire her. The fabric of metal discs hugged and flattered the curves of her breasts and hips. "It moves with you," she said. "It's, like, perfectly balanced. It doesn't sway at all. It gives you momentum."

She stopped in front of the mirror to admire herself, then spun around quickly, so that the discs produced an elegant little tinkle like a gypsy. "But I'll kill you if you tell Troy I said so!"

"Mum's the word," Brad promised.

Chessie was very stubborn, and refused to admit that she had come to like Troy even a little bit since the incident with Aria. She told Brad that she had devised the games to keep Brad and Troy together solely because Brad had a masochistic streak. Who was Chessie to get in the way of Brad's pleasure if he insisted on marrying an ass like Troy?

"Brad, if you want to stick pins under your fingernails, I'll let you do that, too," she assured him. "How do I look?"

"I'd do you."

Chessie looked pleased. She composed her face into an elegant pout, in case she ran into Troy at the altar. Then she lowered herself carefully into Brad's lap. He groaned under the weight of her dress.

"When are you going to give up on that lech and marry me?" she asked.

"One day I'll come to my senses, sweetheart. And pussy will never taste so good."

She cuffed him on the head and announced that she was not getting up until he had provided a thorough catalog of all the straight men they had invited to the reception. She did not want to miss this opportunity to find a husband. Or at least a good lay.

Meanwhile, a steady stream of trucks were arriving from Boston and New York, leaving the Turnpike and rumbling up the two-lane highways and across the covered bridges. They were bearing food and folding chairs and musicians and party favors and each of the hundred details Troy Boston had conjured up for this important day.

Brad and Troy and all of the members of their wedding party—bridesmaids and groomsmen alike—had been running amok all morning among the upstairs rooms of the old inn they had rented for the occasion. It was like a slumber party for adults. All the bedroom doors were wide open and people came and went and dressed and peed and bitched and gorged themselves and humped and waved out the windows as friends arrived.

There was a giddy air of silliness from hangovers and excess mimosa consumption, and splashes of color tarting up the dignified inn with its partridge hunting wallpaper and chill Yankee air.

A team of professional photographers from *Glam!* were capturing the candid flurry of the preparations. They slipped among the happy guests, catching the bras and boxer shorts, the impromptu group hugs, the splash of champagne, and the ubiquitous anxiety of Caroline Treadwell, who—in a rare display of emotion—was proving a less than dignified hostess.

Several times Caroline threatened loudly to go to pieces on the spot from the stress of the occasion, and she nearly decapitated a photographer who had the audacity to shoot a photograph of her less-flattering left-sided profile.

Before the ceremony came the more formal fashion shots. They were taken on a runway that also served as the center aisle, down which the two grooms would walk. The first shoot involved a collection of Troy's that had been inspired by traditional morning wear, with touches that recalled spats and pinstripes and dove-gray waistcoats.

Other collections followed. There were "bad guys" dressed in garb inspired by the roaring twenties, with lots of black and carbines, adopting poses as if they intended to prevent the nuptials. Then the groomsmen appeared in chain-mail business suits that briefly lent the New England air a medieval flavor.

So many bulbs flashed in Brad's face that he was seeing stars all afternoon.

In the middle of one of a dozen takes, Troy complained, "I'm glad I am usually on the other side of the runway."

Brad replied, "I've been in the stars for two weeks." He won a smile from his lover that made all the hassle worthwhile.

The actual ceremony took place under a giant tent set upon the lawn of the inn, at the end of the long runway. The Berkshires rolled in the background, and rows of folding chairs had been set up for the guests. A wall of fir trees lent a solemn sacred air to the festivities far below.

Caroline Treadwell gave away her son. She was bursting with pride as they walked down the aisle, holding her son by the elbow as if he were a trophy. And for the first time since Brad had known her, Caroline looked genuinely happy to orchestrate this exchange between herself and Brad.

The valley itself seemed at peace, brimming with love. After the vows had been exchanged, Brad led Caroline out on the parquet dance floor that had been set up under the tent. He twirled her about the floor to the sounds of the swing band, whose members were all imported from the crowded stage at Wally's Café and playing gratis.

Caroline laughed like a little girl and clung to Brad tightly. She seemed vulnerable for once, not the icy old dame she portrayed herself to be, but the carefree teen she had once been. The band played "The Twelfth Street Rag" and "What Is This Thing Called Love?" When a song came to the end, Bradley would offer to let Caroline go, but each time, she snatched another glass of champagne as if it were jet fuel and insisted on one more dance.

She seemed to think she was being daring. And her eyes were locked on Brad's face. Her body surrendered to his lead. She seemed fascinated by him, transfixed, and maybe the slightest bit fearful.

Suddenly, the calm was punctured by a shout. From nowhere, Aria Shakespeare lunged out of the crowd onto the dance floor. His face was mottled with alcohol, his eyes unfocused.

For a moment, he staggered in a clearing left by the horrified dancers. He pointed at Brad and Caroline, and let loose an inarticulate shout. Then he hurled himself across the dance floor. His dirty platinum hair shimmered. He looked like a lightning strike.

Troy and the other guests were frozen with shock at the noisy apparition.

Brad threw himself in front of Caroline protectively, ready to meet the onslaught. He tensed his fists. He had not been in a fight since he was ten years old.

The *Glam!* photographers began to snap away, creating a dizzying strobic atmosphere as Aria closed the distance, shouting frothing, angry invective. He was wielding a cudgel made from a Club Troy Trojan horse.

At the last possible minute before Aria struck, Caroline suddenly stepped into his path. From a nearby table, she seized two bottles of hot jalapeño-ginger sauce that were meant as a condiment for one of Brad's fabulous culinary creations. With a flick of the wrist, she twisted the tops off the bottles and doused Aria twice. Hot sauce splashed directly into Aria's wide, unfocused eyes. He dropped at Caroline's feet like he had been shot. The cudgel fell to the side and Aria writhed on the floor, trying to claw out his eyeballs.

Turner Page and three shaven-headed gay groomsmen rushed in. They looped a hand under each armpit and dragged Aria off. The moment was over almost before it began. The only sign that it had really happened was Brad's thudding heart and the two bottles of hot sauce in Caroline's fists like a couple of six-guns.

Caroline had a broad smile on her face as she turned toward the photographers. She looked like she must have looked forty years before, as a debutante, with mischief in her eyes and color in her cheeks. For the sake of the cameras, Caroline blew imaginary smoke from the top of each bottle of hot sauce as if it were the barrel of a gun. She stowed the bottles away in the folds of the magnificent gown Troy had made for her.

The guests clapped and roared their approval. They thought that this was just one more marketing stunt for *Glam!*

Before anyone could realize the difference, Troy stepped in and announced dinner was served. The gunfight, he said, had piqued his appetite.

"And by the way," he said, "has someone secured the perimeter?"

Despite the chain-mail business suit he had been forced to adopt and the necessity of escorting Aria to a waiting squad car, Turner managed to pull off the meal Brad had planned without a hitch, hot sauce and all. He balanced his best-man duties with superior restaurant management skills.

The wedding cake was served with chestnut ice cream, apricot and lavender sauce, and candied chestnuts. As a surprise gift to Brad, Troy had arranged with *Food and Wine* to cover each and every delicious element in its fall issue, along with a profile of the groom and chef.

After cake had been downed, toasts were offered and speeches given. In his rumbling baritone, Turner roasted Brad mercilessly, to the happy pleasure of the assembled guests.

Later, as the fever at the reception was coming to full swing, Caroline Treadwell cornered Brad and Troy beneath one of the tent poles. She had been drinking water and had regained that remarkable composure that had withstood three husbands, one Aria, and all her fifty-five years.

She remarked how beautiful "her boys" looked together. And then Caroline allowed Brad a kiss and formally welcomed him to the Treadwell clan.

"I won't," she joked, "even insist that you change your name, though; it's not an absolute requirement." She choked up in the middle of her chuckle.

Troy daubed at her mascara. "For fear," he said, "of allowing her to look like a sentimental old drag queen."

This comment won him a swipe from his mother's white gloves.

Not to mention the fierce looks from a couple of passing drag queens of their acquaintance.

"You two are the ones who are beautiful together," Brad said to his husband and mother-in-law.

Caroline Treadwell put her arm around her son's waist. Next to him, she seemed tiny. Nevertheless, she forcefully and fiercely warned Brad that she would never stop being friends with her son.

Brad smiled and assured her he never intended to get in the way. "As long as we can be friends, too," he added. "I don't want to be on the receiving end of a dose of jalapeño-ginger sauce."

Caroline laughed. She was touched by Brad's invitation. She cupped her hand on his cheek and said, in a voice full of emotion, "Of course we will be."

Caroline's change of heart had been sudden and decisive—and Brad could largely thank Aria Shakespeare. Caroline had been shaken by what she had learned of Aria's shenanigans. Next to Aria, Brad looked like a champion.

Caroline confided to them that, after the Incident (which was how Caroline dignified Aria's attempted photographic extortion), she had conned Aria's mother into a tennis luncheon at the club, which Aria's mother had studiously been avoiding.

As Caroline told the story, with a certain pride in her own resourcefulness, she had plied Aria's mother with Bloody Marys. Once the alcohol had taken hold, Caroline had bullied the poor woman into all kinds of scandalous admissions and revelations.

It turned out that Aria was no longer welcome in his mother's house and had not been for years. Although his mother had procured a job for him at the Design Consultancy, Aria's initial promise proved empty. He was fired for insubordination and habitual tardiness and drug use, and it did not help that there had been rumors of sexual liaisons with clients.

The only reason Aria had been hired by the Consultancy to assist with Club Troy was Caroline's imperious demand. Against the advice of all involved, she had insisted on it. She had trusted his breeding more than she had trusted the other candidate's talent.

"She's lost the faith," Troy joked. "It never really occurred to Caroline that a kid with the right breeding could turn out wrong. Isn't that right, Mother?"

Caroline pointedly refused to dignify the situation with any more commentary. She was only an occasional gossip, and she punished her indulgences in the habit with long embargoes without further elaboration, embargoes she thought of as good breeding.

Brad and Chessie were happy to say that they were not afflicted with such manners. They dished about Aria all night, about what Caroline had learned, and about how she had brought Aria low.

"I still think we should have used the fondue forks," Chessie argued wistfully.

In the end, Brad asked, "Why do you think Aria hated me so much?"

"Oh, it's not all about you, Brad. Aria does not give a shit about you."

"Or me," Troy added, coming up behind them. "Aria was out to make a name for himself, 'while I'm still thin and beautiful so I can enjoy it,' as he used to say. And say. And say."

Brad shrugged and sniffed. "Can you blame him for trying? I'm certainly enjoying it. And I'm thin. And I'm beautiful."

Chessie laughed and took him to dance, and asked what boys he planned to set her up with. Brad looked over her shoulder at his lover, his husband. Despite the hundred people who came up to chat, Troy kept his eyes firmly locked on Brad. It was a sign, Brad thought, that he would never look away.

Behind Troy, the sun had begun to set over the open field. It produced stark silhouettes of ice-cream eaters and a legion of suited gay men resplendent in Troy Boston formal wear.

Toward the end of the night, Brad was not tired at all. In fact, he wished the party beneath the tent would never end. Love was a recipe Brad was going to take to his grave.

"I thought this might be anticlimactic," he confessed, slipping his arm around Troy's waist, beneath his tails. "Since we already did our vows alone, just you and me."

"No, this is important, too," Troy said firmly. He looked Brad in the face. "For everyone else. And for us, it doesn't take away from what we did together. It's just our first chance to reaffirm our vows." He smiled and jabbed Brad in the ribs. "I mean, most couples have to wait until they're fifty. Me and you, we're thin and beautiful, *and* we get to start reaffirming right away."

"Gay boys always do it more fabulously," Brad said. He jabbed Troy back, and they jostled against each other like two boys playing beneath a night full of shooting stars.

about the authors

scott pomfret and scott whittier met, fell in love, and now live together in Boston, Massachusetts. They realized the story of their own romance wasn't the only one out there, so they created Romentics (www.romentics.com) for all gay men who believe in happily ever after.

pomfret, 36, a native of Wellesley, Massachusetts, is a lawyer for the United States Securities and Exchange Commission. His short stories and erotic fiction have appeared in numerous magazines and anthologies, including *Post Road, New Delta Review, Genre Magazine, Friction* (Alyson Books), *Best Gay Love Stories 2005* (Alyson Books), *Best Gay Erotica 2005* (Cleis Press), and *Fresh Men: Best New Gay Voices.* Pomfret has been co-counsel with Gay & Lesbian Advocates & Defenders in a case bringing a constitutional challenge to Massachusetts sodomy laws.

whittier, 29, a native of Poland, Maine, is an advertising copywriter. His commercial work has appeared on radio, billboards, TV, and in print media internationally and has won top honors in the Healthcare Advertising Awards and Admission Advertising Awards. He has published fiction in *Children Churches and Daddies, Playguy, In Touch, Honcho,* and Alyson's anthologies *Just the Sex, Ultimate Gay Erotica,* and *Friction 7.*